STACKS

COOKED
GOOSE

Also by G. A. McKevett
in Large Print:

Death by Chocolate

This Large Print Book carries the
Seal of Approval of N.A.V.H.

COOKED
GOOSE

G. A. McKevett

WHEELER
PUBLISHING

Published in 2004 by arrangement with Kensington Books, an
imprint of Kensington Publishing Corp.

Wheeler Large Print Softcover.

The text of this Large Print edition is unabridged.
Other aspects of the book may vary from the original edition.

Set in 16 pt. Plantin.

Printed in the United States on permanent paper.

Library of Congress Cataloging-in-Publication Data

McKevett, G. A.
    Cooked goose / G.A. McKevett.
       p. cm.
    ISBN 1-58724-589-2 (lg. print : sc : alk. paper)
    1. Reid, Savannah (Fictitious character) — Fiction.
2. Women private investigators — California, Southern —
Fiction.   3. California, Southern — Fiction.   4. Overweight
women — Fiction.   5. Large type books.   I. Title.
PS3563.C3758C66 2004

                            2003062189

A woman is fortunate if, sometime during her life, she finds that one precious friend — another woman who celebrates the good times with her and offers strong, quiet comfort through the not-so-good.

A woman is especially fortunate if that other woman is her own daughter.

This book is dedicated to you

Gwendolynn

For making me
the luckiest mom in the world.

As the Founder/CEO of NAVH, the only national health agency solely devoted to those who, although not totally blind, have an eye disease which could lead to serious visual impairment, I am pleased to recognize Thorndike Press* as one of the leading publishers in the large print field.

Founded in 1954 in San Francisco to prepare large print textbooks for partially seeing children, NAVH became the pioneer and standard setting agency in the preparation of large type.

Today, those publishers who meet our standards carry the prestigious "Seal of Approval" indicating high quality large print. We are delighted that Thorndike Press is one of the publishers whose titles meet these standards. We are also pleased to recognize the significant contribution Thorndike Press is making in this important and growing field.

Lorraine H. Marchi, L.H.D.
Founder/CEO
NAVH

* Thorndike Press encompasses the following imprints: Thorndike, Wheeler, Walker and Large Print Press.

Acknowledgments

Nobody can write a novel alone. Well, this author can't. So I'd like to say a special thanks to some special people who have helped me "cook" this "goose." Thanks, guys . . . and ladies. I appreciate you more than I can say.

Bruce Hald
Mary Phelan, C.N.M.
Officer Dave Birkenhead

and

Officer Bob Costello (ret.)
a great cop,
a wonderful husband and father,
and the best neighbor on Long Island

ONE

December 10 — 4:38 p.m.

"This is just too cool! I can't believe I'm getting paid to *shop!*"

Savannah Reid stood inside the cramped cubicle, generously called a fitting room, and watched while her friend and fellow private detective, Tammy Hart, wriggled into a size zero pair of jeans. Being an overly voluptuous size fourteen herself, it was all Savannah could do not to urp the double chili-cheeseburger and triple thick chocolate malt she had consumed for lunch.

Jealousy was an ugly emotion.

"You aren't getting paid to shop. You don't get to keep any of the goodies," she grumbled as Tammy admired her own teeny-tiny butt in the mirror. "You're getting paid to catch a rapist . . . which we aren't likely to do in the ladies' dressing room, since his m.o. is to nab his victims in the parking lot."

Tammy's enthusiasm for life was only briefly dampened. Bottom lip protruding, she slid out of the jeans and dumped them on the floor. Savannah tried not to notice that the younger, slimmer, disgustingly cellulite-free woman was "not quite" dressed in a purple paisley G-string.

"Have you ever tried wearing a thong?" Tammy asked brightly, pulling on a pair of leggings.

Savannah scowled and shook her head. "Nope. I can't say that I have."

In the mirror Savannah saw two women who couldn't have been more different: an abundantly dimensioned brunette and a blonde with sadly diminishing assets. That was the way Savannah chose to classify them. Savannah was determined to embrace and adore her flesh — all of it — out of sheer rebellion toward an anorexic society that tried to make her feel less than gorgeous because she was thirty pounds over what their charts said she should weigh.

Screw 'em.

That was her motto, and she lived by it.

"Oh, Savannah, you should try wearing thongs. They're wo-o-onderfully comfortable."

"Thanks for the tip, but the idea of butt floss doesn't appeal to me." Savannah picked up the jeans and began to fold them while Tammy slipped into her blouse.

"No, really," Tammy continued, undaunted by Savannah's lack of enthusiasm for the subject. "They make your rear look so cute and —"

"They make *your* rear look cute, Tam. Buttocks the size of mine should *not* be allowed

10

to flap freely in the breeze. It constitutes a public hazard."

She shoved the jeans and Tammy's purse at her. "Are we about ready to go, or what?"

"Sure. Let's boogie out to the parking lot!"

Tammy "boogied" everywhere. And she never — well, almost never — took offense. Long ago, Savannah had decided those were Tammy's two most endearing qualities . . . and her most infuriating ones. Sometimes Savannah genuinely *wanted* to offend this perky, effervescent assistant of hers. But no matter how dark the insult, Tammy Hart continued to shine. With her golden California tan, glossy blond hair, and Miss U.S.A. personality, the girl was the quintessential sunbeam that sometimes required U.V. protectant shades.

Rarely, but once in a while, Savannah hated "perky." Especially when she was dead tired, like today. This gig was "wearing her to a frazzle" as her Georgian grandma would say.

"Did you buy enough loot to look like a serious shopper when you're walking through the parking lot?" Savannah asked.

"Yeah, if I get these jeans, too. They fit really great, don't you think?"

Savannah searched Tammy's face for some sign that she was operating in reality mode. No indication was immediately visible.

"Tammy, it doesn't matter if the jeans fit

or not. As soon as we catch this guy, the job's over, and we have to return all this stuff to the mall. That's why I told you to be sure and save all your receipts. We're undercover here, trying to catch a rapist. It's fake shopping. Got it?"

Tammy sighed and pulled back the cubicle's curtain. "Of course I understand, Savannah. Do you think I'm a bimbo, or what?"

Following her out of the dressing room, Savannah chose her words carefully. "No. I don't think you're a bimbo. But I think that maybe *you* think you are, because sometimes you . . . well . . . you sorta act like one."

Tammy stopped abruptly and Savannah nearly crashed into the back of her. "What kind of psycho-babble is that?"

"See. That's what I mean. A real bimbo wouldn't use the term psycho-babble."

"Gee, thanks. I guess."

At the door they were stopped by the fitting-room attendant, a bleary-eyed, middle-aged woman who appeared to be suffering from Holiday Overtime Meltdown Syndrome.

"Here you go." Tammy shoved three shirts and a dress in the attendant's direction along with the red, plastic tag bearing the number 5. "I'm keeping the jeans."

The woman took the unwanted garments from Tammy and tossed them onto a heap behind her counter. "Merry Christmas," she muttered in the same tone of voice usually reserved for bidding someone a speedy *bon voyage* to Hades.

Savannah was about to return the blessing, when a male voice began to speak . . . from the vicinity of Tammy's chest.

"What are you broads doing in there . . ." The words were gruff and static-fried. ". . . buying out the whole damned store while I'm roasting my chestnuts out here in the parking lot?"

"Oh, my God! What was that?" The attendant's eyes bugged as though she had just witnessed irrefutable evidence of demon possession. Several plastic tags that she had been holding fluttered to the floor. "Did your . . . your bra just say something?"

"Naw," Savannah told her in a lazy, Dixie drawl, "it's just her right boob. Sometimes it has political arguments with the other one about being too far left."

Tammy snickered, but the attendant gave Savannah the same animated look of a stale fish market trout.

"Cute," Tammy whispered to Savannah as they walked away from the woman without further explanation. "But I don't think she got your joke."

"Nope. Sailed over her head like an origami airplane. But she did have a point. Why are we hearing Dirk? He's only supposed to come through on the earpiece."

Ducking behind a rack of coats, Tammy pulled back her shirt lapel and exposed the tiny communication unit taped to her breast. "Dirk's police department reject equipment is fritzing out again . . . big surprise there."

"It's not my equipment's fault," said the voice that sounded like it was broadcasting from a pan of sizzling bacon. "It's the ding-a-ling that's using it. You probably pulled the earpiece out when you were trying on all those clothes."

Tammy traced the thin wire from the plug in her ear, beneath her hair and to the disconnected jack in her bra.

"He's right," she said. Dropping her voice to a stage whisper, she added, "Darn . . . did he hear what I said about thongs."

"Yeah, but he's half deaf," Savannah replied. "He probably thought you said *songs*."

"I don't care what songs you're singing in there," Dirk returned. "Get out here so you can be mugged, raped, abducted, or whatever. I ain't got all day, you know."

Tammy reached down and put her hand over the microphone. "I know he's your best friend, but that guy really gets on my nerves sometimes."

Savannah chuckled and guided Tammy toward the check-out stand. "He gets on everybody's nerves sometimes. Let's buy those jeans and get outta here. He sounds like he's about at the end of his three-inch patience

14

tether. Besides, we've got a rapist who's not exactly spreading holiday cheer. And nabbing his mangy ass would really make my day."

4:47 p.m.

Savannah and Tammy parted ways at the south end of the mall, near Burger King, with Savannah heading for the back parking lot, while Tammy and her carefully chosen purchases took the front.

They had been "mock shopping" all day, but now that the sun had set, Savannah insisted on patrolling the back where fewer shoppers, thick shrubbery and reduced lighting increased the likelihood of an attempted nabbing by the rapist. Tammy had made only a feeble objection; this gig was her first true decoy assignment and she, as well as Savannah, knew her limitations.

The moment Savannah opened the back door and stepped into the late afternoon winter darkness outside, she thought for half a second it was snowing. Then she caught a whiff of smoke and knew the flakes that were falling from the California December sky were ashes, the result of an out-of-control brushfire on the hill. From where she stood she could see, several miles away, the eerie, bloodred line of glowing flames that lit the dark horizon on the east side of town. Like some sort of grotesque, luminous serpent, it wriggled its path up the black hill, consuming a decade's growth of sage, marguerites, and miscellaneous scrub brush.

"It's a little hard to get into the Christmas spirit," she muttered to herself, "when it's eighty degrees and the hills are aflame."

She licked her forefinger and stuck it in the air. The breeze was coming from the ocean, an on-shore flow. That was a good thing, especially for the San Carmelita citizens who lived in the fancy houses with the best views in town — the ones at the top of the semi-charred hill. As long as the wind continued to blow east, they might sleep through the night without that knock at the front door, a fire department representative announcing an unscheduled, emergency evacuation.

Ah, the joys of being an upper-middle-class Californian, Savannah thought, congratulating herself on having the good fortune to be a lower-middle-class private detective. She lived smack in the middle of town, far away from the ocean view lots, with their fire hazards, or the seaside properties, with their potential for high-tide flooding.

Yep. Savannah was damned lucky to be poor. She wouldn't have it any other way.

Switching into her professional "Come-And-Get-Me-You-Ugly-Sucker," mode, she tucked her few packages under her arm and sauntered toward her car, which was parked in the far rear of the lot. She tried to look harried, absentminded, dog-tired and as wimpy as possible. A rapist's idea of the perfect date.

In her peripheral vision she watched an elderly lady climbing into her Cadillac parked in the handicapped space, the young couple pushing a baby stroller with a screeching child inside, and her most likely suspect, a scruffy guy wearing a T-shirt upon which had been scrawled in black marker the warm sentiment, "Shoot 'em all and let God sort 'em out!"

The guy had his head stuck under the opened hood of an equally scruffy, long-past-its-prime Dodge Dart. As Savannah walked by on the way to her classic Camaro, he eyed her so lasciviously that she half expected him to start drooling down the front of his offensive shirt.

"White trash," she muttered as she passed him, echoing her Granny Reid's sentiments about men who couldn't keep their eyes in their sockets when a pair of boobs bounced by.

"What did you say?" Dirk asked in her earpiece.

"Nothing," she whispered. "Just talking to myself. Where are you?"

"By the food court."

"Now, why doesn't that surprise me? And how about you, Tammy? Is your unit working okay?"

"Yeah," came the reply. "I can hear you in my ear instead of in my blouse."

"That's an improvement."

"So, does anybody see our friend?" Dirk asked.

"I don't," Tammy answered. "The most suspicious character I see over here is a Girl Scout selling cookies and a Salvation Army lady ringing a bell."

"Nobody here either," Savannah replied, giving up on the yahoo with the brokendown Dart. Now that he had enjoyed his little "out of body experience" with her, he was back to scraping the corroded terminals of his battery.

"Wait a minute. I see somebody," Tammy said. Savannah could hear the excitement mixed with fear in her voice. This might be for real.

"What is it?" she heard Dirk ask.

Instantly, Savannah whirled around and started back toward the mall. The jerk under the hood gave her an expectant look as she hurried by him, as though hopeful that she had changed her mind.

"A guy in a red and green plaid lumberjack's shirt," Tammy whispered. "With a long white beard!"

The Santa Rapist, as the newspapers were calling him, had abducted half a dozen women from this mall parking lot in the past month. The women had been driven to nearby orange groves, raped and badly beaten. All six victims had claimed the attacker wore a fake Santa's beard as a disguise.

"He's watching me," Tammy said as Savannah rushed back into the mall, past Burger King and out the front door. "He's coming this way."

"Just be calm, sweetie," Savannah told her. "We're on our way. Head for your car, just like we talked about. Open the trunk and slowly, calmly put your bags inside. But don't actually get into the car. Wait for us."

Savannah scanned the parking lot, looking for her assistant, but a big, yellow, Ryder truck was blocking her vision and the streetlamps were situated too far apart for good lighting and visibility.

"Is your car still in the front row, near the road, where we told you to put it?" Dirk asked. Savannah could tell from his huffing and puffing he was running from the food court.

"Yes," Tammy mumbled. "I'm putting the stuff in the trunk. He's about thirty feet away. Watching me. Coming this way."

Savannah broke into a run. She still couldn't see around the damned truck.

"Savannah!" Tammy sounded like she was about to cry. "Savannah, I . . . oh . . . shit! Help!"

"Dirk! The kid's in trouble!" Savannah shouted. "Hurry!"

"I know!" he yelled back, panting. "I'm only halfway there."

Damn him. Great time to take a taco and nacho break, half a mall away!

Savannah threw down her packages and pulled her Beretta from the shoulder holster beneath her jacket as she ran. "I'm coming, Tammy! Hang on!"

Just as she was rounding the front of the truck, Savannah heard a scream that sent her heart pounding up into her throat. It was a shriek of pain and fear — nothing like the fake screams in the movies. This one was for real.

But when she cleared the truck, she saw something that made her heart nearly stop altogether.

Tammy was bent backward over the hood of her Volkswagen bug. A man — just as she had described, with a white beard, wearing a plaid shirt — was bending over her, ripping her blouse open, clawing at her chest.

Savannah let out a roar of rage and threw herself onto the man's back. "Leave her alone, you dirty son of a bitch," she screamed as they both tumbled to the pavement.

She jumped to her feet and with karate expertise landed a solid kick directly to his groin. As he crumpled into a ball of pain, she gave him another chop to the back of his neck with her left hand.

It was only then she remembered she was holding her gun in her right. Proper procedure would have been to level the gun at him and calmly demand he release her assistant.

Yeah, well, screw proper procedure, she quickly decided. Sometimes hands-on, up close and personal contact was the only kind that satisfied the soul.

"Are you all right, honey?" Savannah asked, taking her eyes off her suspect for half a second to check out Tammy, who was still lying across the VW's hood.

"Oh, Savannah . . ." Tammy was fighting for breath. "You shouldn't have. Owww! Oh, damn, that hurts!"

"Hurts?" Savannah looked down at her groaning, moaning Santa lookalike. He was still writhing in the middle of a greasy oil slick on the asphalt pavement, holding his privates. "What are you talking about? What hurts?"

Tammy was tearing at her blouse, pulling the thing off. "It's this stupid microphone it . . . owww . . . it's shorting out or something . . . I . . . owwwwww!"

Dirk ran up to them, his face Christmas crimson all the way back to his receding hairline, sweat dripping from the end of his nose. Perspiration stained his T-shirt with dark circles under the arms and in the center of his chest, making him look even more bedraggled than usual. Dirk was no lightweight himself, and the race had just about done him in.

"What the hell's going on here?" he demanded as Tammy danced around, holding her chest and screeching.

"It's shocking her!" Savannah told him, still holding the gun on her suspect. "Get it off her! Quick!"

Dirk might have been a bit out of shape, but after twenty-plus years on the police force, his reflexes were still sharp. In half a second he had ripped the offending unit and tape off Tammy's chest, leaving her holding her bare breasts in her hands, blushing violently and deeply furious.

"And I suppose you enjoyed groping me while you were at it!" she yelled at him.

"What?"

"You just couldn't pass up an opportunity like that! First you loan us lousy, faulty equipment, and then you molest me right here in front of everybody!"

He stared at her for a long time, then slowly shook his head. "You're a dingbat, you know that, Hart? A first-rate, certified dingbat!"

He picked up her blouse from the ground and tossed it at her. She exposed a breast as she reached up to catch it. Hugging the garment to her, she began to softly cry.

"A nut job," Dirk said, turning to Savannah. "That's who you've got working for you."

"Give her a break, Coulter," Savannah said,

handing him her gun to hold on the fellow who was still wriggling like a caterpillar under a sunlit magnifying glass. She hurried over to Tammy. "Are you all okay, sweetie?"

"No," Tammy said between sobs. "It was awful!"

"I can imagine." She helped her slip on the blouse and button the front as though Tammy were a distraught kindergartner getting ready for a traumatic first day at school. "That nasty ol' thing shocking you and that scumbag attacking you. You must be —"

"Attacking me?" Tammy shook her head and sniffed. "He didn't attack me. He was trying to help me get that thing off my chest. He was just —"

"Oh, damn." The truth hit Savannah with a whollop somewhere in her solar plexus as she stared down at the fellow on the pavement.

He glared back at her with a mixture of rage and confusion in his blue eyes. Blue eyes. White beard. Rosy cheeks — well, his cheeks were sort of green now, but she was pretty sure they had been rosy a second before she had kicked him in the groin.

"You hurt Santa Claus," said a small, wee voice behind them. Savannah turned to see a young boy, watching her with horror on his munchkin's face. "You're in big trouble, lady," he went on to explain in painful detail. "I saw what you did! You kicked Santa Claus right in the balls!"

"Don't say 'balls,' honey. It's not nice," his mother said, pulling her child closer to her and away from the crazed brunette and the other woman who had just disrobed in public. "We prefer to call them by their proper name, testicles."

"Yeah," the kid continued, wide-eyed. "And I saw that lady's chesticles, too! Did you see them? They were hanging right there and —"

The outraged mother clamped one hand over her son's mouth and the other over his eyes as she led him away.

"I'm-m-m . . . I'm-m-m-m . . ." croaked Santa Claus as he struggled to rise.

"What is it, sir?" Savannah graciously offered him her hand. He slapped it away.

A couple of fresh-faced security guards in black, wanna-be-cop uniforms came whizzing up in a glorified golf cart. "What's going on here?" the tallest one demanded as he climbed out of the cart. "Oh, Mr. Wilcox," he said, noticing the man on the ground, "it's a good thing you're here." He consulted his watch. "Your shift starts in three minutes. Are you hurt?"

"I'm-m-m . . . I . . . ack-k-k-k."

"Mr. Wilcox seems to have lost his voice for the moment," Savannah said, trying to sound helpful, even cheerful. "In fact, I think he should probably be taken to a hospital. You said something about his shift. Does he work here?"

"Sure," replied the short one. "He's our five o'clock-'til-closing Santa."

"Oh, shit," Savannah whispered to Dirk, "I really did kick Santa in the balls."

"Definitely classifies as a 'naughty' and not 'nice' gesture," he replied dryly.

Still leaning against the VW, Tammy continued to quietly sob.

"I'm-m-m . . . I'm-m-m-m . . ." Once again, the not-particularly-jolly old elf tried to communicate with the world.

"Oh, Santa. I'm so sorry." Savannah dropped to her knees beside him and clasped his cold, clammy hand between her own. "What is it, sir? What are you trying to tell us?"

"I'm-m-m . . . I'm-m-m . . ."

"That's it. Just take a deep breath and say it."

"I'm-m-m . . . I'm-m-m-m-m gonna . . . sue . . . your fuckin' ass off!"

6:15 p.m.

Having pulled his car deep into the orange grove, well out of sight from the main road, the driver cut the key. He pulled his backpack from the floorboard and yanked the zipper open. Inside he had packed duct tape, thin nylon rope, and a ten-inch butcher knife — the tools of his trade. Rape was a primal act; it didn't require sophisticated, high-tech equipment.

Oh, yes, and the disguise. He was particularly proud of the red hat with its white fur trim and the snow white, luxuriously curly beard. Who said he didn't have Christmas spirit? he thought with a grin as he tossed his keys into the pack and zipped it closed.

When he swung the car door open, the sweet scent of tree-ripened citrus filled his head, triggering memories . . . of last time . . . of the time before . . . and the time before that. Lately, just the smell of his morning glass of orange juice could get him excited and hard.

He glanced at his watch. Six-seventeen. He had to get to the bus stop. The last one ran at six-thirty. Stupid hick town. They folded up the sidewalks at eight.

But he'd be back. In an hour or less, he'd return. With company.

He took a deep breath, smelled the oranges, and felt his blood rush to his groin.

Oh, yeah. He'd be back. And then . . . *party time!*

TWO

"Now down South, where I'm from, we know how to cure what ails a rapist. Yep. We just chop his damned pecker off. Then we string that sucker on a piece of rough brown twine and hang it around the pervert's neck," Savannah told her rapt audience of a dozen women who had assembled at the local library to learn the art of self-defense. "And that usually gets the creep's attention. He's not likely to offend again."

Savannah laughed and her listeners echoed a few nervous giggles. "But here in California," she continued, "y'all are a mite more *civilized.* You catch 'em if you can, lock 'em up for a spell, then let 'em go to do it all again. And that, ladies, is why we need classes like this one."

The group had arrived an hour ago at the library, their clothing and hair all neat and tidy, their faces arranged in pseudo-nonchalant expressions. Unsuccessfully, they had been trying to hide the fact that they were scared to death of the latest threat to their community.

27

Like all Southern Californians, they took in stride the earthquakes, mudslides, occasional riots and seasonal brush fires. But the serial rapist who had been ravaging San Carmelita's women had them afraid to run to the grocery store for a loaf of bread. Only the bravest had ventured outside after dark to attend the meeting at the library.

And after an hour of instruction by Savannah and Tammy, an hour of throwing each other around on the mats spread across the carpeted floor of the Children's Corner, an hour of being told what to expect if they were attacked, the group was a little mussed, a bit disheveled, but in their eyes they had a bold gleam that Savannah welcomed. It told her they were less inclined to become victims than when they had first arrived.

She was moderately satisfied with her results so far. It was a much more productive way to spend the remainder of her fateful evening . . . having been dismissed from the mall decoy gig. After a debacle like that, she would have normally gone home to bury her sorrow in a pint of Ben and Jerry's Chunky Monkey ice cream.

"Walk with your head high," she told them, "your spine straight. Walk with an attitude, girls! A rapist is looking for a victim, not a combatant. We know he's a lily-livered chicken shit or he wouldn't be attacking women."

From the corner of her eye, Savannah saw the research librarian seated at the desk. She winced at the colorful terminology. Savannah ignored her. She had some important points to make, and she had her audience's full attention. "He's a predator who preys on the weak," she said. "Don't give him a reason to think that you're anything other than a raging bitch. A bitch may not be the most popular member of the P.T.A., but she isn't as likely to be attacked as a 'nice girl.' Sad, but true."

A teenage girl, who appeared to be about fifteen or sixteen and had introduced herself as "Margie," raised her hand. Savannah was a little surprised; Margie hadn't contributed a thing since the class had begun. She had sat quietly on the mat, refusing to join in the physical exercises. The girl could only be described as "bristly," due to a dozen unconventionally located body piercings, spiked orange and green hair, and a prickly adolescent attitude.

"Yes, Margie?"

"What do you think he's like . . . this Santa rapist guy?" The fear in the girl's voice belied her bold appearance and expressed the general sentiment of the room. This was the first time anyone had mentioned the real reason they had all signed up for this class. Sure, they were interested in self-defense, but if a maniac hadn't been terrorizing the community, they would have probably all been

29

home watching television sitcoms.

At least the Santa Rapist had jarred them out of their suburban complacency.

"How about that, Tam?" Savannah turned to Tammy, who was sitting behind Margie and the other students on the mat. Having demonstrated her best throwing and ball-busting techniques, Tammy had reverted to being a "girlie girl" and was brushing her long blond hair. Momentarily nonplussed to be caught primping, Tammy quickly ditched the brush, shoving it into her pocket.

"What about what?" Tammy asked.

"What about our friendly neighborhood serial rapist? Can you give us a profile on him?"

Savannah watched, amused, as Tammy's mental disk drive whirred. The young woman was living proof that looking like a blond airhead didn't make you one.

"Generally speaking," Tammy said, "a rapist is an emotionally immature individual, socially inept, with a deep inferiority complex. There are basically two types of rapists," she continued in a practiced, scholarly monotone, "psychiatric offenders and criminal offenders. If he is a psychiatric rapist, he will have an I.Q. that is higher than average, a good education, and may have achieved a high level of success. He lives in a fantasy world, his escape from the normal world where he feels inadequate. He probably

30

knows he's a sicko and may even feel guilty about it. He may worry about his victims and be ashamed of what he does to them."

"Yeah, right," Margie muttered, shaking her psychedelic-colored head.

"Do you have something to add, Margie?" Savannah asked.

The girl shrugged. "From what I read in the paper, he sounds pretty mean, like he enjoys what he's doing."

"I agree," Tammy said. "From what I've read and heard about this rapist, I would classify him as the second kind of rapist, a criminal offender, a sociopath who doesn't care who he hurts as long as he satisfies his own twisted needs. He thinks everyone else is stupid or crazy . . . not him. He's the smart one — at least in his own not-so-humble opinion."

"That's true," Savannah added. "From the victim's reports, we can assume this guy is motivated by his hatred toward women. He's dangerous, ladies. I don't want to scare you any more than you already are, but you need to know as much as possible about the enemy, to be fully prepared."

"What are you saying?" one of the softer, sweeter, Sunday-school-teacher types asked, her eyes bright with fear.

"Exactly what you think I'm saying." Savannah drew a deep breath and decided to be honest with her students. She knew the librarian was listening. The San Carmelita Recreation Department had wanted a much lighter, more upbeat, fun class than the one she was teaching. She would catch hell when the class broke up, but this wasn't the time to chocolate dip the bitter truth.

"His attacks are becoming more and more violent," she told them. "We have to arm ourselves with self-defense skills, criminal knowledge and a generous dose of plain ol' street smarts against this dangerous predator. And then we have to hope to God we don't run into him. Because he's on a frighteningly predictable path. Unless he's caught soon, it's just a matter of time until he kills one of his victims."

8:17 p.m.

Christmas bites, Charlene Yardley thought as she watched one of Santa's overgrown, slightly disgruntled elves lift a chubby-cheeked cherub onto the big guy's lap. The two-year-old shrieked. The toddler's mom yelled, "Hurry up and take the picture, stupid!" to a weary Mrs. Claus behind the camera. The bulb flashed, capturing the precious memory for all time . . . and for the nominal price of $19.95.

Charlene fought back the tears as she turned away from the mall's center with its twenty-foot tree, cotton batting snow, plywood sleigh and gilded Santa's throne. This year *he* would be taking the children . . . her children . . . to see Santa Claus. And even though no one had said so, Charlene knew that *she* would be going along, too. Just one big happy family.

Home-wrecking bitch, Charlene silently added. *May she be impaled on a reindeer's horn or choke on a plum pit in her Christmas pudding.*

As Charlene passed the Victoria's Secret window she tried not to notice the red velvet and emerald-green lace corset and stocking set in the window, tried not to remember . . . what was it he had said that day? Something like, "If you hadn't turned into a fat slob after you had the kids, if you had worn something sexy for me once in a while — like she does — I wouldn't have had to go elsewhere for it."

Okay, he hadn't said *something* like that; he had said *exactly* that. Now Charlene, who had once enjoyed wearing such things herself, couldn't see a lingerie ad or watch a diet commercial without considering suicide . . . or homicide, depending on the depth of her depression at that given moment.

Well, Miss Corset and Garters was welcome to him. It would only be a matter of time until he fooled around on her, too.

They deserved each other.

But the kids . . .

It was Christmas, and Charlene couldn't

believe how much her heart hurt to have to share the children with her soon-to-be-ex and his new honey. Her shoulders ached with the burden of packages she carried under each arm, far heavier than her credit card balance could support. The price of guilt. Guilt for not maintaining a traditional, two-parent home for her son and daughter. The price of not "meeting her man's basic needs" and "making it work."

As she passed through the food court, the buttery, chocolate-rich aroma of Mrs. Fields's cookies beckoned to her, promising a temporary sugar high to lift her sagging holiday spirit.

But what about your diet? she asked herself. *What diet?* her self promptly replied, veering toward the red and white concession. *Like those extra pounds really matter. Like, who's going to see you naked any time soon?*

The very thought of being intimate with a man made her feel sick deep inside. She, who used to *love* sex . . . the whole breathless, sweaty, passionate act. But that had been before she knew how much pain the subject could cause.

Now . . . now her idea of fleshly pleasure was a semi-sweet chocolate chip with macadamia nuts.

A few moments later, Charlene left the cookie stand with her choice in hand and dumped her packages onto a nearby table. Sinking onto the chair, she decided to rest her feet and savor the calories. If she were going to be wearing this cookie on her butt for the next umpteen months, she might as well enjoy the experience.

As the first bite hit her system, she thought of something one of the women had said in her support group the night before.

You'll get it all back, kid, and more. You'll find yourself again.

The quiet voice echoed the words from a remnant of her spirit that had survived the ravages of betrayal.

It'll take a while, but you'll land on your feet.

Charlene Yardley popped the rest of the cookie into her mouth, hefted her children's presents under her arms and headed for the mall exit. Yep, she'd make it through this mess and out the other side.

She might have gotten the wind knocked out of her, but she wasn't down for the count. Not yet. No, Miss Home Wrecker and the worthless s.o.b. she had been married to hadn't scored a KO in this fight. Not yet.

Charlene Yardley lifted her chin a couple of notches, trying her tattered garment of self-respect on for size. Okay, so it needed a little mending. But, basically, it was a good fit.

8:22 p.m.

Over an hour ago he had chosen her. She was the one tonight. Lucky lady.

35

Something about the way she held herself as she walked into the mall's front entrance — head down, shoulders drooped, as though she had recently lost some important battles — told him she wouldn't give him a hard time. And tonight he just wanted an easy, no-frills, minimal-challenge experience.

Sometimes he welcomed the fight, enjoyed the tussle, because, after all, he had the knife; he would always end up on top — so to speak. But it had been a particularly grueling day at work. He was tired. So, in making his choice, he had picked a sheep over a tigress. The only problem was: His sheep was shopping for too damned long!

Lying scrunched into a knot of tight muscles and strained nerves in the rear floorboard of her ancient Pontiac Sunbird, he was cursing the fact that he hadn't picked somebody with a roomier car interior.

But, although the broad with the Cadillac had seemed equally droopy and dispirited, she had locked all her doors. So had the gal with the Mercedes. The Sunbird chick had left the passenger door unlocked, so she had won by default.

That's right, you lucky contestant! Guess what's waiting for you behind Door Number Four!

When he had crawled into the back and shut the door behind him, his excitement level had been feverishly high. But as the clock on the dash clicked off the minutes, his ardor had cooled and his temper heated. Twenty minutes ago he had decided that when the bitch finally did show up, she was going to pay. Big time.

He lifted himself above the backs of the bucket seats, shook the pins-and-needles numbness out of his right arm, and surveyed the parking lot for what seemed like the hundredth time in an hour.

She was coming!

A jolt of adrenaline coursed through him, making his limbs weak with anticipation. Then the flow of energy took a detour due south and concentrated in his groin, where it had the exact opposite effect. Suddenly, it didn't matter how long it had taken; this was well worth waiting for. In fact, the anxiety had made the whole thing better, sharper, more acute, more real . . . the only real moment of his mundane, detached and unreal life.

But as he watched his chosen victim cross the parking lot, he noticed that her demeanor had changed slightly. She didn't look quite as meek and mild as she had before, going into the mall. In fact, she was holding her head in an arrogant, haughty manner that irritated the hell out of him.

Hoity-toity bitch needs to be brought down a notch or two, he thought. *Needs to be shown who's boss.* And what he had planned for her this evening would certainly do the trick.

He noted that she was loaded down with bags, and he wondered if the rear of the car where he was hiding was dark enough. If she tossed the sacks into the back, would she see him?

For a brief moment, he reconsidered his m.o. and decided to alter it next time. This scenario contained too many unknowns, not to mention the uncomfortable wait. But he filed it away — something to consider later when he was reliving this event, moment by delicious moment.

He was relieved when she walked to the back of the car and opened the trunk. His pulse rate rose as he listened to her place the bags inside, then slam the lid closed.

He pulled his knife from the open backpack on the floorboard beside him and gripped it tightly in his sweaty fist. He was trembling all over, but it felt good. It felt great! Control. It was all a matter of control. And he had it.

She unlocked the driver's door, swung it open and slid onto the seat. Tossing her purse onto the passenger's side of the floorboard, she sighed, and he felt that exhaled breath wash through him, hot and moist. Tuned to every nuance of her, he was acutely aware of her perfume, her body's own unique scent, and the underlying smell of chocolate — she had just eaten something like a cookie.

He waited until she had put the key into the ignition and started the car. Without making a sound, without even daring to breathe, he rose onto his knees behind her. His movements were silent, fluid . . . the perfect predator, or so he thought of himself in his deeply self-satisfied moments.

A quick glance right and left told him they were alone in this dark end of the parking lot.

It was time.

His left arm snaked around her from behind. His hand clamped over her mouth. He felt her scream against his palm as he pinched her jaws tightly.

Reaching around with his right hand, he showed her the enormous hunting knife. He felt her terror, like an exotic elixir, pouring through her body and into his. She shook violently and thrashed around, as though she were trying to turn in her seat to see him.

"Don't do it, bitch," he told her in a voice that didn't sound like his own, even to him. This voice was deeper, more guttural, darker and more demonic than anything a Hollywood sound stage could conjure. "Just keep looking straight ahead and don't scream or, I swear, I'll cut your fuckin' throat. Do you hear me?"

He put the blade of the knife against her neck, not caring whether the freshly honed edge nicked her or not. He continued to pinch her jaws tightly until he felt her body go limp in surrender.

"Do you hear me?" he repeated.

She nodded.

Slowly he removed his hand.

He saw her glance at him in her rear-view mirror. But it didn't really matter if she saw him or not. The white beard took care of that.

"Please, don't hurt me," she said in a voice so shrill and squeaky she sounded like a cartoon mouse.

He was highly amused.

"Hurt you? Well, baby, that's up to you. Are you going to be smart, or are you going to be stupid?"

She tried to speak but choked on the word.

"What?" He pressed the knife tighter to her throat.

"I said . . ." She gagged. And he decided that if she ruined this by vomiting, he was going to kill her for sure. "I said . . ." she tried again, ". . . smart. I'm going to be smart."

"That's good. You be smart, baby, and you might even live to give away all those Christmas presents you just bought."

She began to softly cry. "They're for my kids," she said.

He could tell she was trying to keep it together, struggling not to break down. Apparently, she was stronger than he had thought.

"My kids need me," she said. "Please don't hurt me. I'll do anything you say."

"Of course you will," he replied coolly. He was beginning to really enjoy the game. This was it. This was what he lived for.

"You're going to do exactly what I tell you to," he said. "Because I've got the knife. I'm the one in control. Complete control. Don't forget it."

With his left hand he reached down and caressed her breast. Softly at first, tenderly, like a lover. Then he squeezed, tighter and tighter, until he heard her gasp from the pain. He thought of the quiet, deserted orange grove. The rich smell of citrus in the cool night air.

Yes, there was a lot more pain where that had come from.

He could tell already: It was going to be a long, long night.

THREE

Only thirty more feet to the front door, Savannah told herself as she dragged her tired body up the sidewalk to her small, Spanish-style cottage. *Once you're inside, you can fall apart at the seams. You can scream, cry or just quietly pass out, and nobody but the cats will ever know.*
Ah . . . the pleasures of living alone.

As she stepped onto the porch and fingered the selections on her key ring for the one to the door, Savannah tried not to notice that her house was looking as bedraggled these days as she felt.

The chipped stucco had long ago lost its freshly painted, white glow. The bougainvillea bush, which she had named Bogey — after Humphrey — was taking over the front of the place. Any night now, a wandering tendril might snake through her upstairs bedroom window and strangle her in her sleep.

More than once, she had wondered what it would be like to have a man around the house. A Prince Charming, enchanted sword in hand, whacking back the wayward bougainvillea, then climbing through the bedroom window to claim his prize.

Unfortunately, most of the guys she met weren't exactly princes, they weren't notably charming . . . and she hadn't exactly had to bar her bedroom window against marauding, lust-besotted suitors.

Savannah had to admit: Maybe she had been a bit standoffish. Perhaps she should install a functional escalator from the sidewalk, over the porch, to that lonely, second-story window and leave it on "up" all night. Nope. There was no point in playing so hard to get.

But the moment Savannah opened her front door, she abandoned all plans of acquiring a lover. Who needed male attention when feline affection was so readily available, unconditional and uncomplicated?

Two blue-black, furry, live house-slippers entwined themselves warmly around her feet and ankles, vibrating better than any expensive gadget from a Sharper Image catalogue. And these two apparatuses operated, not on batteries, but on cans of salmon-flavored Kitty Gourmet.

"Good evening, Cleopatra, Diamante," she told the regal pair, reaching down to stroke the silky, ebony coats. They each wore rhinestone-studded black collars that glimmered in the dim porch light as they gazed up at her with emerald eyes full of adoration.

"Yeah, yeah, and if I missed a day feeding you, you'd both turn on me like a couple of ravenous jackals," she told them as she tossed her purse onto the cherry piecrust table inside the door. She headed for the kitchen and their feeding bowls, which she was fairly certain — judging from the feverish pitch of their purrs — were licked clean.

They were.

She took a tin of cat food from the cupboard and a can opener from a drawer. So much for immediate self-indulgence upon arriving home, she thought with a tired sigh as she scooped the smelly concoction into the bowls. The cats buried their faces in it, infinitely satisfied.

There, she had done her act of kindness for the animal kingdom. And now . . . a warm bubble bath in the clawfoot, Victorian tub upstairs, a cup of hot chocolate with a splash of Bailey's, a few scented candles and —

The shrill ring of the telephone extinguished her fantasy candles and burst the iridescent bubbles of her imaginary bath.

Irritated, she snatched the phone receiver off the wall. "I'm not here. I never will be again," she told her caller. "Go away."

"Sav-v-van-n-n-ah."

She wanted to hang up. Desperately. But she couldn't pretend she didn't recognize that tear-choked southern drawl. If it had been any of her other eight siblings calling, she would have slammed down the phone without even a nudge of conscience. Even big sisters had to get some credit for time served, now that her batch of younger sisters and brothers were almost all adults . . . at least legally, if not emotionally.

But Vidalia was pregnant. Extremely pregnant.

And as tired as Savannah was, she couldn't be that cruel. You just didn't hang up on a woman who was in a family way. Not one who already had one set of completely adorable, completely undisciplined, five-year-old twins.

Besides, knowing Vidalia, she would only call back.

"Hi, sweetie pie. How's your tummy?" Savannah said as she tucked the phone between her ear and shoulder and reached into the refrigerator for the milk. Even if the bath and candles were a write-off, the hot chocolate and Bailey's were still within arm's reach.

"My tummy is hu-u-u-ge!" The plaintive admission was punctuated with a long, fluid sniff. "And so's my butt. I'm the size of a barn door and gettin' bigger every day. I *hate* being pregnant!"

"Don't worry, honey. Your butt was big before you got pregnant and —"

No sooner had the words left her mouth than Savannah wanted to kick her own ample posterior from there to Sunday. But she had never received any awards for tactfulness, and she was even less diplomatic after a hard day on the job.

Fresh wailing erupted on the other end,

and Savannah felt as useful as a boll weevil in a cotton patch.

"I didn't mean that the way it came out, sugar," she said. "I just meant that we Reid gals are known for being deliciously curvaceous and voluptuous . . . whether we're with child or not."

"Well, Butch says I'm a heifer and if I don't lose all this weight as soon as the baby's born, he's gonna divorce me."

I'd be plum delighted to put a 9mm slug between his beady little eyes and save you the paperwork, Savannah thought. But this time she censored her words before they rolled off her tongue. One major faux pas per evening was enough.

"I'm sure he didn't mean a word of it," she said. "You know how men are . . ."

"Rude, selfish bastards who only care about themselves, who only worry about whether they're gonna run out of beer, and who's gonna win the World Series."

"Precisely."

Another pathetic sniff. "Do you think they're all that way, or just Butch?"

Savannah thought of her bougainvillea that needed chopping, and the proposed escalator construction in her front yard. "There has to be a good one, or two."

"Do you really think so?"

"It's hard to imagine, but there's a lot of them around. I mean, what are the odds they'd *all* be rotten?"

"So, why didn't I marry a nice one?"

Savannah sighed as she poured the milk into a glass measuring cup and stuck it into the microwave. "Because you were in love with Butch." She set the timer and punched the Start button. "You said he had a cute butt and drove his own car. Those were his two major attributes, as I remember you explaining them to me on your wedding day."

"Boy, I was sure dumb then."

"You were young, sweetie, that's all. You —"

"Yeah. I shoulda held out for Bobby Taylor. He had a *new* truck and great shoulders, too."

Savannah's fatigue gauge slid a few notches closer to exhaustion. "Vidalia, I hope you're feeling better now, because I've had a rough day and I really need to just kick back and —"

"Oh, I see. You don't have time for me either. You're so busy with your career and all that more exciting stuff. But that's okay; I understand. Don't you worry about me. No, sirree, Bob. I'll be all right . . . I always am . . ."

A vision materialized before Savannah's eyes: The blessed Saint Vidalia, tied to a stake as flames licked the hem of her robe, eyes lifted heavenward.

It made her want to barf.

As her sister sniffled on the Georgia end, Savannah removed the heated milk from the microwave and slammed the door closed. Mentally, she counted to five, collecting the fragments of her patience before replying. "I'm sure Butch didn't mean to hurt you, Vidalia," she said as she poured the milk into her favorite Old Country Roses teacup and added a generous scoop of cocoa mix. "He's the father of your children and a pretty decent dad. Besides, you married him for better and for worse."

"He's a slob."

"He doesn't beat you."

"And he snores."

"He brings home a weekly paycheck . . . most of the time."

"I have to make him get a haircut and —"

"And he doesn't fool around on you. Stop bitching, kiddo. You've got it better than most. Kiss and make up."

Louder sniffles. "We can't. We haven't had sex for ages, what with my backaches and all."

"Oh, well, no wonder the old boy's cranky," she muttered, pulling an oversized bottle of Bailey's from the liquor cabinet. "Ask him to take the twins to McDonalds for dinner, to vacuum the house, take out the garbage and give you a back massage in exchange for a blow job."

The sniffles stopped. "Do you think he'd do all that . . . just for a B.J.?"

"He's male. He hasn't had sex for ages. It's a done deal."

"Wow, good idea. You give great advice, you know, for a woman who's never had a man in her life."

Savannah grimaced and decided to call a contractor about that escalator. "Think nothing of it," she replied dryly. "Do you feel better? May I go now?"

"Oh, sure. I just heard Butch's truck in the driveway. I'm gonna ask him about . . . you know . . ."

"Good girl."

As she hung up the phone, Savannah was only marginally suicidally depressed. Of her seven sisters, all were married except the youngest, Atlanta. And even the baby of the family had a steady boyfriend who had given her a "promise" ring.

On the other hand, Savannah — the oldest, the matriarch of the Reid clan — was as single as a hag's front tooth.

Of course, that was the way she liked it: uninvolved, uncomplicated, no hassle, no dirty men's boxers on the floor . . . no deep male voice to whisper "Love you, honey," before she went to sleep at night.

It really was simpler this way.

Or so she told herself when an acute case of the "lonelies" set in.

Besides, there were very few mood dips that couldn't be raised by some form of confection.

No sooner had she taken a sip of the chocolate/liqueur concoction than the phone jangled again. Maybe she had blown it with the marital advice. Maybe Butch hadn't gone for the bait after all.

Naw. If Numb Nuts had turned Vidalia down for a B.J., she just hadn't made her intentions clear enough to seep through to his marijuana-dulled brain cells. It was definitely worth another try.

Savannah snatched up the phone. "Sweetie, I know your tummy feels like it's about to explode," she said, "and I'm sure your back hurts something awful, but I'm telling you, oral sex is the perfect solution for what —"

"I couldn't agree more. I'll be right over." Click.

Savannah frowned into the dead receiver, then slowly replaced it.

She sighed. The bubble bath would have to wait. So would the hot chocolate. She had to change the locks, bar the door and cover the windows with industrial-thick plywood.

Who said she didn't have a man in her life?

She had Dirk. Whoopee . . .

And judging from his enthusiastic tone on the phone, he'd be there in less than five minutes. Where was that hammer, those nails?

9:45 p.m.

"I thought I'd treat you to a pizza!" Dirk sounded so pleased with himself as he stood, grinning like a billy goat eating briars, on

Savannah's front porch.

"Dirk Coulter/treat. That's a contradiction in terms," she said, looking for the legendary pepperoni and mushroom pie. By the porch light she could clearly see both of his hands. They were predictably empty.

"Hey, are you implying I'm cheap?" He honestly looked crestfallen; Dirk lived in a world of self-delusion, in which he was generous, optimistic, well-dressed and articulate.

"Dirk, I love you, but you're as tight as my Granny Reid's Sunday-go-to-meetin' girdle."

"Hey, don't even kid about a thing like that . . . mentionin' me in the same sentence as women's underwear."

She grabbed his sleeve and gave it a playful yank. "Come inside and bring your imaginary pizza with you."

He trudged into the living room, his lip protruding in a semi-pout. "I really was going to call and order a pie," he said. "I got this five-dollars-off coupon, and if we don't ask for any toppings and we don't tip the delivery kid — they're always late anyway — it'll only wind up costing me a couple of bucks."

"Gee, you shouldn't have."

"I know. But I thought it was the least I could do, considering your generous offer on the phone a while ago."

"I didn't know it was you."

"That's kinda what I figured, but since

51

you offered, I thought the least I should do was show up in case you changed your mind and —"

"Forget it. It ain't happenin'. How about a beer instead?"

9:50 p.m.

It took nearly five full minutes for Charlene Yardley to realize she was still alive.

When the darkness had closed around her, bringing temporary relief from her nightmare, she had thought she was dying. And she had slipped into that black emptiness willingly, eagerly. Anything to escape. Death had become a friend.

But now Charlene could feel herself rising out of that blissful, womb-like void, in spite of her efforts to stay there. The pain in her torn, battered body, the grave-cold dampness, the residual terror that she couldn't . . . wouldn't name, were claiming her again.

She was re-awakening to her nightmare.

Through shock-dulled senses she tried to determine where she was. But all she could discern were the most elementary of sensations: pain, cold, darkness, a foul taste in her mouth, a vaguely familiar smell.

Slowly, minute by agonizing minute, Charlene realized she was lying on the ground. The taste in her mouth was a combination of dirt and her own blood. The smell was that of oranges, both fresh and rotting, nauseatingly sweet. The wet cold that had seeped through her clothing and into her aching bones was simple evening dew.

It was night. She was lying facedown in an orange grove. Her hands were bound behind her back.

What had happened to her?

Even as the confused, fear-frozen half of her brain asked the inane question, the rational, coming-to-full-consciousness half replied in a language all too clear.

She had been raped and murdered.

No, not quite murdered. But nearly.

Charlene could still see his face as he had dealt her that final blow to the head. Even through his ludicrous disguise, she had seen the wildness, the rage in his eyes.

Yes, he had fully intended to kill her. She had no doubt about that — not then, not now.

Did he think he had?

Where was he?

With that last question, a sense of urgency swept through her, and Charlene Yardley realized that she didn't really want to die after all.

Despite the pain and the spirit-crushing awareness of what had happened to her, she really, really wanted to live.

Far away — she couldn't tell how far — she could hear the occasional, faint, swooshing sound of a vehicle passing. Traffic. A road. Help.

But she had to get to it. Before he returned.

Maybe he was still there. Nearby. Watching her. Waiting for her to move.

Charlene strained to hear any movement, the intake or exhalation of breath. But the night air was filled with the peaceful sounds of the grove: crickets chirping, a frog's croak, the hoot of a distant owl . . . and that promising hum of the traffic.

When a louder, deeper rumble signaled the passing of a truck, she felt the vibrations in the ground beneath her. The road had to be fairly close. If she could only get to it.

She willed herself to rise, but with her hands bound, she couldn't even move. Her limbs refused to obey her brain's commands. Her body seemed no longer her own.

But it *was* hers. The pain told her that much. And if she could hurt, she should be able to move.

For what seemed like forever, she strained at the cord that bound her wrists. At first, it did no good; in fact, her efforts only seemed to make the knots tighter. But as she continued to twist, one way, then the other, she could feel her left hand slipping free. Something wet and slick, maybe her own blood, made it easier. Finally, she wrenched it free.

Now able to fold her right arm, she managed to get it beneath her. But when she tried to rise, to place her weight on it, a pain — like nothing she had ever felt — shot through her, lightning hot, white, blinding.

And when the searing brightness faded, Charlene was — thanks to the overloading and short-circuiting of her sensory receptors — once again, in darkness.

And for a little while longer, her nightmare was on hold.

FOUR

"That old Santa fart didn't mean it when he said he was going to sue me . . . did he?" Savannah stared into the foam of her beer as though it were a fortune teller's crystal ball. After a particularly rough day, the alcohol contained in even one brew could push her paranoia level to clinically certifiable levels.

She and Dirk sat in their usual TV-watching, pizza-eating, beer-drinking positions. Savannah was cuddled into her cushy, floral chintz, wingback chair. Like her, it was a bit overstuffed and infinitely comfortable. On her footstool, Diamante and Cleopatra were curled in black furry balls at either side of her feet. Kitty bookends, she liked to call them.

Dirk was stretched across the sofa. In ancient Roman style, he preferred to conduct his culinary orgies sprawled and horizonal. He had already consumed six slices of his economy pizza. With typical generosity, he had allotted Savannah two.

Dirk sniffed and took a long slug of beer from his bottle, then set it on the coffee table. After seven years Savannah still hadn't trained him to use a glass or a coaster or to leave the toilet seat down. Having Dirk around the house was a bit like owning a husband, Savannah had decided, but without the added fringe benefits of regular sex, lawn care and automobile maintenance. The price without the perks.

"So," he said, "you're worried about getting sued by the Santa with the blue balls. I'd worry too, if I was you. He sounded like he meant it."

Dirk never pulled punches with her. It was his greatest charm . . . and the major reason she often wanted to strangle him.

"How could you tell? Maybe he was just a little —"

"Nope, he meant it. His eyes were bugged out. Way out! That's a definite sign of sincerity. I learned a long time ago from doing interrogations: When the veins in a guy's forehead are poppin', he's usually telling you the truth."

Savannah sighed and thought of all the overdue bills in her desk drawer — scary red-lettered documents threatening to disconnect or repossess some basic creature comfort. The last thing she needed right now was to be sued, by anyone, and especially Saint Nick.

Being a private investigator could prove lucrative from time to time, but more often, detecting provided only a meager existence. Savannah missed the steady paycheck from the S.C.P.D., the medical and dental coverage, the Christmas fund and the all-you-can-eat-and-drink Fourth of July picnic. But she didn't miss the department's lopsided politics or the constant hassle from the suits. Life hadn't been easy as an outspoken, brassy broad who had never quite perfected the fine art of kissing trouser backsides.

No . . . when all was said and done, Savannah was content with her present lot in life; she'd rather be broke.

"So, let Kris Kringle sue me," she said. "I can't imagine that he would welcome headlines that read, 'P.I. Gives Santa Blue Balls.' How's he going to explain that he was ripping a woman's shirt off in the parking lot five minutes before he was going to be sitting on the gilded throne, bouncing kiddies on his knee?"

Dirk took another slurp of suds. "You're right. The mall wouldn't like that either. But they're not going to be hiring you for surveillance again any time soon. That's gonna cause a problem."

"Yeah. It was my only paying gig, and the electric bill's seriously overdue."

"Oh, well, sorry about your cash flow, but I was worried about my investigation. I was hoping you and Fluff Head would help me nab my guy."

"Thanks for your concern," Savannah replied dryly, "and don't call her that. Tammy's a good kid."

"She acted like a nitwit today and opened you up for a lawsuit. Now you're defending her. You're both a bit screwy if you ask me."

"I didn't ask you. And now that you've insulted my employee and me, I'm not going to lift one dainty pinky to help you with this case. You can catch your Santa Rapist without assistance from the bimbos at Moonlight Magnolia Detective Agency."

"You were going to help me . . . even without being paid?"

His jaw and every ounce of flesh attached to it dropped several inches. He couldn't have looked more forlorn if he had just been told that his new cocker spaniel puppy had to have triple bypass surgery.

"You were going to give me a hand with this case . . . for free?"

"That's right, big boy. An honest-to-goodness freebie, for old time's sake and all that. But you had to open your smart mouth and throw it all away. Now ain't that a bite in the ass."

He snapped his mouth closed. A muscle twitched in his jaw.

"So, what's it gonna cost me?" he said. "Exactly how do you want me to suck up?"

She batted her eyelashes at him. "Why, darlin', what makes you think I want you to 'suck up' as you so indelicately put it?"

"Because you're a dame. And dames always want us to suck up. They expect us to kiss their lily white butts and admit what a jerk we've been."

Savannah pictured it for a moment: Dirk on his knees, looking oh-so-humble, her skirt lowered just enough on one side to accommodate the penitent kiss. His lips warm and soft as —

She shuddered.

"Naw . . . that's all right. We'll skip the butt kissing part. Just admit you were a jerk, do some sincere grovelling for the rest of the evening, and we'll call it even."

10:05 p.m.

Angie Perez searched the car's glove box for the box of mints she had stashed there for just this occasion — when her boyfriend, Brett, was bringing her home drunk. Her mom would probably be in bed, but just in case, she'd better not walk through the door reeking of tequila, thanks to the four margarita grandes she'd downed at Brett's brother's house.

Brett had drunk at least five. And he was driving.

Angie had tried to be responsible. She had asked him if they could take a cab or call one of their friends to give them a lift home.

But Brett had been royally pissed at the very idea that she thought he couldn't handle his booze. He was touchy about subjects like how fast he drove, how much he drank, and whether he was the best she'd ever had in bed.

He wasn't. And she was tired of trying to convince him he was.

All in all, Angie had just about had it with Brett; she was seriously considering dumping him. After the Christmas and New Year's Eve parties, of course. Angie knew she was cute. And she was pretty sure that if she gave him the boot on January 2nd, she'd be able to fill the vacancy before Valentine's Day.

"Hey, you're weaving all over the place," she told him when he missed a particularly tight turn on Forest Hill Road. There weren't any forests — just smoldering brush, compliments of the afternoon's fire — and not much of a hill, but Forest Hill Road was the best route for getting across town if you'd had a few too many. Oh, it was poorly lit and fairly curvaceous, winding its way between lemon, avocado and orange ranches. A challenge to drive. But for the most part, cops didn't patrol this stretch after nine in the evening, so it was the choice of the inebriated.

"Slow down, Brett," she said, gouging him in the ribs. "Remember what happened to those sophomores last semester."

"They were idiots. They deserved to die."

Brett had a real way with words, she decided, not to mention his sensitivity.

Yes, he was definitely going to get dumped come January. Being a blond, blue-eyed varsity team quarterback only got you so far.

They rounded a curve and at the edge of the headlight's beams, just ahead on the left side of the road, Angie thought she saw something move. Something white. An animal maybe? A big animal.

It was crawling. Slowly. As though it were hurt.

"Brett. Look at that. Over there."

Brett looked, but he seemed to be having trouble focusing. "What? I don't see nothin'. What are you talking about?"

"There. At the edge of the grove. I think it's a dog that's been hit, or . . . ?"

They drew nearer. Another twenty feet and she could tell what it was.

"Oh, my god, Brett. It's a person. A woman. And she's naked!"

Ordinarily, she would have expected Brett to exhibit an acute interest in a nude female. But instead of stopping, he stomped on the accelerator and his father's ancient Oldsmobile shot forward.

In half a second they had left the naked, crawling woman behind.

"What are you doing? Couldn't you tell she's hurt?" Angie turned in her seat and craned her neck, but she couldn't see much in the red afterglow of the taillights. "Brett, go back! We have to help her!"

"No way. I'm not getting involved in anything like that. Who knows what happened to her? It could have been anything, any kind of trouble."

"That's right. That's why we have to help her. She looks hurt. She may need to go to the hospital!"

Angie punched him in the biceps and tried to grab at the wheel, but Brett shoved her hand away. "I'm not stopping; do you hear me? We've both had too much to drink and I'm driving. If I get another ticket, the judge said he'd suspend my license."

"But —"

"No buts. If that woman got herself in trouble, it's her problem. It's not going to be mine."

At a fork in the road, he slowed a bit and Angie yanked her door open.

"What the hell are you doing?" he shouted. "Close the damned door before you fall out!"

"Stop the car! I'm going to go back and help her, even if you won't!"

He slammed on the brakes, throwing her against the dash. "So, go ahead and get out. I want you out of my car!"

She jumped out before he could change his mind.

"You're stupid, you know that?" he yelled.

"You're really, really stupid."

"Yeah, and you're an asshole."

It was only after she had closed the door behind her that Angie realized her predicament, standing there on a dark road in the middle of nowhere.

"At least call the cops!" she shouted as he pulled away. "Brett, please! When you get home, make a phone call! One lousy call, please!"

But he had already peeled out and amid the squeal of his tires and the roar of the Oldsmobile's eight-cylinder engine, Angie wasn't sure if he had heard her or not.

Even in the dark, with only the light of a half moon, Angie could tell that the woman was badly beaten. Her face was horribly swollen and smeared with something black which Angie assumed was blood. The victim lay on her side at the edge of the road, curled into a fetal position.

"It's okay," the teenager told her, assuming the role of mother/comforter. "You're going to be okay now."

Angie wasn't wearing a coat, only a thin sweater with her new pusher-upper bra underneath. But she quickly determined that this poor woman needed the garment more than she did. She peeled it off and tried to put it on the shivering woman, but she thrashed her arms and hit Angie in the mouth.

Even though the blow smarted and Angie could taste blood from a cut inside her lip, she knew the woman was too traumatized to know what she was doing.

"That's all right," Angie said. "You don't have to wear it. But let me wrap it around you; you're freezing."

The victim quieted down a bit, submitting to being wrapped.

"What happened to you?" Angie asked, casting a few furtive glances at the dark grove behind them. "Who did this to you? Is he still around?"

The woman tried to answer, but her teeth were chattering so hard that Angie couldn't understand her. All she could make out was something that didn't make any sense . . . something about Santa.

Then, it *did* make sense.

Perfect sense.

Angie Perez began to shiver, too, and it had nothing to do with the citrus-scented, cold night air on her bare skin.

This woman was the Santa Rapist's latest victim. And for all Angie knew, the guy was still there in those dark trees, watching, listening. For all she knew, he wasn't finished for the night. And she was here on this lonely road, shivering in her bra, with his shattered victim at her feet.

For all Angie knew, Brett had been right, after all, and she was stupid, putting herself in a position like this.

The woman on the pavement groaned and tried to mouth some words through her swollen, bleeding lips.

Angie bent closer and stroked her hair. She could feel dirt embedded in her scalp and something wet and sticky . . . probably more blood. "What is it?" she asked her. "What are you trying to say?"

"Th— . . . thank . . . you."

Tears sprang to Angie's eyes and, although she was still fully aware of her dangerous situation, she wouldn't have chosen be anywhere else at that moment.

"You're welcome," she said. "You're very, very welcome."

She looked right, then left, up and down the empty road and whispered a prayer of thanks that God had brought her here tonight and allowed her to help one of His children who was so badly in need. Then she quickly added a request that stupid, asshole Brett had found an ounce of compassion in his heart and made that phone call.

10:14 p.m.

"How about all the registered S.O.s in the area?" Savannah asked, knowing what Dirk would say. He was a good cop who knew the basics, like checking out any local sex offenders. Most rapes were committed by repeat

66

offenders. And law enforcement figured that the average rapist attacked at least fourteen victims before getting caught.

A very nasty habit.

"We've got a couple of possibles," Dirk said, munching the last piece of cold pizza. "But they're both chicken hawks, and kiddie pervs don't usually cross over to attacking full-grown women."

"True. What have you got from the victims? Any common acquaintances?"

"Nope. No link, except that they were all snatched out of the mall parking lot."

"That's got to be bad for mall business. It's probably a downtown merchant trying to divert some of the Christmas sales."

"Hey, I hadn't thought of that."

"I was kidding. Sorry, a bad joke." Savannah thought about the victims and their families for whom Christmas would never be the same. For years, the city of San Carmelita would be different; fear changed everything. Soberly, she said, "You're looking for a guy who's probably in his late teens to mid-thirties, attractive and —"

"Attractive?"

"Sure. Haven't you noticed? Most rapists are good-looking dudes who wouldn't have any problem picking up a woman. But I suppose having the woman's consent would ruin the fun."

"I never understood rape mentality." Dirk

shook his head thoughtfully. "When a woman says, 'No! Oh, God, no!' it's a real turnoff for me."

Savannah stared at him for a moment. "I'm so glad to hear that, Dirk." She cleared her throat. "As I was saying . . . an attractive young man, above average intelligence and a decent job and his neighbors think he's a great guy."

"Gee, that narrows it down."

"Oh, yeah . . . and he likes to dress up like Santa."

"Mmmm . . . if he got off by dressing like *Mrs.* Santa or the elves . . . then we'd have something."

10:28 p.m.

Through a haze of semi-consciousness and pain, Charlene Yardley could hear the male voice . . . his voice. He was back.

"Don't move. Lie still," he was saying.

Large hands . . . a man's hands gripped her shoulders, holding her down. She fought against him as she swam her way to the surface of full consciousness. "Do you hear me? Be still," he told her as he pinned her to the cold wet ground.

Not again! She wouldn't let him do it again. She would die first. "No!" she screamed, but her own voice sounded weak, barely a croak in her throat. "Get away . . .

away . . . from me."

The fingers tightened, pinching her flesh that was already bruised. "You're going to hurt yourself," he said. "Don't move."

Another voice in the darkness. Softer, like an angel's. A woman. "It's okay," she said. "You're safe now. He's just trying to help you."

Charlene tried to open her eyes. But one was so swollen she couldn't see out of it, and the other felt as though it were on fire.

The man over her looked different from her attacker. This man wasn't wearing a beard or red hat. He was young and clean shaven, and his hat was dark. She was dimly aware of lights flashing over him, over them — red lights, blue lights.

She was still lying on the ground, and he was kneeling over her. Behind him was the girl with the angel's face, the girl who had come to her first . . . was it hours ago?

"I'm a police officer, ma'am," he was saying in a gentle, consoling tone. "My name is Officer Dunn. I've called an ambulance for you. It's on its way."

Charlene started to cry as she realized her rapist hadn't come back to kill her after all. Help had come. The help she had prayed for.

"My arm," she said. "I think he broke my arm." Every word, every movement of her mouth brought stabs of new miseries.

"I'm sorry, but that's why you need to lie still," he said, "or you might make it worse. We'll get you to a hospital right away, and they'll give you something for the pain."

The girl moved to Charlene's other side and knelt in the dirt. Her dark hair spilled around her pretty face as she bent over and took Charlene's hand in hers.

"Here. Hold my hand," she said. "Everything's going to be all right. You'll see." The girl's fingers were warm and comforting, and the touch went straight to Charlene's heart.

"He . . . he hurt me," she said between sobs.

"I know. There, there . . . it's okay." The girl stroked her hair as she had before, and even though the teenager was only a few years older than her own kids, Charlene felt as vulnerable as a child.

"I . . . I thought he killed me, but then I woke up."

The police officer released his hold on her and peeled off his jacket. He handed it to the girl. "Here," he said, "put this on. We don't want our Good Samaritan freezing to death."

As the girl slipped into the coat, he turned back to Charlene. "I hate to have to ask you questions at a time like this, ma'am, but I need to know: Did you get a good look at the man who attacked you?"

Charlene forced herself to speak in spite of the pain. "No, wore a beard . . . red hat, like Santa."

The policeman nodded. "Was he a white guy, black . . . latino?"

"White, I think. Was dark and . . ."

"About what size?"

"Wh— . . . what?"

"Was he tall or short?"

"Don't know. Bigger . . . than me. Can't talk now . . . hurts to breathe."

"That's okay. We'll take your statement later." He patted her shoulder, but his eyes were scanning the scene. Standing, he pulled a flashlight from his belt and began playing the powerful beam back and forth across the ground in ever-widening swaths. "You just rest," he said. "It's all over now."

"No," Charlene whispered. "Not over."

The girl leaned closer, placing her ear near Charlene's mouth. "What did you say?" she asked.

An emotional abyss swallowed Charlene Yardley and she felt herself falling, tumbling headfirst into an ever-darkening blackness. "This . . . will never . . . never be over."

FIVE

"Paranoia over the Santa Claus Rapist reached new heights this evening," the channel seven newscaster announced as blithely as if she were hawking corn dogs at a ball game, "when a local shopping mall Santa was viciously attacked by an over-zealous member of mall security."

Savannah's eyes bugged and her jaw dropped as she stared at the screen. "Oh, man . . . tell me this isn't happening."

"It's happening," Dirk replied with a sniff and a snort, then he took a long last chug from his beer bottle.

"You're a lot of help." Savannah covered her eyes with her hands, but peeked through her fingers. "Tell me when it's over."

The anchor's far-too-cheery account continued over footage of the mall's front lot where the incident had occurred. "In a display of true holiday spirit, Henry Wilcox, a.k.a. Kris Kringle, was attempting to aid a young woman in the parking lot, when an unidentified —"

"Unidentified," Savannah whispered, "thank God."

72

"— mall guard administered a swift kick to Mr. Wilcox's groin. Wilcox's doctor says that, due to the delicate nature of his injuries, Mr. Wilcox will be unable to perform his duties as Santa for the remainder of the holiday season."

Dirk nodded solemnly. "Yeah, with nuts the size of basketballs, you wouldn't want kids squirming around on your lap."

"Shut up, Coulter," she snapped, glaring at him through her fingers. "You don't need to state the obvious."

"It's over."

She dropped her hands. "Gee, thanks."

"I told you, that dude's gonna sue you. You can't mess with a man's gonads like that. You hit a guy where he lives and he'll come after you, one way or the other."

The phone rang and Savannah groaned. "That's probably him now." She stepped into the kitchen and plucked the receiver from the wall. "Hello. Yes, this is Savannah Reid." She listened, frowning. "No, no comment."

She hung up and trudged back to the living room where she plopped into her chair. Dirk gave her a questioning look. "A reporter from the *Star*," she said, "wanting to know if I'm the unidentified guard. I'll be front page headline by morning."

He smirked. "It won't be the first time."

"I know. It's getting harder and harder to remain a *private* detective in this town." She heard something vibrating and jumped up from her chair. "What the hell's that?"

"You're sure strung tight. It's just my butt buzzing." He reached down to his belt and unsnapped his pager. Peering at the display, he muttered, "Shit."

"Who is it?"

"Captain Bloss. And he's used the 666 code."

"Mmmm . . . 666." She raised one eyebrow. "Those are some pretty ominous digits. What do they mean?"

The thought occurred to Savannah that, all of a sudden, Dirk looked even more tired than she felt. No easy feat.

"They mean," he said, "you're going to get bumped from tomorrow morning's headline. That son of a bitch has raped another one."

11:27 p.m.

When Savannah and Dirk arrived at the crime scene, the orange grove looked as though it had been invaded by a flock of alien spacecraft — a dozen squad cars lining the sides of the road, blue and red lights flashing eerily.

Savannah pulled Dirk's old Buick onto the shoulder near the center of the hubbub. As they climbed out of the car, she saw Patrolman Mike Farnon and his partner Jake McMurtry, two of her favorite ex-compatriots.

Mike's round face glowed when he spotted

her. "Hey, Savannah!" he shouted. "Haven't seen you since the Fourth of July barbecue. You're looking good."

She gave him a dimpled grin and a wink. "Ah . . . you silken-tongued laddie, you're just sayin' that because it's true."

Jake slapped her shoulder, hard enough to hurt. She accepted the gesture as a compliment, establishing her as "one of the boys." "What are you doing here?" he said. "Don't tell me you're this old fart's date." He pointed at Dirk, who was still strolling around, checking out the scene.

"No, but he was the designated drunk at our late-night beer and pizza orgy," she said. "Somebody had to drive him here."

Dirk joined them, wearing his "I Mean Business, Suckers" scowl. "So, guys . . . what've we got?"

Jake nodded to the nearest radio car and a teenage girl who sat, shivering, in the backseat. The door was open and her feet were hanging out. A large jacket — a cop's uniform coat — was draped around her shoulders. "The girl over there . . ." he said, ". . . the pretty Latina. She and her boyfriend were driving by about 2200 hours and spotted the victim crawling, naked, by the side of the road. The girl got out to help her. The boyfriend drove on . . . didn't want to get involved."

"Nice guy," Savannah muttered.

"Yeah, right. But he did call it in when he got home."

Dirk gave an unimpressed grunt. "So, the mayor will pin a rose on his nose."

"Is the victim at the hospital?" Savannah asked.

"Yeah, the ambulance just left."

"How is she?"

Jake looked like he might be feeling a bit queasy. "Not great. Her arm's broken, maybe some ribs."

"And her face is pretty mashed up," Mike added, looking equally sick.

"Were you two the first to respond?" Dirk asked.

"Not the first. We were on a possible liquor store burglary over by the high school. Titus got here first. He'd just come on duty."

"Where's he?"

"He's been searching the grove since we got here." Mike pointed into the orchard where a lone figure was combing the ground with a flashlight beam.

"Did he string the tape?"

"Yeah. He had the perimeter set up when we arrived."

"Good man." Dirk waved a hand toward the teenager in the backseat of the patrol car. "Has anyone questioned the girl?"

"I think Titus talked to her, but we told her you'd want to speak to her, so she's been waiting around."

"Whose jacket is she wearing?" Savannah asked.

"Titus gave her his. Seems she put her sweater on the victim. The kid was freezing when he got here."

"Thanks guys," Dirk said. "Keep these people back behind the line, especially the reporters, and let me know when Bloss gets here."

Dirk headed toward the unit and Savannah followed.

"What makes you think the captain's coming?" Jake called after them.

"Are you kidding?" Savannah replied over her shoulder. "We've got television cameras here, and Bloss is still working on his fifteen seconds of fame."

Savannah felt a mini-surge of affection for Dirk as she watched him drop to one knee beside the open car door to talk to Angie Perez. His street-worn face softened, and he dropped the brusque, tough guy tone of voice when he interviewed victims or traumatized witnesses.

After being his partner for seven years and his friend for ten, Savannah knew all his secrets . . . like that he would get teary-eyed over an abandoned puppy. And the guy couldn't be all bad if he liked cats.

She leaned over the open car door and listened as he spoke to the distraught teenager. "Your name is Angie, right?" he said.

The girl nodded.

"I hear you did a good thing, helping the victim," he said as he fished a tattered tissue out of his jacket pocket and handed it to her.

"I don't know how much I helped," the girl replied between sniffs. "I hope she's going to be okay. Have you heard how she is?"

"No, I haven't," Dirk said. "But I'll call the hospital in a little while and I'll let you know, okay?"

"Thanks."

"And how about you?" Savannah asked her, touched by the teenager's concern for the victim. Who said kids didn't have a heart these days? "Are you going to be okay, sweetie?"

"Yeah. I guess so." Angie dabbed at her eyes and the dark streaks of mascara dripping down her cheeks. "I mean . . . I don't know why I'm crying. I wasn't the one who . . . That poor lady."

Savannah reached over and stroked the girl's hair as though she were one of her younger sisters. "You're crying because you have a heart, kiddo, and it hurts to see something like that."

"I guess you guys get used to it," she said, hiccuping, "but that's the first time I've ever . . ."

Dirk looked down and brushed some dirt off the knee of his jeans. "We don't get used to it either," he said quietly, "if that makes you feel any better."

He waited while Angie blew her nose and composed herself, then he said, "Do you feel up to telling me what happened?"

"I already told the policeman, the one who got here first and helped me with the lady."

"I know. I'm sorry, but if you could go over it again, I'd really appreciate it."

As the teenager began to relate the details of her experience, Savannah noticed a crowd of spectators beginning to form at the periphery of the scene. Leaving Dirk to question his witness, she walked slowly along the edge of the group, studying each face. Many times, the perpetrator of a crime returned to the scene and watched the aftermath unfold, mentally wallowing in the carnage he had created. Savannah had learned, long ago, to search the spectators for suspects.

One young man in particular caught her attention. He was a young, blond fellow, about Angie's age, wearing a football letterman's jacket and a guilty-as-hell look on his handsome face. He was staying well to the back of the crowd, his eyes trained on the patrol car where Dirk was questioning Angie.

As Savannah approached him, she decided to take a verbal stab in the dark and see if she could draw a little blood. She smelled the booze on his breath as she leaned close to him and said, "Your girlfriend's doing her duty as a citizen. Why don't you be a man and go do the same?"

"What?" He turned to Savannah and glared at her with as much concentrated focus as his bleary vision would allow.

She decided his confusion was as fake as a five-dollar alligator-skin purse.

"You heard me," she said, "and you know exactly what I'm talking about. You're Angie Perez's boyfriend, the one who called this in. At least tell them what you saw."

He glanced around furtively and lowered his voice to a stage whisper. "Get away from me, lady. I didn't see anything. I don't know what you're talking about."

Savannah shrugged. "Have it your way," she said as she walked away. "But if that detective who's talking to Angie has to come to you rather than vice versa, he's not gonna be his usual charming self."

She walked to her car, opened the trunk and took out a small camera. Systematically, she began to take pictures of the crowd, working from one end of the group to the other. Dirk would comb them later, identifying as many individuals as possible.

"Hey, Reid! What the hell are *you* doing here?" said a male voice with an irritating, nasal twang directly into her right ear.

Savannah braced herself and turned to face the one human being she despised most in the world. As far as she was concerned, Captain Harvey Bloss had worked hard to ascend to that high-level position on her personal shit list. In the interest of fair play, she had bestowed the honor judiciously — no one deserved it more.

"Now, what do you suppose I'm doin', sugar?" she said, far too sweetly. "I'm gawking, like everybody else. Fortunately there's no law against that."

Bloss gave her a drop-dead look that matched her own degree of animosity. "Get out of here, Reid," he said with a long, liquid snort that made Savannah shudder. "You've got no business hanging around a crime scene."

Bloss wasn't a particularly attractive man, even without the disgusting mannerisms. He wasn't overweight, but he had a pudgy, bloated look about him that indicated, perhaps, a lack of sleep and excessive alcohol consumption. He peered at the world through squinted, suspicious little eyes, and the only time he actually made eye contact was when he was trying to intimidate someone.

But, mostly, he just irritated the crap out of her and she loved returning the aggravation. Having the opportunity to irk him made her day.

She lifted one eyebrow. "Excuse me? This is a public street I'm standing on and, thanks to you, I'm now Jane Q. Public, so I'm right where I belong."

"Go home, Reid."

"Go to hell, Bloss. Go directly to hell. Do not pass Go, do not collect two hundred dollars."

"How juvenile."

She wrinkled her nose as though she had just caught a whiff of a week-old road-killed skunk. "Yeah? Well . . . nanny, nanny, boo, boo. And your mother dresses you funny, too."

Bloss gave her a condescending look that made her want to slap him stupid, then he walked away, heading for the car where Dirk was questioning Angie.

Lucky Dirk, she thought as she watched Bloss, mentally calculating the length of the proverbial stick up his butt. Why else would someone walk that stiffly? Or maybe it was a simple case of deficient dietary fiber.

She heard a girlish giggle behind her right shoulder. The titterer stepped forward, and Savannah recognized the outlandish orange and green spiked hair. It was the punked-out kid from her self-defense class.

"Oh, hi, Margie," she said, embarrassed that she had appeared so unprofessional in front of a student. "Sorry you overheard that. I don't usually talk to law-enforcement officials like that, but I sorta hate that guy."

"Me too. What did he do to *you?*"

"It's a long story. What do you mean, you hate him, too? What did Captain Bloss do to you?"

Probably had her arrested for drugs or shop-lifting, Savannah thought, as she checked out the leather clothing, trimmed with metal studs and the pierced lip, cheek, nose and eyebrows. Then she reminded herself that not every kid who dressed like a weirdo was a criminal . . . just lacking in taste.

"He left me and my mother for another woman," the girl said, "when I was ten years old."

Savannah's jaw dropped half way to her chest. "What? Bloss is your dad?"

"Yeap. Sucks, huh?"

Savannah shook her head, trying to rearrange her scrambled brain waves. "Wow! I didn't even know he had a kid."

Margie laughed, but there wasn't much humor in the sound. "That's a scary thought, huh? A jerk like him procreating? My mom should've had him spayed on their honeymoon."

Savannah studied the teenager's face. Her expression was belligerent, but, beneath all the exaggerated makeup, her eyes were full of sadness. "Not necessarily," Savannah said. "You seem like a nice kid."

"Naw, I'm a brat. Ask anybody who knows me."

While they had been talking, Bloss had made his rounds and returned with Officer Titus Dunn in tow. Bloss fixed his daughter with one of his classic glares which was, un-

83

doubtedly, intended to instill fear and intimidation. Margie glared back, the picture of adolescent rebellion.

"What the hell are you doing here?" he asked her.

"You need to hire somebody to write you some new lines," Savannah muttered, recalling his earlier greeting to her.

Titus started to grin, but swallowed the smile when Bloss shot him a warning glance.

"I was looking for *you*," Margie told her father, her demeanor as bristly as her hair.

"How did you know I'd be here?" he snapped.

"I was in the kitchen when you took the call. I heard you say where you were going, so later, I decided to —"

"What do you want?"

"Money," his daughter returned, her tone turning as curt and hostile as his.

"Why?"

"Does it matter?"

"Hell, yes, it matters."

She sighed and rolled her eyes heavenward. "I'm going out with Meg, okay?"

"Where?"

"Don't know yet, but I need some cash."

"No."

Margie's face flushed angrily. She stuck out her open hand, ramming it against her father's chest. "Give me the fucking money!" she screamed. "No-o-o-ow!"

84

Savannah glanced over at Titus, who was also watching the bizarre exchange with amazement. Neither of them dared to breathe.

Having been raised Southern style, at the end of a hickory stick, Savannah couldn't comprehend such blatant defiance.

Bloss glowered at his daughter for what seemed like an eternity as his face turned as dark as hers. He was huffing and puffing like a disgruntled bulldog, his meaty fists clinched at his sides.

But the girl didn't budge.

Finally, he reached into his pocket and pulled out his wallet. "There!" He tossed a handful of bills at her. "Now get out of here, and stay with your friends. Don't go anywhere alone."

Margie gave him a sarcastic, self-satisfied smirk and walked away, clutching her cash to her chest.

"When are you coming home?" he called after her.

"When I get damned good and ready," she yelled back as she climbed into the driver's seat of a new, ice-blue, BMW convertible nearby.

The Roadster took off, spinning its wheels in the roadside gravel. Savannah cleared her throat and shook her head thoughtfully as they watched the car disappear around a curve. "Well, well . . ." she said, ". . . darned kids these days. Sometimes, they just won't do ya proud."

SIX

December 11 — 12:30 a.m.

If Savannah and Dirk had been concerned about the latest rape victim's security, all their worries evaporated when they saw Officer Morton O'Leary stationed outside her hospital room. King Kong himself couldn't have charged through that door, even with Godzilla as a backup.

When Savannah and Dirk passed through, Savannah flashed O'Leary a friendly, open smile and received only a perfunctory grunt in return.

Six-foot-four, three-hundred-pound Officer O'Leary's steel-trap mind might have been a tad rusty in the hinges, but he took his job as first line defense very seriously. And if his sheer bulk weren't deterrent enough, he carried a .357 Magnum as a side arm and a billy club the size of a California redwood. No one got past Morton O'Leary; no one even tried.

Once inside the private room, Savannah and Dirk saw a sweet-faced nurse who was sitting on a chair beside the bed, watching over her charge with obvious concern.

"How is she?" Dirk asked as he looked down at the woman who was lying still, eyes closed, her head swathed in bandages, her right arm in a cast. Both of her wrists bore the dark, tell-tale lines, indicative of having been bound. The lower half of her face, that showed below the wrappings, was grotesquely swollen and splotched with patches of red, black, and purple bruising.

Savannah winced, unable to even imagine how that sort of beating would have hurt. The victim looked like someone who had been involved in a violent traffic accident. But her situation was all the more horrific because it had been some sick individual's intention, not Fate's intervention that had put her here.

"She's asleep," the nurse said. "She has been for the past hour."

"Has she said anything?" Savannah asked, thinking that the woman's face was so badly contorted that she would surely be unrecognizable to her loved ones. It would require plastic surgery to put her right again. And those were just the physical injuries. The emotional scars would be permanent.

"She just told us that her name is Charlene Yardley," the nurse replied. "And she asked us to call her ex-husband."

"Did you?" Dirk asked.

"Yeah." The nurse lowered her voice and added, "He wouldn't come, the jerk. But he gave me her sister's number. I called her, and she's on her way."

"I wanted to ask her some questions," Dirk said, "but if she's sleeping, I . . ."

"She needs the rest, poor baby." Savannah patted Charlene's hand, noting the torn nails and skinned knuckles. Apparently, she had put up some sort of defense. "That bastard really put her through the mill."

Charlene's eyelids flickered. "Mama?" she whispered through cracked, puffy lips.

Savannah leaned close to her. "What, honey? Did you say something?"

"Mama?" she murmured again.

Savannah shot a quick look at Dirk and the nurse. Dirk gave her a nod. "I'm right here, sweetheart," she said. "You're going to be fine. Everything's going to be just fine."

Charlene's eyes fluttered again and this time she opened one just a crack and looked up at Savannah. When she closed it, tears slid down both her cheeks and she began to cry. "You aren't my mom," she said between sobs.

Savannah's heart ached. "I wish I were," she said softly. "Your sister's on her way here to see you."

"Oh, great . . . that's all I need. My sister's stupid and a drunk."

Savannah gulped. So much for close family ties. "Do you want me to try to find your mom for you?"

At the suggestion, Charlene only cried harder. "You can't," she said. "My mama's dead."

"Oh, I'm sorry." Having struck out twice, Savannah was reluctant to swing a third time, but she had to ask, "Why did you think I was your mother?"

"You . . . you sound like her."

"Oh." The light dawned. "Was your mom from down South?"

"Savannah, Georgia."

"Well, if that ain't a coincidence. My *name* is Savannah. Is that close enough?"

At least Charlene had stopped crying. That was a step in the right direction. So, Savannah decided to press a little further. "This detective who came in with me . . . his name is Dirk Coulter . . . he needs to ask you a few questions. Do you feel up to it?"

At the mention that a man was in the room, a look of fear crossed Charlene's battered features. "No," she said adamantly. "I don't want to talk to him."

Dirk took a step back from the bed. "Van, maybe if you do it . . ." he said.

Savannah nodded and stroked Charlene's fingers. "Do you feel like talking to me?" she asked in her most beguiling tone. "Just for a couple of minutes. If you get too tired, we'll quit."

She hesitated, then said, "Okay."

"Did you see the man who attacked you?"

"Yes . . . well . . . sorta."

89

"What did he look like?"

"He wore a beard, a big white one, like Santa. But it was fake. It slid around when he was . . . you know . . . when he was raping me."

Savannah glanced over at Dirk, who was suddenly all ears. "When the beard slipped," she said, "did you happen to see his face?"

"Not really. Not enough to tell anything."

"Do you know if he was Caucasian, or black, or Hispanic, or — ?"

"The other policeman asked me that, too."

"I'm sorry, but I have to ask again. Just in case you might remember something else."

"It was dark. But I think he was white."

"What else was he wearing, besides the beard?"

"A black shirt, like a sweatshirt . . . and I think . . . jeans."

Savannah thought for a moment. "Did the shirt have any words or pictures on it?"

"No."

Of course not, Savannah thought. That would have been too easy. Oh, well, it was worth a try. Your average criminal wasn't known for his high intelligence quotient and more than one had been nabbed because he had committed his particular crime dressed in a T-shirt that said something like, "Dudley Trucking — Bowling Champion 1979."

"Could you see the color of his hair?" she asked.

"No. He was wearing a red and white hat, like Santa Claus."

"How big a guy was he?"

"Bigger than me and a lot stronger." She began to cry again. "He . . . he really hurt me."

"I know, honey." Savannah felt tears well up in her own eyes. She glanced over at the young nurse, who was biting her lower lip. "But you've got great doctors and nurses here," she told her. "They're taking good care of you."

"But what if he comes back?" Charlene asked. She was trembling so hard that Savannah could feel the bed shaking as she leaned against it. "What if he comes here to the hospital and tries to kill me again?"

"He can't," Savannah told her. "No way. Right outside your door is the biggest Irish cop you've ever seen, and he's packin' a gun the size of a Sherman tank. Ain't nobody comin' through him, I guarantee it. You're safe now, Charlene. Really."

She continued to sob. "But I don't feel safe."

Savannah didn't have the heart to tell Charlene Yardley that one of the worst things her attacker had done to her was to rob her of the simple, human joy of ever feeling safe again.

"I know you don't," Savannah said, "but we're going to catch that bastard for you and

91

put him away so that he can't ever hurt you or anyone else again. I promise."

Charlene turned her face away, but she gripped Savannah's hand even harder. "He . . . he . . ." She struggled with the words. "He did awful things to me," she finally said, as though she were confessing some deeply personal, mortal sin.

Savannah returned the squeeze. "I know. I'm so sorry."

She began to cry even harder. The sound was like that of a wounded animal, and everyone in the room shuddered. "He made me do things to him, too," she told them. "He said he'd kill me if I didn't."

"That's okay, Charlene," Savannah said. "You only did what you had to, what anyone would have done under those circumstances."

"If my mama had seen me there in that orange grove, she . . ." Charlene released Savannah's fingers and covered her face with her hand, as though trying to blot out memories that could never be erased. "Oh, God," she said, "I'm glad my mother is dead and won't ever know what he did to me, and what he made me do to him."

"Your mama would have wanted you to do whatever was necessary to stay alive. And that's what you did," Savannah told her firmly, then she softened her tone. "You were a brave girl, Charlene. A strong, brave girl. And now everything's okay, sweetheart. You're safe and everything's going to be all right."

Pulling the sheet higher around Charlene's shoulders, Savannah said, "You try to go back to sleep, honey. Just close your eyes and try not to worry about anything. Atta girl."

After several minutes, Charlene had stopped crying, and her breathing was slow and rhythmic. Finally, Savannah stepped away from the bed and walked over to Dirk. "Come on," she whispered to him. "Let's go get that damned sonofabitch and nail his dick to the nearest wall."

Half-awake and half-asleep, Charlene heard what the woman with the soft, sweet, Southern accent whispered. And, after hearing her, Charlene felt a bit better.

Mama had said she was going to get the bad guy and make him pay for what he had done to her little girl. And Mama sounded like she really meant it, too.

8:39 a.m.

After several hours of dirt combing — searching the crime scene for the most minute particle of evidence — Dirk, Savannah, and Officer Titus Dunn had decided it was time for some nourishment at a local pancake house.

The waitress, who filled out her hot pink uniform to perfection, eyed Titus as she sidled by, a coffeepot in her hand and a twinkle in her eye. "You need a refill?" she asked him, ignoring Savannah and Dirk, who sat across the booth from the patrolman.

Savannah was only mildly irked. After all, Titus was the quintessential tall, moderately dark, and delectably handsome hunk who spent most of his spare time lifting weights at the gym. While Dirk was . . . well . . . Dirk was Dirk. And she, herself, probably wasn't the waitress's preferred gender.

But, on the other hand, there was no excuse for a customer suffering from low blood sugar or caffeine deprivation in a pancake house.

"Excuse me, Adrienne," she said, reading the name tag over the waitress's left boob. "I need another Danish — cherry and cream cheese — and some more coffee," she said, waving her hand in the woman's line of vision. The waitress tore her eyes away from Titus for a second. "And do you have some half and half?" she added. "This blue water just doesn't cut it."

Adrienne shook her head slightly, as though coming to consciousness after a long, deep slumber . . . or maybe a short, intense fantasy. "Sure," she muttered. "Coming right up."

"Two Danish rolls and four cups of coffee for breakfast," Dirk said, shaking his head in mock disgust and doing that "tsk, tsk" thing that made Savannah want to box his jaws. Dirk turned to Titus. "You can tell — this one's really got the old girl shook up."

Titus laughed and turned golden eyes rimmed with long black lashes to Savannah. Her heart did a pit-a-pat. "What's he saying, Savannah?" Titus said in a voice as deep as his shoulders were broad. "Do you eat more when you're upset?"

"No, I eat less," she said, giving Dirk an evil eye. "Normally, I'd have a short stack of hotcakes to go with the rolls, and a slab of ham on the side."

Titus chuckled, revealing a smile that should have been used on recruitment posters for the S.C.P.D. Half the force would have been women. "We miss you, Savannah," he said affectionately. "It's just not the same at the station without you." He nodded toward Dirk. "And this guy mopes around with his chin draggin' on the floor. It's like he's got an acute case of permanent PMS."

Savannah nudged Dirk in the ribs with her elbow. "Ah, Dirk's always been a downer. He considers it his mission in life to keep us optimists adequately depressed."

Dirk scowled. "I'm not a downer; I'm a realist."

"You're a Gloomy Gus who's only happy when he's pooping in somebody's ice cream."

Titus grimaced and looked down at the

eggs and link sausages on his plate. "Oh, man . . . now there's a visual I could have done without."

"Me, too." Dirk gave her a look of disgust mingled with respect. "Van, you're the only chick I know who can out-gross a guy."

"Why, thank you, darlin'. That's high praise, indeed, coming from a foul-mouthed, dirty-minded adolescent like yourself."

Adrienne arrived with the coffee, half and half, and Savannah's Danish. As she dumped a healthy — or unhealthy, depending on the point of view — portion of cream into the coffee and stirred it, she wondered when Charlene Yardley would be able to eat solid food again.

"Speaking of disturbing visuals," she said, "I can't get the victim's battered face out of my mind."

"No kidding," Dirk said, slathering more butter and syrup on his tall stack of blue-berry flapjacks. "She looked like a semi had run over her, backed up, and made a second trip."

"She looked pretty awful out there in the grove, too." Titus shook his head, and he had a sad, distant expression on his face. "I don't understand how one human being can do something like that to another one . . . and somebody they don't even know."

"Well, we assume it was a stranger attack, but we aren't sure," Dirk said, chewing and talking at the same time — a habit Savannah had tried for years to beat out of him. Dirk was a fairly old dog, and keeping your mouth shut when you eat must be classified as a new trick.

"Is she going to be all right?" Titus asked.

"Probably," Savannah replied. "Her arm is broken, she has a concussion, and she needed a lot of stitches for the lacerations on her face and head. The sonofabitch really did a number on her. May he rot in hell."

"When I talked to her there in the grove," Titus said, "she told me she thought he was white, and he was wearing the Santa Claus disguise. That's about all she could tell me."

"That's all she had for us, too," Dirk said, replenishing his mouthful. "Nothing to go on."

"Yeah, her memory's about as worthless as the crime scene." Savannah's fatigue began to catch up with her as her tummy filled. Food . . . and now sleep. That would improve her mood considerably. The simple pleasures of life.

"I can't believe," she said, "we searched that long and didn't come up with anything except a few more of those damned curly, white hairs. That's a piss-poor payoff for the backache I've got."

"But at least we've got the hairs," Titus said, "and we know it's the same guy who did the other women. That's something."

"So . . . we've got a nondescript, probably white, Santa Claus who's molting," Dirk grumbled. "Big friggin' deal. He's gonna keep on raping and plundering — will probably escalate to murder before long — and we're never, ever, gonna catch him."

Savannah felt her own mood barometer drop fifteen notches. "Like I told you," she said to Titus, "Dirk makes sure that no one's morale rises above Suicide Level One."

"Hey, what can I say?" Dirk shrugged and gave her a lopsided smile. "It's my job to make sure everybody around here understands the situation. And the situation is: We got a very sick guy on the loose . . . and when it comes to nabbing him . . . we got diddly-squat."

SEVEN

After breakfast, Savannah drove Dirk back to her house to get his car, where he had left it the night before. As they stood beside his old Buick in her driveway, saying good-bye, Savannah noticed that Dirk was wearing what she called his "sorta-sappy" look. It was the expression he donned when he was feeling sentimental, but, being Dirk, didn't want her to know.

"Listen, Van," he said, nudging a rock in the dirt with the toe of his scuffed sneaker that looked worse than usual, thanks to their stint in the muddy orange grove. "Before you go, I just want to say that I really appreciate your help, last night and today. Workin' with you, it was kinda like old times."

She chuckled. "Yeah, except in days of yore I got paid."

His sappy look quickly changed to indignation. "You aren't suggesting *I* pay you, are you?"

"You? A man who reuses coffee filters? A guy who could read a newspaper through the best towel in his bathroom?"

He bristled. "Hey, are you insinuating I'm cheap or somethin'?"

"Who, me? You, cheap? Never."

He wasn't convinced his case had been made. "I bought you pizza last night . . . kind of," he argued, "and breakfast this morning. Basically, I've fed you for the past twelve hours."

"So? It was the least you could do." She propped her hands on her hips and tossed her head. "Let me remind you, good buddy, that if it hadn't been for you, I would have been snoozing away in my comfy bed for eight of those twelve hours."

"Well . . . like I said, I appreciate what you did, especially talking to that Yardley gal there in the hospital and —"

"Yeah, yeah, I know you appreciate me . . ." She waved him off. She could only take so much sentiment Dirk style. "So shut up already. Any time."

"*Any* time?"

He looked far too eager. She decided to backpedal. "Well . . . almost any time. When?"

"How about later this afternoon or tonight? I gotta go over the victim files. And I always get bored and fall asleep if I have to do it by myself."

"Paperwork? Forget it. I gotta sleep this afternoon and give another one of those self-defense classes at the library tonight. Sorry, old chum, but you're on your own. Maybe to-morrow . . . unless a real, live, paying job comes along."

She socked him on the shoulder, then started to walk away.

"Listen," he called after her, "I'll try to get you some dough for the time you're putting in on this one. Maybe I'll write you up as one of my snitches or something. I'll call you Trixie Delight or Ample Samples."

She stepped up onto the porch as he climbed into his Buick. "Gee, thanks. But I know how much you pay your snitches. Don't bother; five bucks doesn't buy much these days. Just keep me in pizza and Danish."

"Sure thing. I got more freebie coupons where that came from."

"I'll bet you do. Go get some sleep; you look like I feel. And that's not a good thing."

When she walked into the house, she was a bit startled and dismayed to see the blinds thrown wide open, sunshine pouring in. New Age jazz was playing on the stereo — *cheery* jazz. Tammy, the indomitable morning person, had struck again.

"Good morning," trilled a joyful greeting from the kitchen. Tammy bounded into the room, holding a glass of carrot juice in one hand and a large quartz crystal in the other.

Savannah considered making a sarcastic comment about the kid "stroking her rocks" again, but that would only lead to a lecture about crystal power or some other hocus-pocus goofiness.

"Don't give me any of your 'good morning' crap," Savannah mumbled as she tossed her purse and keys onto the piecrust table beside the front door. "It isn't morning until I've slept."

Tammy giggled. "Oh, oh . . . our mistress is feeling a little testy," she told Diamante, who was sunning herself in the open window. She held out some pink slips of paper to Savannah. "Here you go . . . messages."

Savannah refused to take them. "Go away. Leave me alone."

"Your sister, Vidalia, called."

Heading for the stairs, Savannah stuck her fingers in her ears and sang, "La, la, la, la, la-a-a-a. I can't hear you. I'm going to take a hot bubble bath, and then I'm going to bed."

"She was crying."

Savannah paused, one foot on the bottom step. "Of course, she was crying. She's seven months pregnant. All she does is cry or eat. Lately, she's been crying and eating at the same time . . . and complaining about how much weight she's gained."

"She says she's going to leave her husband."

"Vidalia's always threatening to leave Butch. But she won't. He's the one who's buying the Ben and Jerry's Cherry Garcia ice cream she's gorging herself with and the tissues she's boo-hooing into. She may be pregnant and depressed, but the girl isn't stupid."

Savannah continued on up the stairs, dragging her body that was becoming more weary with every step.

Still obnoxiously cheery, Tammy called after her, "Well, this time I think she means it. In fact, she mentioned something about leaving him and coming out here to spend Christmas with you."

Suddenly energized, Savannah nearly tumbled over herself getting back down the stairs. "What? What did you say?"

"And she mentioned something about bringing some twins."

"Oh my God!" Savannah choked on her own spit and couldn't speak or even breathe for a moment.

"Who are the twins?" Tammy asked, so innocently, with such casual indifference. She could afford to be nonchalant. She didn't know.

"The twins are my niece and nephew," Savannah said. "Redheaded, freckle-faced five-year-olds."

"How cute!"

"Cute, my ass. Those cherub-faced gargoyles could guard the gates of hell. They're holy terrors, I tell you! The worst! Where is Vidalia's phone number? Dear Lord! I have to stop her before she starts packing!"

★ ★ ★

She was too late.

"Vidalia just hightailed it out of here and took my young'uns with her, she did," Butch told Savannah when she called from her phone in the bedroom. "And here it's just a few days before Christmas. I tell you, Savannah, that girl's done gone plumb whacko on me. Worse than the last time she was pregnant, and you know what a nut-job she was then."

Good old Butch, Savannah thought as she sat on the edge of her bed and kicked off her shoes, he'd never win the "Sensitive Husband of the Year" Award. But Vidalia wasn't a particularly easygoing gal either, even when she wasn't pregnant, let alone when she was "big as a barn."

"Maybe she just went to the grocery store," she said hopefully.

"She packed six suitcases."

"The mall perhaps?"

"She told me flat out she was going to California. Says she's gonna live there with you in your spare bedroom, her and the twins and the new baby. Now what do you think of that there?"

"I think I'm going to be sick." She collapsed across the bed, which had begun to spin as though she had consumed a six-pack of beer on an empty stomach.

Staring up at the ceiling, she cursed Fate for making her the oldest of nine siblings . . . the big sister they always ran to when their lives were in shambles . . . or when they *perceived* their lives were a mess. Usually, they weren't half as bad off as they seemed to think they were. In her line of work, Savannah had seen worse . . . much worse.

"Did it occur to Vidalia to give me a quick phone call and ask if it would be convenient for her and her offspring to live with me right now?" she said, more to herself than Butch.

"Who knows what's between her ears? I'm plumb worn to a frazzle tryin' to figure that girl out. If it wasn't for the babies, I'd just say 'Good-bye and good riddance.' "

"Come on, Butch, you don't really feel that way."

"Right now, I do. She's more trouble than she's worth."

"Is she driving here in her condition?" Knowing the usual state of Vidalia and Butch's domestic economy, she assumed her sister wouldn't have been able to swing air fare.

"Nope, the car's in the garage. Your brother Macon is overhauling the engine for me. She took the bus."

Savannah gasped. "The *bus?* She and the twins are riding a bus from Georgia to California? That's crazy."

"Crazier than a bedbug, that's your sister."

"She's not that crazy, even when she's pregnant. She must have been hoppin' mad. You two must have had a hell of a fight. What was it about?"

"About?" he answered quickly. Too quickly. "It weren't about nothin'."

"What did you do to her?"

"Not a blamed thing. She just got on her high horse and —"

Savannah sat up suddenly. "Did you hit her? 'Cause if you raised a hand to my little sister, I'll get hold of you, boy, and turn you ever' which way but loose."

"I never hit a woman in my life, and you know it, Savannah. Though lately I been thinkin' that's what Vi needs, a good paddlin' on the behind. It might get her to thinkin' what's what."

All the wind went out of Savannah's sails, and she sagged like a wet sheet on a clothesline. "When will they be arriving?" she asked, too tired to breathe.

"Best I can figure, three or four days. You call me when they show up, you hear?"

"I hear. I'll call." She sighed. "Hell, I probably won't even bother with the phone. You'll just hear this long, plaintive wail and . . ."

7:30 p.m.

"Okay, ladies, it's time to join the real

world, cruel as it may be," Savannah told her class as they exited the library's front door and entered the poorly lit parking lot. "Everybody got somebody to walk with?"

They paired up like third grade students on a field trip, but they weren't nearly as chatty or jubilant. No sack lunches, no big yellow bus waiting for them. Just a dark, shrubbery-lined parking lot dotted with ominous shadows.

"Here's your chance to practice what we've been preaching . . . parking lot safety," she said, searching the shadows herself. The town bad boy preferred shopping malls, but you never knew when he might wax literary and start hanging out at the local library.

"What's the first thing you do, Tammy?" she asked her assistant, who was bringing up the rear.

"Make sure you've got your keys ready in one hand, and if possible, some sort of weapon in the other," Tammy responded.

"That's right. And remember, almost anything can be used for defense, even an old, battered copy of *Wuthering Heights*. I once knew a young lady who was walking through the park on her way home from school when some perv flashed her. She smacked him on the dicky-do with *War and Peace* and changed his gender."

A few giggles cut the tension for a moment, but it quickly returned. Savannah turned deadly serious. "Like I told you earlier inside, it's when you're getting in and out of your car that you're the most vulnerable. And this is true, whether there's a psycho on the loose or not. Angie . . ." She turned to Angie Perez, who had joined them for the first time tonight at Dirk's suggestion. The scared teen hadn't required much coaxing. "What are you going to do on the way to your car?" Savannah asked her.

"Look everywhere. Make sure nobody's following me. Check for anyone hanging around beside my car or even lying under it."

"And, Margie, what do you do if you see anything at all suspicious?"

"Turn around and go back into the store," she replied, all of her cockiness temporarily on hold. "Ask security to walk me out or call a cop."

"Good girl."

Margie beamed, and it occurred to Savannah that the girl must not receive a lot of adult praise or validation. No wonder she was such a brat.

"And once you're at the car?" Savannah continued.

"Look in the back floorboard before you even open the door, and make sure that sonofabitch isn't waiting for you," said Denise, the previously prim and proper librarian.

Savannah smiled. "You're darned right. And once you're inside the car?"

"Lock the doors right away," Margie supplied. "And don't waste any time getting going."

"I think you've got it! Use what you've learned . . . not just now but *all* the time. Be careful and be safe until we meet again. And, in spite of all this, try to enjoy the holidays."

As Savannah watched her vigilant students file out to their cars, employing all of her suggestions, she should have felt good. At least, they were better informed, less likely to fall prey to the predator.

But she didn't feel good.

And she wasn't sure why.

Tammy walked up to Savannah and slid her arm through hers. "What's wrong?"

"Don't know."

Savannah didn't take her eyes off the lot, watching each woman as, one by one, they got into their cars and pulled away. Finally, the last one drove off, leaving only half-a-dozen empty cars in the lot.

"I've just got a creepy feeling," she said, searching the shadows.

"How creepy?"

"Very."

"Maybe it's nothing."

"Maybe."

She walked Tammy to her car, and Tammy waited until Savannah was inside her Camaro before the two women drove away from the lot together.

"Maybe Tammy's right; maybe it's nothing," Savannah whispered to the empty darkness around her as she headed home.

But inside, deep in her psyche, where Savannah stored things like feminine intuition and gut-level instincts, she knew damned well . . . it wasn't nothing. It was something. She just didn't know what or who.

He had been sitting in one of the "empty" cars in the library parking lot, watching the women exit the building. Slouched low in the seat, his window rolled down a crack, he had been able to hear some of what had been said.

Their comments amused him. Their caution was so misplaced.

Because he had changed his m.o.

So what if the average criminal followed the same pattern, crime after crime, until he was caught? *He* wasn't your average criminal. Not by a long shot.

He was smart — at least in his own, not-particularly-humble opinion. He was flexible. He knew when it was time to shift some things around. No problem.

The end result would be the same. He'd still wind up in an orange grove with the woman of his choice. And then . . . party, party!

This time he had chosen a bit more carefully. He watched his quarry as she stood and chatted with the others, unaware that he was watching, unaware of the role he would play in her life very soon.

Yes, this time he intended to do a number of things differently.

He would study his victim more thoroughly. He would stalk her a little longer, savoring the hunt. And when the time came, he would fulfill some of his darkest fantasies, dreams that, until now, had only been in his mind. But he would bring them into reality. Live every moment in the flesh.

This time, he was going to rape her, beat her, hurt her, as he had before.

But this time, she was going to die. The ultimate fantasy fulfilled.

"You've got twenty-four hours," he whispered, as he watched her drive away, out of sight, but only for the moment. He didn't care where she was going now; he knew exactly where to find her when he wanted her. This time he had really done his homework.

"That's right, baby, twenty-four hours . . ." he repeated, then added, ". . . more or less."

EIGHT

Charlene Yardley had drifted off to sleep long ago, but Savannah continued to sit in the chair beside her hospital bed, reading from the worn fairy-tale book she had brought from home. Although Savannah's own mother had spent more evenings carousing in honky-tonks than reading to her children, Savannah had gone to sleep many nights with the sound of her Granny Reid's gentle voice in her ears.

Although child psychiatrists might have objected to Granny scaring her granddaughter witless with tales of cannibalistic witches, cross-dressing wolves, and cinder girls whose only ambition was to charm a prince into supporting them for the rest of their happily-ever-after lives, such tales were part of a Southern girl's upbringing.

Savannah betted on the fact that Charlene Yardley's mom had read her to sleep with such stories, and the tears in Charlene's eyes had proven she was right.

Once, half an hour ago, Savannah had slipped out to make a phone call to Dirk.

They had already spent the afternoon together, going over the victims' files. But when
she had told him she was at the hospital and
had something new, he had said he would be
over as soon as possible. She had decided to
wait until he arrived to discuss her latest
finding with him.

He didn't disappoint her. Five minutes
later, he stuck his head into the room and
seeing the sleeping Charlene, tiptoed over to
the side of the bed.

"Thanks for coming," Savannah whispered,
laying the book aside. "I couldn't wait to
show you this."

"Yeah, I wanna see it," he replied. "But
you may wanna show me and then get the
hell outta here."

"Why?"

"The captain was standing by my desk
when you called. When I hung up, he wanted
to know what you had told me. I described
the bruise, like you did, and he got all interested . . . said he was gonna drop by himself
to look at it."

"Since when does Bloss take an interest in
the details of a case?"

He shrugged. "Mostly when it'll irk your
butt."

"Yeah, no kidding."

Charlene stirred and moaned slightly. They
waited until she was completely still and her
breathing was slow and even before Savannah

nudged Dirk closer to the bed.

"Have you got your penlight?" she asked.

He pulled the small flashlight from his pocket and handed it to her.

Flipping on the small switch, she leaned over the sleeping Charlene. Shielding half of the light with her hand to keep it out of the woman's eyes, Savannah directed the beam on the lower part of Charlene's right cheek.

"Take a look at that," she said, "just above her jawbone."

He leaned close and squinted, then he quirked one eyebrow. "I'll be damned. You're right," he said. "Did you ask her about it?"

"Yeah. She has no idea how it got there."

"Hmmm . . ."

Charlene stirred again, and Savannah snapped off the flashlight. "Come on," she whispered. "Let's talk outside."

She gave Dirk back his light, scooped up her storybook, and followed him out of the room.

They walked down the hall several yards, to get out of earshot of the formidable Officer Morton O'Leary and a couple of nearby nurses who were chatting over some patient charts.

"You were right," he said again. "That's one helluva patriotic bruise. A star — distinctive as can be — and some stripes. How the heck do you suppose she got that?"

"Yeah, what are you talking about, a star?"

said a nasal, twangy voice behind them that set Savannah's teeth on edge. She turned to see Captain Bloss, who had just rounded the corner, coming from the elevator bank. Apparently, he had overheard Dirk's comment; he was all ears — except for his bulbous, varicose-veined nose and little piggy eyes.

"The victim has a very distinctive bruise on her cheek," Savannah said, swallowing her distaste and resisting the overwhelming urge she had every time she saw the cursed man to spit in his eye. Granny Reid would not have been proud.

"It looks like a . . . star?" he asked.

"Yeah," Dirk interjected. "A five-pointed star with some long, spaced out stripes beside it."

"That's pretty weird." Bloss sniffed loudly and wiped his nose with the back of his hand. Deliberately, he turned away from Savannah to face Dirk. "What do you make of it, Coulter?"

Dirk shrugged. "Don't know. I just saw it. Like you said, it's weird."

Savannah decided to talk, whether she was being addressed or not. "I think the rapist slapped her, wearing a ring with a prominent star on it. The stripes are where his fingers struck her. Some of our other victims were sure he was right-handed. If he was facing her when he backhanded her, the marks would be on the right side of her face. That's where they are."

Bloss studied her thoughtfully for a long moment, then gave her a sarcastic smile that made him, if possible, even less attractive. Her palms itched to slap the look off his face.

"Well, well," he said, "too bad you're not still on the force, Reid. You're quite the little Sherlock Holmes."

"And you, Bloss, may shove it . . . sideways . . . with barbed wire wrapped around it," she said, as coolly as though she were delivering a stock market report. Turning to Dirk, she said just as casually, "You know where I am if you need me."

"Thanks, Van," he said. "I never would have noticed that bruise and it could be important. I owe ya."

She knew he was saying all that because Bloss was standing there. Dirk never missed a chance to make her look good in front of the stupid brass who had fired her. And he had never forgiven Bloss for breaking up their partnership. God bless him.

"You bet you owe me, big boy," she said in her best Mae West impression. "An extra large pizza, and this time I get toppings and a six-pack to wash it down with. Bloss here's buyin'."

As she sauntered away, she could feel Bloss's eyes boring into her backside. Gran would have been proud. She'd put him in his place and hadn't even spit between his eyes.

Gran had done her job well; Savannah was a true Southern belle, a lady through and through.

Well . . . except for that part about telling him to shove barbed wire up his rear end. Sideways.

7:12 p.m.

As he crouched in the oleander bushes beside her garage, he decided that the rear floorboards of cars hadn't been all that uncomfortable by comparison. At least, there hadn't been ants in those cars, and they hadn't smelled like tomcat piss.

He'd been here for more than half an hour, and his patience was wearing thin.

She should have been home ten minutes ago . . . at the latest. Where the hell was she, anyway? He'd make her pay for holding him up like this.

And it wasn't just the discomfort or the inconvenience. He had studied the household and knew the comings and goings. If she didn't get here soon, there would be a greater risk of intervention by a third or fourth party.

On the other hand, the added risk made it all the juicier. Danger, and its accompanying adrenaline rush, had been his favorite narcotic for quite some time. A lot of people fantasized about rape, he surmised. But few had the courage to actually act out those fantasies.

That was what set him apart from the others. They were just dreamers; he was a doer.

He figured he wasn't any worse than anyone else. Others fantasized, he performed. That didn't make him bad, just ballsy . . . and a lot smarter than the average Joe, because he got away with it.

Only time would tell if he could get away with murder, too.

7:17 p.m.

As Margie Bloss drove her new BMW Roadster down Harrington Boulevard, heading for home, she briefly entertained the fantasy of turning the car north and just driving, driving, driving, until she hit San Francisco.

She had never been to San Francisco, but she had seen the postcards. And, from what she'd heard, she was pretty sure she'd like it.

Anywhere was better than her dad's house. Mostly because *he* was in it. Sometimes.

If there was one thing Margie Bloss hated — and she hated a lot of things about her parents — it was coming home to an empty house. And in her sixteen years, she had come home to find her house empty far more often than she had been greeted by a parent at the front door.

For a few years, she and her mom had

lived next door to her best friend, Meg. Megan's mom was one of those stay-at-home types who baked cookies from scratch and sewed all the kids' Halloween costumes . . . stuff like that. She had been in the kitchen, dishing up hot chocolate chippers from the oven when Meg and Margie had come home from school every afternoon. And she had let Margie hang out at their house until her mom got home from work . . . even if it was pretty late . . . and it often was.

But then, Meg's mom could afford to stay at home; she was still married to Meg's father. *He* hadn't fooled around with other women and got his butt kicked out of the house, like Margie's crummy dad.

A few weeks ago, Margie's mom had married Crummy Husband Number Three. Numero Tres and Margie had hated each other on sight, when Mom dragged him home from the bar that first night, and their relationship only deteriorated from there. Days before the wedding, he said, "I'll be damned if I'm going to support some punk with pink hair and a ring through her nose. The kid cleans up her act, or she's out!"

So, Margie did the only thing she could under the circumstances . . . she dyed her hair orange and green, and got her tongue pierced, too.

He had kicked her out. And Mom had let him.

To hell with them both, she decided.

Worse yet, they had shipped her off to her dad's. Talk about going from bad to worse. Oh, sure, he had bought her the Roadster, and it was a pretty cool car.

But it didn't make up for years of coming home to an empty house and waiting, hour after hour, for your parent to arrive . . . a parent who, if honest, would admit wishing that you weren't living there.

As she pulled into the driveway and pushed the button on the remote garage-door opener, she didn't know whether to hope her dad's car would be inside or not. Her dad . . . or being alone . . . what a lousy choice.

He was gone.

Okay, fine. She'd blast out his stereo and smoke a joint right in the living room. He wouldn't smell it when he did come home; he'd been smoking cigarettes for so long that his nose didn't work.

Maybe she'd shoot up some heroin, too, just to irk him, and invite some boys over for an orgy.

Except that Margie didn't do that sort of thing. No hard stuff. She might smoke some pot once in a blue moon. She might drink a little and let a boyfriend feel her up if she really, really liked him. She might yell at her folks to get what she wanted from time to time, but Margie liked to think that, basically, she was a lot better kid than they gave her credit for being.

She had friends who were a lot worse.

As she pulled her Roadster into the dark garage, she was careful not to hit the trash cans on her right or the water heater on the left. Whether she wanted to admit it or not, the car was pretty special to her, and she wanted to keep the paint and body perfect for as long as she could.

When he had given it to her, her dad had made some smart-mouth remark about how she would probably wreck it the first month. She would show him how wrong he was . . . how responsible she had become since she had turned sixteen. It was time the old man realized, she wasn't a kid anymore.

Making sure the car was securely in Park, she cut the key and grabbed her purse from the seat beside her. Just as she was opening the door, she thought of what Savannah had said about being careful when you got in and out of your vehicle. Savannah was pretty cool; Margie wished she had a mom or at least a big sister like Savannah to talk to, to do things with. That would be —

The rest of the thought vanished the instant she saw him, a man-shaped shadow, slipping beneath the garage door just before it slid closed.

He was inside! With her! And the door was closed!

It's your dad, her mind whispered frantically.

And she tried with all her might to believe it.

He forgot his keys or something. Yeah, that's it.

But that wasn't it.

And he wasn't her father.

Through the garage's one small window, the streetlamp shone in, just enough for her to see the snowy, curly beard, the silly hat with the white fur trim.

She opened her mouth to scream, but the cry froze there, choking her, and all that came out was a strangled, gagging sound.

"Don't!" he said as he moved closer to her. "Don't scream, don't say anything, just do exactly what I say. Because if you don't, I'm going to kill you. Do you understand?"

Margie nodded as a wave of pure terror washed over her, icy cold, from head to toe. When the jolt of adrenaline hit her knees they nearly buckled beneath her.

"I said, 'Do you understand?' " he repeated. His voice had a harsh, cruel tone to it. "Answer me, or I'll kill you right here and now."

"Yes." She gulped and nodded her head vigorously. "I understand you."

And she did. She understood him much better than he probably realized.

Margie wasn't a stupid girl. She had lied and been lied to many times before, and she was streetwise enough to recognize manipulation when she heard it.

And she knew deep in her gut — just as she had known that this intruder wasn't her father the instant he had entered the garage — whether she did as she was told or not, this guy intended to hurt her.

Then he was going to kill her.

NINE

"Tammy, I can't believe you did all this. Bless your little pea-pickin' heart." Savannah gave her assistant a hug as she surveyed her "child-proof" guest bedroom, stripped to the bare minimum in anticipation of the arrival of the twins from Hades. "You put away the china knickknacks," she said, "and my porcelain doll and the antique satin pillows . . ."

"And your nasty books that were stashed under the nightstand," Tammy added with a smug grin.

"You mean, my ladies' erotica?"

"That's what I said . . . your smut."

Savannah put on an indignant face and crossed her arms over her abundant chest. "I'll have you know, Miss Tammy Smartie Pants Hart, that some of that is considered classic literature."

"Aw, pooh. It's unadulterated filth, and you know it. You should be ashamed of yourself, having that stuff in your house."

"So, let me guess: You've stashed it in your tote bag, and you're taking it home with *you* tonight?"

Tammy shrugged, then nodded. "I thought it was the least I could do . . . for your sake, of course."

"Of course. How very thoughtful. Whatever would I do without you?"

Tammy picked up her tote bag and headed out the bedroom door with Savannah following. "You'd be embarrassed when your sister discovered what a pervert you are, reading pornographic materials like that."

"There's nothing in those books she hasn't done herself; she is pregnant, you know."

Tammy grinned slyly. "I thumbed through a couple of pages, and I don't think most of the sexual practices in those books even lead to pregnancy. 'Unnatural' is the word that comes to mind."

Savannah pointed to the head of the stairs with her left hand and gave Tammy a gentle shove with her right. "It's getting late, kid," she said. "Don't you have a home of your own to go to?"

"As a matter of fact, I do need to be going." Tammy started down the steps, then gave Savannah a playful smirk over her shoulder. "I think I'll hit the sack early tonight; I need to catch up on my reading."

7:47 p.m.

Margie was shaking so badly that she could hardly drive. But he was sitting in the passenger's seat of her Roadster with the tip of a huge knife pressed against her ribs, so she had to do the best she could.

"Turn right at the next intersection," he said, poking her with the blade for emphasis, "and be sure to make a full stop at the sign. We don't want you breaking any laws or any cops pulling us over, now do we?"

He was leading her through dark, back roads. So the hope that anyone might notice him sitting beside her, wearing a Santa costume, was next to nil. Besides, he was slouched down in the seat, and when they met another car, he ducked down below the dash.

She could tell he was taking her to the edge of town. To the orange groves. Not far from where her dad had been investigating the rapist's last scene, when she had dropped by to ask for money.

For just a moment, she thought of how her dad was going to feel when he saw her body, lying there on the ground, beaten, cut up, dead. Margie was a cop's kid, and she had sneaked plenty of peeks at crime scene photos over the years. Eight by ten, full color pictures.

Now she wished she hadn't.

She and her dad might not get along; they might never have been close, like a father and daughter should be. But he was still going to feel really, really bad when he saw her.

Suddenly, she hated the man sitting next to

126

her. And the hate made her feel stronger, not quite so weak and vulnerable, so she nursed the feeling, allowing it to grow inside her.

"So . . . baby . . . do you know who you're riding around with?" he asked her.

She despised the snide tone in his voice. He was actually proud of himself, the bastard.

"Yeah, I know all about you," she replied, equally sarcastic. "You get your kicks by raping and beating women. You're a real fuckin' celebrity."

He hit her on the side of the head so hard that she nearly lost control of the car. It was all she could do not to smack him back, start crying hysterically, or both.

"Watch your language," he said. "I don't approve of women cussing . . . especially kids. You're a smart-mouth punk who needs to be taught a few lessons."

Margie swallowed the retort that rushed to her lips. She had to be smart. This guy was looking for any excuse to hurt her. The realization that he actually enjoyed causing her pain was like a blast of ice water through her body, alerting every nerve and cell to the mortal threat she was facing.

This felt like a bad dream, but it wasn't. This was real. And she had to keep her wits about her if she was going to find a way out of the nightmare alive.

Summoning every particle of courage and

experience she had gathered in her brief life, Margie shifted into "cop's daughter" mode. Her dad hadn't really talked to her that much about crime, or the potential of being victimized, but she had absorbed some secondhand knowledge by watching and listening when her father thought she was tuning out.

She studied her kidnapper in her peripheral vision, trying to gather all the information she could in spite of his disguise.

He sat several inches higher than her in the seat, and when they had been standing face-to-face in the garage, she had come up to about chin level on him. Under his bulky black sweatshirt, he looked to be in good shape, neither fat nor skinny, just medium.

His hands were large. So was the knife he was holding. It looked like something you would take hunting, if you were expecting to do hand-to-hand combat with a grizzly bear.

As they passed beneath a streetlamp, she caught the glint of a ring on his finger. It was big, like some sort of class ring, and had a gold star in the middle of the setting.

That rang a bell, somewhere in her distant memory. She had seen a ring like that before, but she couldn't recall where or when. And there wasn't time to think about it now, because they were getting farther and farther out of town . . . closer to the place he had chosen.

Very soon her nightmare was going to get much worse.

"Turn left up there," he told her, pointing to a dark road that veered off the main one about a quarter of a mile ahead.

There were no other cars in sight. Any dim hope she had been entertaining that they might cross paths with a cruising police unit evaporated.

Margie realized that no one was going to help her get out of this one. If she was going to live, or die horribly, it was all up to her and this maniac sitting next to her.

And she wasn't about to leave her life in *his* hands if she could possibly avoid it.

"Tell me something, kid," he said, again, using that mocking tone that she hated. "Are you a virgin, or are you an experienced woman?"

For half a second, her memory returned to the backseat of Tommy Morrison's classic Mustang . . . and to Jerry Whitley's basement family room the night of her sixteenth-birthday party. Then she shoved any honest answers to the question aside and tried to figure out what he wanted to hear.

Any guy who didn't approve of women *saying* "fuck" probably wouldn't approve of them doing it, either.

"Well?" he said, poking her on the upper arm with the point of his knife blade.

She felt it nick her skin and a small warm,

liquid trickle flow down the back of her arm. He had cut her. And he had done it so casually, as though it were nothing at all to him.

Her shaking got worse.

"Yes," she told him. "I'm a virgin."

He laughed. "Yeah, sure. And I'm Santa Claus."

The road they were on became more and more narrow. On either side was nothing but orange trees. Row after row, leaves and round fruit, shining silver in the moonlight.

"All right," he said. "See that driveway up there, on the other side of that big water tank? I want you to pull the car into the drive. Nice and slow."

Margie's heart had been pounding before, but now it felt like it was about to jump out through her throat. She could hardly hear what he was saying for the pulse throbbing in her ears.

Time slowed to a surreal crawl as a hundred thoughts streaked through her brain. But the thought that stuck was something Savannah had said in their defense class: "Even if you take all these precautions," she had told them, "you may still find yourself in a potentially life-threatening situation. And you may have to do something bold, something dangerous and extraordinary to get out. You may have to risk your life to save it. Only *you* will be able to make that decision. Go with your instincts."

And Margie's instincts told her that if she and this guy got out of the car together and walked into that orange grove, she would never walk out again.

For half a second, she thought of her pretty new car and how careful she had been not to even get a scratch on it. Then she thought, *To hell with that! This asshole's not going to rape and murder this punk kid if I can keep him from it!*

Margie rammed the gas pedal to the floor and steered straight for the water tank.

7:50 p.m.

No sooner had Savannah settled her weary body into the Victorian, clawfoot tub full of fragrant bubbles, than the phone rang.

"Someday I'll learn not to bring you in here with me," she told the cordless phone as she lifted it from the top of the hamper and pushed the On button.

"Whoever this is, I'm not very happy with you," she said into the receiver.

The rich, throaty chuckle on the other end made Savannah smile from ear to ear and forget all about the intrusion.

"Gran!" she said, "I take it back. You're the only person on the planet who's welcome to call me anytime, day or night."

"Let me guess . . ." her grandmother replied in an eloquent Southern drawl as soft as

131

Georgia peach fuzz, ". . . you're taking a bubble bath, roses or gardenia. And you probably have a few votive candles lit and —"

Savannah laughed. "You know me too well."

"I taught you everything you know about being a woman."

"That's true," Savannah replied, "but I'm still waiting for you to teach me everything that *you* know."

"Now, darlin', you can't handle that much knowledge . . . not just yet. It's too much power for one so young."

"I'm over forty."

"You're half my age. You're a baby."

Savannah sank lower into the bubbles and felt the past week's tension melt away, thanks to the silky warmth of the water and her grandmother's soothing presence that could reach three thousand miles and rejuvenate her spirit.

"You know, Gran," she said, "I'd like to think that when I'm your age I'd have half your vinegar."

She heard a ladylike sniff on the other end. "Hell, child. You'd have been lucky to have half my vinegar last week. Are you ready for Christmas?"

"Ready for Christmas?" Some of Savannah's stress returned with a rush. "A lot's been going on around here. I haven't even started yet. And you?"

"All done . . . except for you. What would

you like Santa to bring you?"

"A big, handsome hunk, wearing a sprig of mistletoe for a mustache."

"Mmmm . . ." Gran considered the request thoughtfully for a moment. "I think that could be arranged. I'll run over to the old folks' home and see if I can scare up somethin' for you."

"Gee, thanks."

"Hey, some of those fellas are pretty spunky. They're always chasing me around."

Savannah grinned. "You'd better run fast. You know what they want."

Another sniff. "I know what they want, all right. They're after my pension check, but I'm gonna spend it all by myself. I already raised one man — your grandpa, may he rest in peace — and that's enough toil and trouble for any woman."

Savannah lifted a handful of suds and watched them glisten, iridescent in the candlelight. "Have you heard, I'm going to be having company in a few days?"

"Of course I've heard. In a town this size, we know what everybody had for supper last night and we've got an opinion on the subject."

"So, what's your opinion on this subject?"

"Butch is a jackass, and your sister doesn't have the sense the good Lord gave a goose, God love 'em both. And now they're gonna afflict you with their malarkey. You're just lucky, I reckon."

"And are the twins still as adorable as always?"

"Even more so. Do you have a freshly recharged fire extinguisher?"

"Ah, I think I do —"

"And something you can use for a tourniquet?"

"Do you really think I'll need —"

"And do you have enough money stashed away for some major home repairs because by the time they leave, you're gonna need a new roof and carpeting."

Beep.

"Excuse me, Gran, but I've got another call coming through." Savannah sighed, surrendering all hope of that relaxing bath. "Can you hold for a minute?"

"I suppose, but remember, I'm eighty-six; I could kick off any minute now."

Savannah punched the Flash button. "Hello."

The instant she heard the sobbing on the other end, she knew someone was in bad trouble. "Savannah, it's me, Margie, Margie Bloss."

"Yes, of course, Margie. What's wrong?"

"I got away from him. He was going to kill me, but I wrecked my car and ran away."

Savannah sat, bolt upright, in the tub, splashing water all over the floor. "The rapist?"

"Uh-huh. The Santa guy."

"He attacked you?"

134

"No, I mean, he got into my car with me and made me drive out to the orange grove, but I got away and —"

"Margie, calm down, sweetheart, and tell me where you are." She vaulted out of the tub, yanked a towel off the rack, and began to frantically dry off.

"I'm at a phone booth," the girl said between gasps. "I ran all the way here and I can't breathe."

Savannah raced across the hall to her bedroom. She tucked the phone between her ear and shoulder and pulled a pair of sweatpants and a T-shirt from her dresser drawer. "That's because you're scared. Honey, try to take a couple of slow, deep breaths. Come on, do it with me. In . . . really slow . . . now out . . . that's it. Again. And again. Now tell me where you are."

"I told you. I'm in a phone booth."

"I know, but where is the phone booth?" She struggled into the clothes and pulled on a pair of sneakers. "Are you near a store or —"

"A service station . . . a Mobil. But it's closed. There's no one around."

"A Mobil station . . . orange groves . . . is it the one on Turner Canyon Road?"

"I think so."

"Where was the rapist, the last time you saw him?"

Margie laughed, but it was the sound of hysteria. "He was flying across my car. I ran

135

it into a water tank as hard as I could. I think it knocked him out. I didn't hang around to find out. I got out of the car and ran like crazy."

"Good girl! You did great, Margie. I'm very proud of you. Is the phone booth where you are, well lit?"

"Yes. When I opened the door, the light came on."

"Well, I want you to hang up and get out of the booth. Look around you. Is there any place you can hide . . . beside the building . . . in some bushes?"

"There's a pile of old tires next to a truck."

"Get between those tires and the truck and don't move until I get there. It'll take me about five or six minutes."

Savannah raced down the stairs and snatched her purse, gun and keys from the hall table. "As soon as we hang up, I'm going to call the police for you," she told the girl. "Maybe they can get there first and —"

"No! Don't call the cops! That's why I called you. I don't want to talk to my stupid dad yet." She began to cry again. "I just want to see you first, not him."

"Okay, okay. I'm on my way. Now hide and hang tight until I get there."

No sooner had Savannah turned the phone off than it rang again. Gran.

She punched the button again. "Gotta go,

Gran," she said as she ran out the door. "Emergency."

"I understand. I'll pray for you."

"Thanks, love you."

"You, too."

As Savannah sprinted down the driveway to her car, she said a couple of quick prayers herself. One to thank God for a grandmother who was astute enough to know, from three thousand miles away, when her grand-daughter needed a prayer. And one for Margie . . . that the good Lord above would keep that rotten bastard away from the kid until Savannah could get to her.

TEN

8:02 p.m.

On the way to the gas station on Turner Canyon Road, Savannah called Dirk on her cellular phone. When he didn't answer at work, she gave him a ring at home. His sleepy "hello" told her he had hit the sack early, trying to make up for the sleep deprivation of the past forty-eight hours.

Too bad. If she couldn't enjoy a simple bubble bath, he sure as hell didn't get snooze time.

"You'll never guess where I am," she told him as she sped toward the edge of town and the agricultural area of the county.

"I don't care where you are," he grumped.

"He nabbed another one."

Mentally, she could see Dirk perk up like a bloodhound catching a whiff of raccoon scent. "Where? When?" He certainly didn't sound sleepy now.

"Just now, out on Turner Canyon Road. But forget about *where* and *when*. Ask me *who?*"

"Ask you *who?*"

"That's right. Ask."

138

"Okay . . . who?"

"Captain Bloss's teenage daughter, Margie."

"No shit!"

"Absolutely not a smidgen. But she got away from him before he could rape her, or worse. She called me at home and I'm on my way right now to pick her up."

"Where? Where are you going? Where is she?"

She could hear him rushing around, throwing on clothes, just as she had done a few minutes ago.

"I'll tell you, but you can't question her until I get her to a hospital or back to my house. She's shook up and she said she didn't want me to call the cops until we've had a chance to talk."

"Yeah, right. Where is she? Where are you picking her up?"

"I'm not telling you unless you promise not to butt in."

"Butt in, my ass. I —"

"Or your ass either. I don't want to see any part of you, Coulter — heads or tails — until I give you the thumbs-up. Promise."

"All right," he mumbled.

"She's hiding at the Mobil station on Turner Canyon Road. She says she wrecked her car nearby with him in it. Hit some sort of water tank. That's how she got away from him."

"So, there's nothing to stop me from lookin' for the car and him in that area, while you check her out."

"Absolutely nothing."

The phone clicked and the line went dead.

Dirk never had been one for sentimental good-byes.

8:05 p.m.

Savannah pulled her Camaro into the dark, empty lot of the service station a couple of minutes later, her eyes scanning the area for signs of life . . . or, more specifically, lowlife. Besides a scared Margie Bloss, Savannah was looking for one rapist/woman beater who she would love to plug between the eyes with a 9mm bullet.

Savannah knew that some people might have considered her cold-blooded attitudes toward criminals less than compassionate or humanitarian. But she didn't give a damn what the liberals thought about her politics. When they had scraped up the shattered remains of innocent victims' lives from bedroom floors, city streets, and back alleys, then they could talk to her about understanding and pitying the underprivileged, abused perpetrator.

She reserved her compassion for their victims. And right now, she was hoping this latest crime victim would be basically intact,

140

emotionally as well as physically.

When she thought of Charlene Yardley, bruised and broken, on that hospital bed, she shuddered to think what could have happened to young Margie.

Having pulled the Camaro close to the pile of tires and the truck that Margie had described, she put the car in Park but left the engine running, her headlights trained on the dark area beside the broken-down, rusted truck.

So far, she saw neither hide nor orange and green hair of the girl.

With her Beretta in her right hand, she opened the car door and got out. "Margie!" she called. "Margie, it's Savannah. Come out, honey."

At first, she heard nothing. Then there was a rustling off to her left, a shuffling sound, and a soft curse as someone banged into something metal.

She readied her weapon, pointing it upward, but prepared to lower it if she saw anything resembling a Santa beard and hat.

"Margie, if that's you, say something," she said, every nerve torquing tighter as she waited for a response.

Finally, just as she was about to lower the Beretta, she saw a white, frightened face appear in the car's bright lights.

"Hi, kiddo," she said, infinitely relieved to see the girl alive and relatively whole. "I hear your date turned out to be a first-rate creep and you need a ride home."

The next minute Savannah's arms were full of a sobbing and sniffling, cut and scraped, dirty and exhausted — but infinitely grateful — teenage girl.

"Come on, darlin'," Savannah told her, helping her into the car. "It's all over now, and I'm gonna take care of you. Don't you worry about a thing. I'll take it from here."

8:22 p.m.

"I told you I didn't want to go to a stupid hospital!" Margie yelled in her loudest, most completely outraged, adolescent voice as she sat on the edge of an emergency room gurney, wearing a shapeless, pale blue, tie-in-the-back and show-your-bare-butt gown.

The kid was definitely not a satisfied customer of the Community General Hospital of San Carmelita. And Savannah couldn't really blame her.

First, they had ignored her, keeping her waiting while they tended to more immediate, life-threatening situations. Then they had scrubbed the grit out of her deeply scraped knees and elbows . . . a very painful process, judging from the bloodcurdling yowls she had produced.

Next, they stitched one particularly deep cut on her upper shoulder, the only wound directly inflicted by her attacker. The other damage had been done during the automobile wreck or while she was running through the orange grove to safety.

Finally, the hospital staff had added insult to injury.

"Do you know what they want to do to me?" Margie demanded, bristling with indignation.

"Yes, I have an idea," Savannah replied as she sat on the gurney beside the girl and placed her hand on her shoulder. "Do they want to do a rape test examination?"

"Yeah! That's what he said . . . that smartass young doctor with the major attitude. He said I don't have a choice, that I *have* to let them do it."

"No, you don't have to. But I do want to talk to you about it."

"There's nothing to talk about!" She shrugged Savannah's hand off her shoulder. "I told them, the guy didn't rape me. What's the matter with that stupid doctor? He acts like he thinks I'm lying!"

Savannah paused, choosing her words carefully. "Don't take it personally, Margie. The doctor doesn't even know you, so he doesn't know if you would lie or not. A lot of women do lie about rape, because they're embarrassed, or they feel guilty, like it's their fault they were attacked. That's completely false, but it's a common feeling."

143

Savannah watched Margie's face for any telltale signs of those commonly held emotions of guilt or embarrassment. All she saw was plain old anger. The kid wasn't ashamed; she was just extremely pissed.

"That young doctor strikes me as a bit arrogant, too," Savannah continued, "and if you say he's an asshole, I'll take your word for it. But I really think he has your best interests at heart about the rape exam."

"I'm not going to let them do it. I didn't get raped, but I've been through enough already tonight. I saw that kit thing they had there on the tray. I'm not going to let somebody comb through my pubic hair and stick giant cotton swabs up my . . . you know."

"Yes. I know." Savannah stood and faced Margie straight on. "If you swear to me that he absolutely, positively, didn't sexually assault you, I'll tell Dr. Wise Guy to take a hike."

"The creep absolutely, positively didn't do me. I promise."

Savannah nodded. "Okay, Margie. I believe you. I'll go talk to the doc."

"Make sure he knows where the city pier is," Margie said as Savannah walked away, "and don't mention that the end of it fell off during the last big storm."

The kid'll be all right, Savannah thought as she went to find her young friend's least favorite physician. Minus the green and orange

144

hair and the disrespect for her elders, Margie Bloss reminded Savannah of another girl who had been the same age and temperament about thirty years ago down in peach and pecan country.

The kid had spunk. And kids with spunk almost always landed on their feet.

Unless, of course, they landed on their heads.

9:41 p.m.

As Savannah watched Margie sitting at her kitchen table, stuffing her face with ice cream, hot fudge sauce and whipped cream, Savannah decided she and the kid had even more in common than she had originally thought.

Savannah had heard of people who simply couldn't eat when they were upset. But she filed them away in the same category as "morning people" and those who claimed that running five miles a day gave them energy — Certifiably Bonkers.

At least she and Margie Bloss weren't afflicted with such silliness, she concluded as they ooo-ed and ahhh-ed over their frozen confections.

"I guess I should try to call my dad and tell him what happened," Margie said between spoonfuls. "I feel kinda bad for not calling him earlier. I just didn't want him to make a big deal about it."

After having taken a long, hot shower with rose-scented gel in Savannah's romantic bathroom and slipping into Savannah's thickest, softest terry robe, Margie looked like a normal teenager, almost. With the harsh makeup washed away and her hair brushed straight to her shoulders and the multi-piercings removed — except for three in each ear — she could have passed for any other kid with orange and green hair.

"Don't feel too bad," Savannah told her. "I've been calling your house, the station, and his cell phone since we first arrived at the hospital. The staff there was calling him too, trying to get permission to treat you, but he was nowhere to be found. Which reminds me . . . as far as Community General is concerned, I'm your loving aunt."

Margie's mouth popped open, revealing an unattractive mixture of ice cream and hot fudge. She jumped up from her chair. "You called my dad?" she shouted, her pale face flushing red with fury. "I don't believe you did that when I distinctly told you not to!"

"Well, Missy, I don't always do what I'm told," Savannah replied calmly, studying a spoonful of her dessert, "especially when the one giving the orders is young enough to be my daughter." She took the bite, savored it with closed eyes, then pointed her spoon at Margie's bowl. "Sit down and eat your ice cream. It's melting."

Margie stuttered and sputtered, then did as she was told. "But you promised not to call the cops," she protested in a whining voice that irritated Savannah more than the kid's temper.

"I did not," Savannah said as she rose and walked to the microwave. Opening the door, she took out the jar of recently-zapped fudge. "I told you that I wouldn't call a unit to pick you up from the service station, that I'd do it myself. Once you were with me, all bets were off. Do you want some more hot fudge?"

Margie hesitated, obviously weighing the advantages of additional hot fudge over the desire to continue the argument. "Yeah, I'll take some more fudge, and ice cream, too."

Savannah rewarded her with the chocolate and a smile. "Now that's my kind of girl . . . eats like a stevedore."

Margie returned the grin and for a moment the bristly adolescent disappeared and a delightful little girl shone through. "I like Chunky Monkey," she said. "It's my favorite."

"Mine, too."

Margie watched with acute female interest as Savannah replenished her own bowl. "Do you ever have . . . like . . . a weight problem?"

"Nope. I decided a long time ago, there's a lot more to me — and to being a woman — than some numbers on a scale." Savannah replaced the fudge in the microwave and walked across the kitchen to the refrigerator. "More whipped cream?"

"Sure." Margie cast an only-moderately-sly sideways glance at Savannah's amply rounded figure. "My dad says you were fired from the police force because you were overweight."

Dumping the remainder of the cream into her own bowl, Savannah said, "Yeah, and your dad's full of . . . well . . . let's just say your father and I have different versions of that story."

"I'd like to hear your version."

Savannah licked the whipped-cream spoon and dropped it into the sink along with the empty bowl. "Naw. It's old news, while what happened to you tonight is front-page headline material." She returned to the table and sat down. "Let's talk about that."

Before Margie could reply, the doorbell rang.

Savannah rose to answer it. "That's probably Dirk," she said.

Margie wasn't pleased. "You mean, Dirk Coulter, your old partner?"

"He's not all that old, but —"

"He's a cop! I told you not to call the cops."

Savannah sighed. "Been there, done that. So, neither one of us is particularly good at taking orders." As she left the kitchen, she added over her shoulder, "And, just for the record, that's closer to the real reason why I got canned."

She looked through the peephole and saw a wet, pink, slimy tongue. Yeap, it was Dirk.

"Hi," she said, swinging the door open and ushering him inside. "We're in the kitchen, pigging out with Ben and Jerry. Wanna bowl of ice cream?"

As they passed through the living room, he peeled off his battered bomber jacket and tossed it onto the sofa. "What flavor is it?" he asked.

She gave him a withering look. "Free . . . your favorite. Do you want some or not?"

"Do bears sh—"

"Hush." She pressed her finger to her lips and nodded toward the kitchen. "There's a minor in the house."

"I'm not going to say nothin' her foul-mouthed father don't say," he whispered.

"Sh-h-hhh."

She led him into the kitchen, where Margie still sat at the table, wearing a whipped-cream-laced scowl.

"Margie," she said, "have you met Detective Dirk Coulter?"

"I think so . . . a long time ago." She couldn't have been less impressed.

"Ms. Bloss, how nice to see you again," Dirk said with all the respect due royalty. He pulled out a chair and sat across from her. Savannah took her seat at the head of the table.

"You were just a kid," he continued, "the last time I saw you . . . at a Fourth of July picnic, I believe. What are you, about twenty-two now?"

Savannah resisted the urge to gag. Dirk knew when to spread it on thick . . . mainly, when he wanted to get as much information as possible out of a disgruntled, female witness.

It was working. Margie fluttered her lashes as demurely as a Southern belle. "No," she said. "I'm just sixteen."

"Really? You look much older."

More fluttering. A shy smile. "Oh, well . . . thanks, Detective."

"We found your car where you . . . ah . . . *left* it," he said, "smashed into that water tank."

Tears clouded the teenager's eyes, but she blinked them back. "The Roadster's a write-off, isn't it?"

Dirk nodded. "Afraid so. But it was a pretty smart move; it got you away from him."

"I guess it's too much to hope that you found him dead inside the car," Margie said bitterly.

"Way too much, I'm afraid."

Savannah set a bowl of ice cream in front of Dirk and handed him the jar of hot fudge. Years ago, he had been demoted from "guest" to "family." If she could buy it, he could damned well serve himself. "No sign of Santa?" she asked.

"Not even a curly white hair," he said, sounding tired. "Of course, we had the car towed to the impound lot. We'll go over it with a fine tooth comb tomorrow morning when it's daylight."

"Does my dad know what happened to me yet?" Margie asked.

"Not as far as I know. We put out an APB for him, so I'm sure he'll show up soon."

Margie gave a disgusted sniff that didn't cover the hurt in her eyes. "He's probably hanging out in a sleazy motel somewhere with some bimbo. That's usually what he was doing when my mom couldn't get in touch with him."

Dirk looked embarrassed. Savannah had noticed, years ago, that Dirk took it personally when members of his own gender screwed up. And she had decided that was somehow endearing.

"Well, whatever he's doing," Dirk said offhandedly, "I'm sure he'll get the message soon. How about your mom? Have you talked to her yet?"

Margie shook her head. "Savannah already offered to call her. But she's gone to Italy this month with her new husband. I don't know how to get hold of them . . . wouldn't really want to anyway."

"Hm-m-m-m." He picked up the ice cream and dumped twice as much into his bowl as Savannah had originally given him. "Then why don't we just see how big a dent we can make in this carton of ice cream," he said, "and we'll talk about the guy who grabbed you tonight."

"Dent, my eye." Savannah shook her head, mentally wishing her Chunky Monkey a fond farewell. "By the time Coulter finishes an ice cream carton, it's as totalled as your car. Sorry, Margie, bad joke."

She left the table and walked to the coffeemaker where she threw in some water and a hearty, Louisiana chicory blend. It was going to be a long night; all that sugar would need a caffeine chaser.

Margie and Dirk continued to chat companionably, and Savannah wondered at the seeming compatibility between these society misfits. In polite company, neither would have been considered charming. Maybe that was the common ground.

Just before she left the two of them, and headed upstairs, she told Margie, "I'm going to try to get your dad again on the phone, while you tell Dirk all the gory details."

As she walked upstairs and into her bedroom, Savannah whispered a prayer of gratitude that, at least this time, the details weren't nearly as gory as they might have been.

She had an idea where she might get in touch with Bloss. The comment Margie had made about the cheap motel and a bimbo had stirred an inkling.

Cops — like plumbers, bankers, and doctors — were creatures of habit. And some of those habits weren't particularly commendable.

In her years on the force, she had seen far more "fooling around" than she had wanted to, and a lot of it had taken place at the Blue Moon Hotel on the outskirts of town. Experience had shown her that San Carmelita's doctors took their honeys to the Grand Marquis on the beach for nooners. Lawyers preferred Casa Presidio in the marina. But cops fancied the understated, underpriced ambiance of The Blue Moon for their peccadillos.

"Hello," she said when the front desk answered, using her breathy, phone-sex voice that she usually reserved for undercover prostitution stings. "I need to speak with one of your guests. His name is Bloss."

"There ain't no Bloss stayin' here," said an oily-sounding guy.

"I see." She dumped the sexy tone. Why put out if it wasn't working? "Could you please check again," she snapped. "He and his 'wife' might be listed under 'Smith' or 'Doe.'"

"I'm sorry." The asshole didn't sound exactly suicidal to her. "We don't have any guest listed with the name Bloss, Smith or Doe. Is there something else I can do you for?"

"You can tell the good captain that his

daughter has been in a traffic accident, and he needs to get over to Savannah Reid's house as soon as possible."

"I told you, he isn't here."

"Yeah, yeah. Just give him the friggin' message, would you? Do a good deed; it's Christmas for Pete's sake."

She slammed the phone down, hoping he still had it to his ear.

When she was walking down the stairs, she could hear Margie chatting away in the kitchen, even more animated than before.

The moment she entered the room, Margie jumped up from her chair and hurried to her. "Savannah, I just remembered something else," she said, grasping Savannah's arm.

"What's that, darlin'?"

"I just told Dirk . . . and he thought it was pretty important . . . the rapist dude . . . he was wearing a ring. A big one. When he whacked me on the head, it really hurt."

Savannah led her back to her chair. "That is important. I should have asked you about that. Which hand was he wearing it on?"

"His right one, the one he was holding the knife with."

"What did it look like?"

"It was big, like a class ring. In the middle was a dark circle and inside that was a big, metal star."

Dirk gave Savannah a knowing look, which she returned.

"If I give you a piece of paper," she said to Margie, "can you draw it for me?"

The girl shrugged. "I'm not very artistic, but I'll try."

Savannah took a legal pad and pen from the drawer beneath the phone and handed them to her. "Here, just do the best you can."

Several minutes later, they had a fairly decent sketch of a man's ring. With satisfaction, Savannah noted that the style and shape of the ring in Margie's drawing could have caused the bruising on Charlene Yardley's face.

"For someone who isn't very artistic, that looks pretty good to me," Dirk said, still buttering the kid up. She beamed, reveling in adult male praise.

"Do you think it's a fair representation of what you saw?" Savannah asked her, just making sure.

"As best I can remember. I was really scared and it was pretty dark . . . but . . . yeah, it looks like it."

"Great." Dirk tore the yellow sheet from the pad and studied it carefully. "We'll have Charlene Yardley and the other victims look at it," he said, "and see if they remember seeing it, too."

Again, the doorbell sounded. Savannah's two cats, who had just ventured into the kitchen and buried their whiskers in their food dishes, ran for cover.

"Hmmm . . . Now whoever could that be?" she said as she sauntered to the front door. She had a good idea who her guest was, and she was in no hurry to let the Big Bad Wolf into her humble cottage.

"Why, Captain," she said, flashing him her most saccharine smile, "how nice of you to grace my doorstep with your auspicious presence."

Shoving the door open, he barged into the room. "Cram it, Reid." He paused and glanced around the living room. "Where's my daughter?"

Savannah couldn't resist a little verbal jab. "You must have gotten my message," she said sweetly. "I hope I didn't interrupt anything important."

He stared at her blankly for a moment, then glowered, his little piggy eyes squinting even tighter. "Where the hell's my kid?" he demanded.

"Well, if you're going to be snotty about it." She waved a hand toward the back of the house. "Kitchen. There."

He stomped past her, pushing her aside. She considered giving him a karate chop between the shoulder blades, but decided on sarcasm instead. "Do come in and make yourself at home," she muttered as he marched through her living room and into the kitchen. "Just take off your coat and throw it in the corner. Don't see why you won't stay a little longer."

Bloss ignored her and headed straight for his daughter, who was cowering in her chair.

"What's this shit about you wrecking your new car?" he snapped.

Dirk gave a Savannah a look and whispered, "So much for not swearing around minors."

Anger replaced the look of fear on the teenager's face. "Hi, Daddy," she said dryly. "It's nice to see you, too."

"Is it totalled?"

"Yes, the car is smashed to smithereens. And I'm fine, thanks for asking."

Savannah could hear the pain behind the girl's sarcasm, and she had to bite her tongue to keep from interfering.

"I've made one damned payment on that car." His voice rose along with the florid coloring in his puffy cheeks. "One payment! And you've already smacked it up! I can't believe it! What kind of idiot are you?"

Savannah had had enough. She stepped between the captain and Margie. "That's enough, Bloss," she said quietly.

"Who the fuck are you to tell me 'That's enough,' when I'm talking to my own kid?" he shouted.

Dirk stood, too, but Savannah shot him a "Stay Out of It" look. Bloss was still Dirk's boss, and there was no point in him getting canned, too.

157

"You're in my home," she told Bloss, still reining in her temper. "And Margie is a guest in my home. That makes it my business. And, besides that, I'm just trying to stop you from saying things you'll regret and making a complete as . . . I mean, fool . . . of yourself, Captain . . . sir."

In spite of Savannah's silent admonition, Dirk took a step in the captain's direction. "Your daughter," he said, "wrecked her car to keep from being raped and murdered. He was in the car with her. That's how she got away from him."

"He was . . . you mean, the rapist? Oh, my God." The bluster went out of Bloss, apparently, along with the strength in his legs. He sat down hard on the nearest chair and wiped a hand across his eyes. For once, his daughter had his full attention. "Did . . . did he — ?"

Margie gave her father a cold, bitter smile, and for a moment, Savannah could see a strong family resemblance. Margie was Bloss's daughter, after all . . . not a heritage to boast about.

"No, he didn't rape me," Margie told her dad, "but if I hadn't acted like an idiot and wrecked my new car — the car you've only made one payment on — I'm sure he would have."

Bloss's scowl deepened. He turned to Dirk, who was returning to his seat. "When did all this supposedly happen?"

"Supposedly?" Margie's eyes filled with tears. She slammed her fist on the table. "What do you think, Daddy, that I made this all up? You think I wrecked my car and made this up to . . ."

"It wouldn't be the first time you've lied to me," Bloss returned. "It's not like you're above it."

Dirk cleared his throat loudly. "It happened, sir. I'm sure about that. It was approximately 1930 hours this evening. He was waiting at your house, slipped into the garage when she came home, and forced her to drive out on Turner Canyon Road. That's when she smashed the Roadster into a water tank and ran away from him. She called Savannah, and she picked her up at the Mobil station out there."

"Did you get him?"

"Afraid not. By the time we got there, he was gone."

The captain sat quietly, absorbing the facts, then he seemed to soften. He turned to Margie. "Did you get hurt? Have you been to the hospital?"

"Savannah took me. I just got some scrapes and bruises. And a couple of stitches on my shoulder where he gouged me with the tip of his knife."

She pulled the robe aside, showing him her bandage. He gave it a cursory glance.

"Good," he mumbled, "that's good."

"Your daughter showed a lot of smarts and courage, Captain," Savannah said. She walked over to Margie and put her hand on the girl's uninjured shoulder. "If she hadn't, it might have turned out a lot differently."

"I know that." Suddenly Bloss looked fifty years old going on eighty. He shook his head and sighed. "I know what could have happened. Shit. This sucks. My own kid. That guy's nuts."

"I think that was a given," Savannah said, "even before he came after Margie."

"Did you get a good look at him?" Bloss asked the girl.

"Not really. He was wearing that Santa stuff."

"She gave us pretty much the same limited description as the others gave," Dirk interjected. "The only thing new was this." He took the drawing from his pocket and unfolded the paper. Spreading it on the table in front of the captain, he said, "The guy was wearing a ring like that, a big one with a star in the middle."

When Bloss saw the drawing, he looked like he had been hit in the solar plexus. Savannah watched him, fascinated by his reaction. She recalled that he had seemed upset at the hospital when she had told him about the star-shaped bruise on Charlene Yardley.

"Are you sure, Margie?" Bloss asked her.

"Are you absolutely certain he was wearing something that looked like this?"

"Sure, I'm sure. What do you think, I just made it up, too? Give me a break."

Savannah couldn't resist. "Captain, what do you think about the ring? Does that particular design *ring* a bell with you?"

He gave her a deadly look that told her more than his curt, "No." Turning his back to Savannah, he asked Margie, "Do you think he knew who you are . . . you know . . . that you're my kid?"

"I don't know. He didn't say anything about it either way. But I guess he did. I mean, he knew where I lived. He must have known it was your house, too." She shrugged. "Or maybe he just picked out anybody . . . any house."

Bloss stood abruptly. "Come on. Get your stuff. We're going home."

"Home?" Margie looked horrified at the very idea. "I'm not going back to that place. No way!"

"Do what I'm telling you. Get a move on."

"No! He knows where to find me. He'll come after me again!"

"Don't be stupid. I'll be there, too. He's not going to get to you without coming through me first."

What an egotistic jerk, Savannah thought, mentally loping his swelled head off with a dull machete.

"I'm not going," Margie said. "I want to stay here tonight with Savannah. I feel safe here."

"Are you saying I can't keep my own kid safe?" Bloss bellowed.

Margie gave him a withering look. "Well . . . you didn't. I was almost killed tonight, and where was my big protective father?"

"That isn't fair; I didn't know. How could I have known he was going to come after you?"

"You could be home once in a while when I get there. Just once in a while, Daddy. They couldn't even get hold of you when I needed you in the hospital. I didn't want you there, because I knew you'd blame me for wrecking the car." She paused, only a second, to catch her breath, then went at him again. "But even if I had wanted you, they couldn't find you. They left messages for you everywhere, even an APB, and they couldn't find you. You're never, ever, around when I need you."

"You've got a lousy attitude, you know that. You're ungrateful, just like your mother."

"Excuse me, Captain," Savannah said in her most controlled, authoritative voice, trying not to convey the fact that she wanted to rip his tongue out and shove it in his left ear. "I hate to interrupt this family discussion, but we've all had a tough day, especially

162

Margie. Why don't you just give it a rest? She's welcome to sleep here in my guest room, and you two can resume your argument tomorrow morning after she's had a good night's sleep. Does that sound like a plan?"

He thought about it longer than she had hoped. Finally, he turned to his daughter. "Is that what you want, Margie?"

"Yes."

"Fine," he snapped. "If you don't want to come home with me, so be it. I'll send somebody over tomorrow morning to get you."

"Gee, thanks," Margie replied.

"You," Bloss said, pointing a finger at Dirk, "come with me. I want you to take me out to the crash site and fill me in on what you've got so far."

"Good night, Margie, Savannah," Dirk said graciously as he rose to follow the retreating Bloss. "You girls did good."

"Thanks." Savannah gave him an appreciative smile. Dirk could be sweet when he had a mind to be.

"Yeah, thanks," Margie said, equally grateful for the seldom heard encouraging word.

Once the men had exited the house, Savannah offered Margie a cup of hot chocolate. Not too surprisingly, she accepted.

While Savannah was heating the milk, Margie doodled on the legal pad, uncharacteristically quiet.

"What's on your mind?" Savannah asked her.

"I was just thinking what a jerk my dad is. You hate him, too, huh. I can tell."

Savannah weighed the wisdom of being honest against diplomacy. She decided to hit somewhere in between. "He's not my favorite person on the planet. But he did a good thing by having you, so he can't be all bad."

"He doesn't care about me."

Savannah chose a colorful Alice in Wonderland mug from her cupboard. "I'm sure he does," she said as she stirred hot milk into the cocoa mix. "Some fathers just aren't that good at showing it."

"Does your dad love you?" Margie asked, watching Savannah squirt a swirl of whipped cream from an aerosol can on top of the cocoa.

"Don't know. Never really knew him. He was a trucker . . . on the road about 364 days a year. Once a year he dropped by to get Mama pregnant. Then he'd take off again. We were mostly raised by my grandmother."

"I don't like very many men. Some of the boys my age are all right. But the older ones, like my dad . . . they're all creeps."

Savannah shaved some chocolate curls onto the top of the whipped cream and sprinkled on a bit of cinnamon. "They're not all creeps. Dirk's cool. He farts and burps too much, but basically, he's all right."

"Yeah, Dirk's cool," Margie reluctantly conceded as Savannah handed her the overloaded mug.

"And I know a few others who are definitely worth the air they breathe," Savannah said as she poured herself a cup of the Louisiana brew. She sat across the table from Margie. "But just a few. Two . . . maybe even three."

"But women are better."

Laughing, Savannah lifted her mug and Margie returned the toast. "Women are definitely better. Wa-a-ay more better."

ELEVEN

December 13 — 2:16 a.m.

"Savannah . . . pssst . . . Savannah."

Savannah fought her way to consciousness from a deep, much needed and deserved sleep. Gran was right, there was no rest for the weary. By the dim moonlight shining through the lace curtains, she could see her favorite flannel pajamas standing in the bedroom door. Margie was wearing them.

"Yes, dear?" she said groggily.

"I had a really bad dream." Margie sounded and looked like a forlorn five-year-old who was afraid of the thunder. But Savannah reminded herself that this teenager's recent nightmare had been far more traumatic than the usual lightning storm.

"I'm not surprised," she said. She sat up in bed and turned on the nightstand lamp. "Do you want to come in here and tell me about it?"

"Well . . . not really. I don't want to talk about it. Or even think about it. I was wondering if . . ."

"Yes?"

"If you'd think it was just completely weird

if I asked you if . . ."

"If . . . ?" Savannah had a good idea where this was headed.

"If I could sleep in here with you."

Savannah chuckled. Now, how had she guessed that one? "No. I don't think it's weird at all. Climb in." She pulled back the comforter on the other side of the queen-sized bed, fluffed the pillow, and patted the mattress invitingly. "You don't hog the covers, do you?"

"Sometimes." Margie laughed and climbed in beside her, looking grateful and infinitely relieved.

"Well, don't, or I'll kick you out. And stay on your own side."

"Okay."

Savannah turned out the lamp and lay down. She pulled the blankets up around her chin.

Margie did the same, flouncing around like a banty hen making her nest. When she was finally settled, she sighed and said, "You're cool, Savannah. I wish you were my mom or my big sister."

"I can be your big sister if you want," she said, touched by the girl's honesty and vulnerability, rare in an adolescent. "Heck, I'm a big sister to half of Georgia . . . what's another sister or two?"

"You've got a lot of brothers and sisters?"

"There are nine of us. I'm the oldest."

"Wow. I'm an only kid. They say that

167

makes you spoiled, but I think it just makes you lonely."

"I think you're right."

Savannah stifled a giggle.

"What's so funny?" Margie asked.

"Lying here with you . . . it reminds me of a little song my granny used to sing to us at bedtime."

"Sing it to me."

"Naw. You don't know what you're asking. Believe me, Granny Reid sings a lot better than I do."

"I don't care. I want to hear it."

Savannah took a deep breath. "Okay, here goes":

Two little chil'uns, lyin' in bed,
One 'most sick, and the other 'most dead.
Call for the doctor. The doctor said,
"Feed them little chil'uns some short'nin'
    bread."

"Wait a minute." Margie flopped onto her side, facing Savannah, and propped up on her elbow. "Does 'chil'uns' mean children?"

"Of course. Don't you speak Southern?"

Margie laughed. "I guess not. And what's short'nin' bread?"

"Something you wouldn't want to eat. Here's the second verse":

Two little chil'uns, lyin' in bed.

168

One turned over, and the other one said,
"You peed in my wa-a-rm pla-a-ce.
You peed in my wa-a-rm place."

Margie socked Savannah on the shoulder. "That's a silly song."

"Maybe so, but those are the house rules: Stay on your side, don't hog the blanket, and —"

"And don't pee in your warm place."

"Or anyplace else for that matter."

"You got it."

Savannah gave her an affectionate nudge with her elbow. "Good night, sleep tight, and don't let the bedbugs bite."

"You have *bugs* in your bed?"

"It's just a quaint, Georgia nighttime blessing. Hush and go to sleep."

"Okay. Thanks, Savannah."

"No sweat."

9:10 a.m.

"Good morning, ladies. Coulter Limousine Service." Dirk stood in Savannah's doorway, wearing a smile that could only have been accomplished by sleeping with a coat hanger in his mouth the evening before. A night owl, like Savannah, Dirk felt basically the same way about morning people as she did: They should be shot at sunrise, when they were at their obnoxious perkiest.

Savannah ushered him into the living room, where she and Margie were sipping coffee, munching donuts, and watching Bugs Bunny cartoons on television. Although Savannah had slipped into jeans and a sweatshirt, Margie was still wearing her borrowed p.j.'s and robe. They looked like the remnants of a pajama party.

Margie was only mildly pleased to see Dirk. "So, you're the one my dad pawned me off on," she muttered. "Lucky you."

"Actually, he didn't pawn you off on anybody. I volunteered for the job," he said, sweeping off an imaginary hat and bowing low. "Driving a couple of beautiful women around the town isn't such a bad way for a guy to make a buck. Are you about ready to go?"

She sagged as though every bone in her body had just melted. "Let me get dressed."

After watching the girl trudge up the stairs, Savannah turned to Dirk. "Boy, you're sure laying it on thick. What's up?"

He grunted, plopped down on one end of the sofa and reached into the bright pink donut box for a cream horn. "The old man wants me to dump her off at Casa Presidio in the marina."

"Will he be there?" She sat beside him and finished off her coffee.

"Are you kidding?" He bit off a third of the pastry in one bite and talked while he chewed, dribbling powdered sugar down his chin. Years ago, Savannah had realized that her attempts to civilize this rough-around-the-edges bachelor were only going to be moderately effective. "If Bloss wouldn't take the time to drive his own daughter around this morning, do you think he's going to spend the day baby-sitting her?"

Savannah couldn't believe it. This was low, even for a slug like Bloss. "Are you telling me that poor kid has to sit in a hotel room alone all day, after what happened to her last night?"

"Seems so." He shoved in another huge bite.

"Well, that stinks. *He* stinks. She's going to be hurt and mad as hell, and I don't blame her."

"Me, either. That's why I was hoping you'd come along for the ride . . . you know, and get her settled into the room."

"Settled, my butt. You want someone else there to defuse the bomb when she blows."

"That too. Will you ride along?"

He crammed the last third of the cream horn into his mouth and chewed noisily while he waited for her answer. He didn't look particularly worried or anxious; he knew how Savannah felt about neglected kids, having been one herself.

"Sure," she said.

He lowered his voice, leaned closer to her

. . . and the donut box . . . and nabbed a lemon-filled one. "And there's another reason why I want you along. Something's come up. I want you to run out to Titus Dunn's place with me."

"Titus? Why?"

Before he could answer, Margie reappeared, wearing the same soiled T-shirt and shorts she had worn last night. She looked vulnerable and forlorn.

"Okay," she said. "I'm ready. Where are we going?"

"Well, I . . ." Dirk half-choked on the jelly donut.

A look of horror crossed her face, quickly replaced by fury. "My dad didn't tell you to take me *home*, did he? I mean, I can't go back there. Not yet!"

"No, of course not," Savannah interjected; Dirk was still gagging. "Your father arranged for you to have a nice room down on the beach at the Casa Presidio."

Margie glared at Dirk. If looks could have killed the messenger bearing the bad tidings, he would have been a corpse. "A hotel?" she shouted. "He's having you dump me off at a lousy hotel?"

"Ah . . . that's what he said, yes," Dirk admitted, looking miserable. "Well, he didn't say the 'dump' part."

"Is he or anyone else going to be there?"

"No-o-o-o . . . not right away."

172

"Then he's *dumping* me. Why couldn't he just let me go to one of my friends' houses? Then I could at least be with somebody who cares about me."

Her eyes flooded with tears and her chin trembled. Savannah wanted to take her in her arms and give her a tight hug, but she didn't think the girl would welcome an affectionate gesture when she was so angry.

"He probably thought you'd be the most safe and comfortable in the hotel," Savannah offered, knowing how lame it sounded.

"You're wrong," Margie said, heading for the door. "I don't know why he wants me at a rotten hotel, but it doesn't have anything to do with what's best for me or what I want. He doesn't think about me at all." She stomped to the door and yanked it open. "Come on. Let's go."

Savannah reached into the coat closet for her purse and gun as Margie marched down the driveway toward Dirk's old Buick. "I wish I could argue with her," she said sadly, "but . . ."

"Yeah." Dirk nodded as he followed her out the door. "I hear ya."

9:55 a.m.

"I've seen Sadder Sacks in my day, but that kid takes the cake," Dirk told Savannah as they drove away from the Casa Presidio

173

and headed inland toward the foothills, that were charred from the previous brushfires.

"Sacks, cakes, you're mixing your metaphors," Savannah said absentmindedly as she stared out the passenger window and tried not to see the vision of Margie's woebegone face when she had told her good-bye only moments before.

"Mixing my whats?"

"Never mind. You're right. She was really bummed."

"That was pretty nice of you, Van, offering to go over to her house this afternoon and pick up some of her clothes and makeup stuff."

"Hey, a girl can't live without her 'stuff,' especially a teenager. Besides, somebody's gotta give the kid some attention. I was afraid if I didn't, she'd split. She may anyway."

"You think?"

"Maybe." A chill swept over her when she thought of how the night's events might have concluded. "I hope she stays put, behind locked doors, at least for a while."

"You figure he might be looking for her?"

"Who knows why a sicko like that does anything?"

They rode along in silence until Savannah noticed that Dirk was heading out of town to a small, neighboring community called Two Trees, named for a pair of enormous oaks that crowned a nearby hill. She recalled when Titus Dunn had moved from the beach to this area years ago.

"By the way," she said, "I didn't want to ask in front of Margie, but what's this about Titus? Why did you want me to go by his place with you?"

"He's missing."

"Missing?" The chill she had experienced went even deeper. "What do you mean, 'missing'?"

"I mean he didn't report to work last night. He was supposed to come on duty at 1800 hours, but he didn't show. In eleven years on the force, he's never done that before."

"Did anybody try calling him at home to see if he's sick or — ?"

"I did. At least five times. Just got the answering machine."

"How about his girlfriend, Christy? Has she heard from him?"

"Seems she's gone to Seattle to take care of her mom who's dying of some terminal illness. We didn't wanna shake her up if there's nothing to this. She's got enough on her plate as it is."

"No kidding. That's too bad. I always liked Christy. She and Titus are a nice couple."

"Yeah."

Savannah pictured Titus as he had been the last time she had seen him at the pancake house. He had been so pleased to have been the first on the scene of Charlene Yardley's attack, so happy to have been able to offer the victim some help and comfort.

"You don't think anything's actually happened to him, do you?" she said.

"Do you?"

Officer Titus Dunn. Punctual. Reliable. A good cop. Not showing up for work or even calling in? Had something happened to him? "Maybe."

"That's what I thought," Dirk replied, his tone as grim as the expression on his street-worn face. "Maybe."

"Do you think it might have anything to do with this case?" Savannah waited, hoping he would say, "No." Dirk had good instincts; if he thought Titus was okay, perhaps he was.

"It might have something to do with the rapist," he said. "It might not. Either way, I think Titus is in trouble."

Savannah's heart sank. Not the answer she had been hoping for. "Me, too."

TWELVE

When Dirk and Savannah came to a stop in front of the small, but well-kept cottage, she was surprised to see how many improvements Titus had made to the property. A carport had been added, flower bed planted, a lush lawn nurtured, and the hedges were meticulously trimmed.

"The place looks great," Savannah said as they climbed out of the car. "Looks like Christy's got a green thumb."

"No, actually, that's Titus. He's quite the gardener. How long has it been since you've been here?"

"Oh, gosh . . . at least five years. I was still on the force. Titus and Christy had just started going together, and they gave a barbecue."

They headed up the cobblestone sidewalk which was lined with a royal blue carpet of Crystal Palace lobelia, dotted with clusters of sweetly scented paperwhite narcissus.

"I remember that barbecue," Dirk said. "It was in July or August."

"Of course you remember, darlin'. Free

177

food, free beer. It was probably the high point of the social season for you."

Dirk stopped in the middle of the sidewalk, his hands on his hips. "You know, Reid, I'm getting tired of your 'cheap' cracks."

She shoved his shoulder as she walked past him. "Don't be so cheap, and I won't crack. Buy me dinner sometime, big boy, and see how friendly I get."

He followed her, wearing his grouch face. "Ah, you're just messin' with my head," he said. "I took you out to The Bench for your birthday and you didn't exactly come across afterward. In fact, you've never come across . . . not even close."

She gave him a withering look. "You don't exactly woo a girl. All-you-can-eat miniature meatballs and buffalo wings at a sports bar's happy hour ain't exactly my idea of a birthday bash."

"You chowed down on the pretzels and the peanuts, too," he offered in rebuttal.

"You said you were taking me out for a meal. I was starving." She shook her head, disgusted. "And to think I got all dolled up in my pearls and little black dress for you."

He dropped the grumpy facade and winked at her. "You looked pretty damned good in those pearls, too . . . as I remember."

She returned the flirtatious grin and added an extra waggle to her walk. "Fortunately, your taste in women is better than your

178

choice of restaurants and cuisine."

"What's my cousin got to do with anything?"

"Not a thing. I'm just messin' with your head again."

She pointed to the black, late-model Jeep in the driveway. "That's his Cherokee, huh?"

"Yes, but I think he drives a 1968 Charger, too," Dirk said, glancing around the otherwise empty drive.

"Maybe it's in the garage. Wanna look?"

He shook his head and stepped up onto the porch. "Let's see if he answers the door before we go pokin' around."

Savannah joined him on the steps and watched and waited as he rang the doorbell several times. "Hmmmm," she said. "Maybe our boy went fishing for the day or into L.A. for a gardening expo."

"Wouldn't that be nice. Not likely, but nice." He jiggled the knob, but the door was locked. "Let's try the back," he said.

Before they reached the rear door, they saw the first signs of trouble. Savannah knelt down and pointed out some dark, red-black drops on the cement walkway leading from the back of the house to the driveway.

"Not a good sign," she said, feeling her stomach lurch. The thought of a fellow cop coming to harm still made her sick, even if she wasn't officially one of the fellows anymore.

"Not good at all," Dirk muttered as he hurried to the door. He turned the knob and the door swung open. "You know any cops who leave their doors unlocked?"

"Not a one."

"Me neither."

Dirk drew his weapon, and Savannah did the same. Carefully, he took a few steps inside. She followed. They were in a small, tidy kitchen with freshly starched curtains at the window and a bowl of fresh fruit on the table. The answering machine on the counter was beeping and the light flashing. Savannah glanced at the message indicator. Five calls.

"Titus?" Dirk called, his pistol pointed at the ceiling, every muscle and nerve tense and ready for use. "Hey, Titus," he yelled louder as he walked slowly toward the door leading to the living room. "Are you home, buddy?"

"It's Dirk and Savannah," she added, close behind him. "Yoo-hoo, Titus?"

They had taken only a few steps into the living room when they saw the carnage: the sofa overturned onto its back, the glass coffee table shattered, the television knocked off its shelf and lying on the floor with its picture tube broken, a mirror on the wall cracked and books and knickknacks scattered everywhere.

But those things didn't bother them nearly so much as the blood. Lots of it. Splashed across the wall, puddled on the beige carpet, smeared on furniture. It was everywhere.

"Oh, shit," Savannah muttered, shaking her head.

"This is bad," Dirk replied, his voice husky. "Oh, man. This is really bad. I'll check the bedroom."

"I'll get the bath."

They met a minute later in the hallway.

"Nothing?" Savannah asked. She could tell by his face that he hadn't discovered a corpse. Thankfully, neither had she.

"Nobody," he said. "But there's more blood in there."

"In the bath, too. Looks like somebody tried to wash up. You'd better call it in."

Dirk holstered his Smith and Wesson and took a cell phone from his inside coat pocket. He punched in some numbers. His face looked so gray that Savannah wondered briefly how long it had been since he'd had a physical. This line of work was tough on anyone, let alone an aging detective who subsisted on donuts, pizza, and beer.

"Coulter here," he said into the phone. "I'm at Titus Dunn's house in Two Trees. He's not here, but the place is trashed and there's blood everywhere. Looks like he put up a hell of a fight."

As he talked, Savannah continued to search the room that had, until recently, been the cozy living room of a cop who liked to garden and loved his girlfriend and barbecued ribs. Now it was a crime scene.

Maybe even worse.

"Hey, Dirk," she said, interrupting his call.

"Hold on," he told his party on the other end. "What is it, Van?"

"There's a bullet hole here in the wall behind the front door, and blood spray on the paneling."

He hurried over to examine the neat round hole and the not-so-neat pattern of splattered blood, signifying that a human body had sprung a major leak in that immediate vicinity.

"Shit," he said. Then, into the phone, "You'd better send Dr. Liu and a couple of techs. I'm afraid we've got a homicide scene here."

THIRTEEN

Savannah had left the scene to collect Margie's "stuff" from her house — using the girl's key rather than pick a police captain's lock — and deliver it to the perturbed and bored teenager. By the time she returned to Titus Dunn's cottage in Two Trees, the property had been converted into a miniature city, inhabited by Dr. Jennifer Liu, the county coroner, and her crew of crime technicians.

Savannah stepped over the yellow tape that was cordoning off the area, and walked up to the first technician she recognized, Eileen Brady. Eileen was on her hands and knees, collecting one of the blood drops from the driveway with a cotton swab. "Hi, Eileen," she said, trying to blend in and not make it too obvious that she was an average citizen, not an authorized person, blithely invading a crime scene. "Is Dirk still around?"

"He left a few minutes ago to get a bite to eat." Eileen laughed and shook her head. "Seems nothing ruins that guy's appetite."

"How true. I've seen him help fish a two-week-old decomposing corpse out of a lake and, half an hour later, eat a quarter-pounder with cheese. Go figure. I see the meat wagon; where's Dr. Liu?"

Eileen pointed with her bloody swab. "Inside the house."

"Thanks."

Savannah strolled on into the house, keeping an eye peeled for Bloss or any other members of the S.C.P.D. brass who hated her.

There were several.

She hated them right back.

Not seeing anyone on her mental hit list, she ventured inside the house, where she saw a beautiful, petite, and ultra-feminine Asian woman, who looked the exact opposite of the funereal coroner stereotype.

Dr. Jennifer Liu brushed her long, glossy, black hair away from her face with one gloved hand as she rose from where she had been kneeling on the floor. "Hey, Savannah! How nice to see you. Did you bring me some Godiva chocolates?"

"Sorry, Dr. Jen, I didn't know it was that time of month. PMS again?"

"It's always that time of the month. You should know that."

Long ago, Savannah and Dr. Liu had discovered they were soul sisters, and the common bond between them was a love of chocolate. Usually, when Savannah visited the doctor's autopsy suite, she was looking for answers, and from the beginning, Dr. Liu had established the price of her bribe — a Snickers bar if it was a mundane inquiry, Godiva if it was something heavy.

"So," Savannah said, watching Dr. Liu move from one ruined object in the room to the next, making notes and sketches on a yellow legal pad, "how's it going?"

"Slow. Methodical. Careful." Jennifer looked sad. "Especially when it's one of our own."

On the other side of the room, Savannah could see Cindy Oleksiak, who was also collecting blood samples. Savannah recognized the process as a quick and effective method of typing the specimens.

"Is all of this Titus's blood?" she asked Dr. Liu.

"We've tested samples from in here, the bedroom, and the bathroom," she said. "They're all the same type: A Negative."

"His type?"

Dr. Liu nodded. "Afraid so. It's a fairly uncommon type. Of course, we won't know for sure until we do the DNA tests. That's going to take a while."

"Do you think he was murdered?"

The doctor glanced around and lowered her voice. "Honestly? Yes. I think so. There's a lot of blood here. And that was a .357 slug that we took out of the paneling. Judging from the blood spray on the wall, it went through a body first . . . about chest level. It would have done a lot of damage."

Savannah digested that information a moment or two before she could speak. "Why do you suppose they removed his body?"

"Who knows? But there are blood drops leading through the kitchen, out the back door, to the driveway. Like Hansel and Gretel, they left a pretty clear trail."

"We saw some of those drops earlier. Dirk said Titus keeps a classic Charger in the garage."

"It's gone. They've put out an APB on him and the car."

Savannah's brain searched for a happier, less tragic explanation. "Maybe he was wounded and left on his own, tried to get to a hospital and passed out along the way . . . something like that?"

"Anything's possible." She gave Savannah a cheerless but understanding smile. "To be honest, I'm afraid that's wishful thinking," she said. "I doubt someone who had been that badly wounded and had lost that much blood, would still be able to get around on their own, let alone drive an automobile."

So much for happily-ever-after endings, Savannah thought. "I suppose you're right. It's just that . . . well . . . Titus is a sweetheart and . . ."

"I know. We're all pretty fond of him. This is going to be terrible for Christy. She's so in love with him. I hear they just got engaged last month."

"And her mom's terminally ill. Poor girl.

186

Like they say, 'When it rains . . . you might as well start building that ark.' Has anyone told her yet?"

"Dirk made the call just before he took off for lunch. She can't leave her mom. Asked him to keep her informed."

Savannah glanced around the shattered remains of the room that said so much about what had happened inside those walls, and yet revealed so little. "Did you find anything else that might point a finger at who did this?" she asked.

Dr. Liu smiled. It was her cocky, almost arrogant, grin that she got when she had something good. She reached into her lab coat pocket and withdrew a small plastic bag that was sealed and labeled. She stuck it under Savannah's nose. "I thought you'd never ask. Take a look."

At first, Savannah thought the doctor had handed her an empty bag. Then she caught her breath. "Wow! Is this what I think it is?"

Inside the bag were three hairs. Coarse, silver, curly hairs.

"I won't know for sure until I get them back to the lab and under a microscope, where I can compare them with the ones taken from the rape victims. But I'm ninety-nine percent sure it'll be a match."

Savannah felt the adrenaline rush to her knees, and they turned to warm gelatin. "Where were they?"

"On the carpet right there, about three and a half feet from where the victim would have been standing when he was shot."

Savannah fingered the bag thoughtfully. "Does Dirk know about this?"

"Nope. I found them after he'd left," she said proudly. Looking over Savannah's shoulder, she peered out the window. "But I'm pretty sure that's your old partner, pulling in the driveway right now. You can tell him if you want. I'm sure it'll make his day . . . or ruin it."

Savannah hurried out the door and met Dirk on the lawn. He had a McDonalds' large Coke in his hand, and a sated look on his face. "Hi," he greeted her. "Did you get the teenybopper's junk to her?"

"I left her happy and sassy, lying on the bed, watching soaps. Oh, and she's discovered the wonders of room service. That kid's appetite is almost as monstrous as yours and mine. Bloss is going to have to take out a second mortgage just to pay her tab."

Dirk snorted. "Good. Serves him right." He nodded toward the house. "How's Dr. Liu doin' in there?"

"Bad news and good . . . well, at least interesting, news."

He frowned. "What's the bad?" Good ol' Dirk. He knew how to embrace the dark side of the moon.

"The blood is most likely Titus's," Savannah said, hating how the words tasted in her mouth. "And there's so much of it that he's probably dead."

Dirk's face dropped. "That's about as bad as bad news gets, all right. What's the good?"

"Good or bad, depends on how you look at it. But she also found what she thinks are some hairs like the ones from Santa's beard."

"No way! Why would that sonofabitch go after Titus? He likes to rape women, not kill cops."

Savannah shrugged. "Maybe Titus saw something at the scene, something the rapist didn't want him to talk to anyone about."

"But Titus already said he didn't find anything that night, or the next morning either."

"Perhaps he saw something but didn't realize it was significant until later. I don't know; it's just a thought."

He shook his head and took a long swig of Coke. "Oh, man . . . this is too bizarre. A serial rapist who goes from mall abductions and rapes to kidnapping a police captain's daughter, to shooting a cop. Just what kind of weird is this?"

Savannah sighed, feeling old. "The kind of weird . . ." she said, ". . . that keeps you awake at night."

11:14 p.m.

As Savannah stood beside her sofa, looking

down at Dirk, sprawled across it, his mouth hanging open and drool oozing down his chin onto one of her best throw pillows, she wondered if the fried liver and onions had been such a good idea, after all.

He had seemed so discouraged when he had dropped by this evening. Sitting at her kitchen table, a beer in one hand and the other hand buried in a plate of chocolate chip cookies, he had dumped his whole rotten day on her.

After he had left Titus's house, he had spent the rest of the afternoon interviewing the previous rape victims, asking them about the star-studded ring. No one remembered it specifically, although two said their attacker might have been wearing something like that.

Nothing like concrete evidence to make a detective feel warm and fuzzy.

Dirk had been anything but fuzzy, sitting there at the table, shoving his face full of cookies. Taking pity on him, she had offered to make his favorite dinner: liver, fried with bacon and onions, mashed potatoes and gravy. The guy had real down-in-Dixie taste buds.

Unfortunately, he had the cholesterol level to match. And seeing his inert form stretched across her sofa, she was afraid that meal might have put him right over the edge.

But she wasn't terribly concerned — as long as he was drooling. To the best of her knowledge, corpses didn't drool. But she'd have to ask Dr. Jennifer sometime, just to make sure.

When the phone rang, she hurried to answer it, before the racket woke him. He hadn't had a real night's sleep since the case had begun, and she hoped the snooze would improve his mental focus . . . and maybe even his grouchy disposition.

"Hello," she said softly as she took the cordless phone into the kitchen.

"Is Coulter there?" the nasal voice on the other end barked at her. This hatred she harbored for Bloss was quickly turning to full-fledged loathing. She could almost feel her hackles rise.

"Why?" she replied just as curtly.

"Because I have to talk to him."

"Maybe he is, maybe he isn't."

"Put him on the phone."

She stuck her tongue out at the phone. "Say, 'Pretty please, with sugar on it.'"

"Fuck you, Reid. Get Coulter. It's important."

She grinned. His goat had definitely been gotten. She was finished with the game. "Only because you asked so nicely."

She walked into the living room, phone in hand, then thought of something else she wanted to say. "Oh, by the way, I think the way you're neglecting your daughter is shameful," she told Bloss, "although it's perfectly in keeping with your usual lack of sensitivity and complete absence of character."

"Shut up about my kid, you dumb bitch." Ah-ha! She had struck a nerve. Might as well irritate him just a little more while the gettin' was good.

"A bitch, maybe," she said, "but dumb? How would you know? Stupid Head."

"Get Coulter!"

"Pee-Pee Brain."

"Now! God damn it, Reid, you'd better . . ."

"Yeah, yeah, yeah."

She walked over to the couch and nudged Dirk in the ribs. "Hey, Sleeping Beauty. Bloss is on the phone," she told him, loud enough that the captain would be sure to hear, "and he's got his panties in a wad about something."

Sure enough. A few more obscenities drifted from the receiver in her hand.

Dirk looked suspicious. "Did you say something to piss him off?"

She batted her eyelashes. "Me? Why, of course not. You know how I just *adore* that man."

"Right." He sat up, ran his fingers through his hair and took the phone. "Coulter here." He listened. Savannah pretended not to as she rearranged the books and magazines on her coffee table. "Really? When? Where?"

Whatever it was, he was wide awake now. He made a scribbling gesture in the air and Savannah quickly supplied him with a tablet and pen. He began to write. She looked over his shoulder and read something about rocks and the beach. She had never been able to decipher his chicken scratches.

"Did they say who they were? What else?" He threw down the pen and reached for his sneakers, which he had kicked off and thrown beneath the sofa. "Okay," he said, pulling them on. "I'm on my way out there right now." He gave Savannah a funny look. "No, of course not, Captain. I wouldn't think of taking Reid with me."

When he hung up the phone and reached for his coat, Savannah grabbed hers, too.

As they rushed out the door, she said, "So, where are we going?"

"To that big, stone jetty, just north of the pier."

She locked the door behind them, then ran to catch up with him as he hustled to his car. "Why?"

"Because some anonymous caller just phoned the station."

"And?"

He paused for a moment, his hand on the Buick's door handle. He looked a tad green. "And they said that's where we can find Titus Dunn's body."

FOURTEEN

December 14 — 8:16 a.m.

Dirk sat on the end of the pier, his sneakers dangling over the edge, looking about as miserable as Savannah had ever seen him. She walked out to him and sat next to him, ignoring the fact that she would probably get seagull poop or fish bait remnants on her good linen slacks. Friends didn't concern themselves with such things at times like this.

"Don't jump," she said, nudging him with her elbow. "It isn't worth it. The water's damned cold this time of year."

"Oh, I don't know," he mumbled. "I hear that drowning ain't all that bad."

She gazed thoughtfully out at the horizon where the morning sky was clear, cloudless, blue . . . the typical California sky. "I don't trust information about dying," she said. "Like, how do they know for sure? The people who have really gone through with it aren't around to talk about it. The rest of them are guessing."

"I suppose Titus knows what it's like to die."

She glanced over her shoulder at the jetty and the stretch of beach between the rock

194

formation and the wooden pier. The area was swarming with cops. Dr. Liu and her team were hovering over the classic Charger they had found, parked in the beachside lot. It had been empty. Thank God.

Except for a generous amount of blood splatterings, smudges and smears.

Hordes of spectators lined the yellow tape that marked the perimeter. Some were equipped with cameras, microphones, and pushy attitudes that identified them as media.

Everybody wanted a piece of the action.

"We can't be sure Titus is dead," she said, trying to believe her own words, "until we find the body."

"Where the hell is it? We looked all night." He waved a hand at the assortment of uniformed cops, plain-clothes cops, off-duty cops. Everyone and their brother was looking for any sign of their fallen comrade. "Dammit, Van," he said, "half of the force . . . hell, more than half . . . was out here looking all night. And we got zip, zilch."

"We've got a little more than zip or zilch. There's the Charger."

He cast a depressed look at the car and winced. "So, the blood is probably his, the same as the house. We already knew he was hurt. So, that's nothin' new."

Savannah marveled at how Dirk could put a negative spin on anything. But this time, he wasn't without justification.

195

"And somebody wiped the car down pretty good when they were through with it," he continued, "so we don't have any prints to go on."

She was determined to find the proverbial glass half full, or at least not bone dry. "That tells us something," she offered.

"What? That his attacker has good house-keeping skills?"

"Maybe. But mostly, it tells us that Titus was inside the car, bleeding, and whoever shot him must have been with him in the car, probably drove him here, took him out of the car and wiped everything down."

"Then where's his body? If they dumped him here, where the hell's the corpse?"

"If it was lying on the jetty rocks, like the caller said, it may have been washed away before we got here. There was a high tide last night."

"There's a happy thought; we may never know what happened to him, let alone who did it."

She draped one arm across his broad shoulders. "Buck up, babycakes. It ain't over yet."

She heard footsteps on the pier's wooden planks, coming toward them. When she turned to see who their visitor might be, some of her depression turned to irritation. Captain Harvey Bloss. Just who she needed to see right now.

He had shown up a couple of times during the night to annoy the searchers, pretending to be in charge, but getting in the way. Each time, Savannah had ducked out of sight, rather than risk another confrontation. She didn't want to fight; she was too tired to be feisty.

"It's El Capitan Muy Loco. Whoopy-do. Want me to just go ahead and jump?" she asked, pointing to the water that splashed against the barnacle-encrusted pilings below. "Now might be a good time to find out if drowning's a nice or crummy way to go."

"Naw. Stick around. If he gives you any guff, he'll be the one going for a dip. I'm not in the mood to put up with his b.s. right now."

Dirk looked like he might actually welcome a verbal clash. When he was that tired and discouraged, he didn't always use the best judgment — unlike Savannah who didn't have to be tired or discouraged to abandon good judgment.

"Don't get on Bloss's bad side," Savannah warned him. "Believe me, having been there myself, I can vouch for the fact that it's not a place you want to be."

"I thought I told you to stay away from crime scenes, Reid," Bloss said, dispensing with his usual unpleasantries.

"What crime scene?" She donned her most irritating pseudo-innocent face for his benefit.

"This is a city pier. The only things murdered here are some red snappers and worms."

"Are you telling me you weren't running around down there?"

Dirk stirred, as though about to jump into the conversation, but Savannah squeezed his forearm. "Am I telling you that, Captain? No. I'm not telling you that . . . or anything else, for that matter. As far as I'm concerned, you and I aren't speaking."

"Actually, we are speaking. We have some business to discuss. Privately."

He gave Dirk a dismissive nod, which clearly irked the heck out of him. Dirk turned to Savannah. "Van?"

"Sure. No problem," Savannah said, looking up and down Bloss's less-than-impressive physique with contempt. "If push comes to shove, I can take 'im. *He'll* be the one going over the edge."

Once Dirk was out of earshot, she asked Bloss, "Business? What kind of business?"

"Actually, it's more of a favor." He looked like he was about to choke on his own spit.

"A favor? *You're* going to ask *me* for a favor? How fun! I get to tell you to go hell in a handbasket! Go ahead, ask. I can't wait."

"I want you to let Margie stay at your house for a few days, until this case is resolved. I'm concerned for her safety, and I think she'd be better off there than the hotel."

"Oh." Her emotional hot air balloon came tumbling to earth. She would do it. She had to. But she wasn't going to let him off that easily. "So, tell me why I should do anything for you?"

"Not for me. For Margie." His patience was on a very short leash and it quickly reached its end. "Don't bust my balls about this, Reid. Believe me, it's not my idea. It's hers. For some reason, which I can't understand, she likes you. She's throwing a fit to stay with you."

"Tell me the truth about something."

"What?" He looked unhappy, uncomfortable. Briefly, she wondered why.

"Is she in danger? Do you know something I don't?"

"She was kidnapped and —"

"I know. But she got away. Do you have any particular reason to think he might come after her?"

His usually florid face blushed even redder. She could tell she was really pissing him off. She couldn't be more pleased.

"Look, Reid," he snapped. "You know as much about this case as I do. I just figure it's a good idea at this point for her to stay at your place. I can't keep paying for a hotel room and all that room service."

"Oh, I see," she said sarcastically. "It's an issue of economics."

"It's an issue of my daughter getting on

199

with her life. She won't stay cooped up in a hotel room anymore."

"And you need a baby-sitter."

"I'll pay you."

"How much?"

He named an amount that was larger than she had anticipated, a sum that would make a tidy difference in her overdrawn bank account.

"That's not nearly enough."

He upped his offer by fifty percent. But she was feeling perverse.

"I don't want your damned money. I want you to bring a couple of bags of groceries over — all her favorite stuff."

"I don't know what she likes."

Savannah shook her head. "What a sorry excuse for a father you are. Ask her. Tell her to make a list and you go shopping and you deliver it to my door. I want to make sure she's got everything she wants to eat. Nobody's ever fainted from hunger in the Reid household."

"Obviously."

"Up yours."

"So, you'll pick her up right away and take her home with you?"

Savannah nodded. "And you'll drop off the groceries this afternoon?"

He agreed. As he walked away, he said over his shoulder, "Watch out for her, you hear? I don't want anything happening to that kid."

As Savannah watched him leave, she lifted one eyebrow and mumbled, "You'd better be careful, Captain. There for a second, I thought I saw a flicker of humanity."

Then she reconsidered. "Naw."

9:42 a.m.

When Margie opened her hotel-room door and saw Savannah standing there, she nearly "cut a rug" as Savannah's Granny Reid described the little dance done by extremely happy people.

"Savannah! Hi!" She threw the door open wide and practically pulled Savannah inside. "I thought it was my dumb dad. Come on in."

"You should have looked through the peephole first, and then you would have known who it was," Savannah told her. "And you oughta stop calling him your dumb dad."

"Why? He is."

"Because it confuses me . . . makes me think you've got a smart one around somewhere."

"What?"

"Never mind." Savannah sat on the edge of the bed that was littered with deflated potato chip bags, an empty pizza box, makeup and lots of new clothes that looked like they had been purchased at the gift shop downstairs. Yeah, Harvey Bloss was going to have a four-figure bill to pay. And it couldn't have happened to a more deserving guy.

"The point is," Savannah continued, "he's still your father, and where I come from, you don't talk that way about your elders . . . no matter what their I.Q. . . . or lack thereof."

Margie plopped down on the other side of the bed and put on a sourpuss. "I thought you came by to see me, maybe to hang out. But I guess you're here to lecture me about respecting my parents."

Savannah grinned. It was always fun to make somebody's day. "No," she said. "I came by to spring you outta this joint. The parole board granted you a pardon."

Margie jumped up from the bed, scattering bottles of blue and black nail polish. "No kidding?"

"I kid you not, kiddo. Get your stuff packed."

"All right!" Then she looked suspicious. "Where am I going? Not back to my house."

"Nope. Back to *my* house."

"He's going to let me stay with you? He actually agreed to that?"

"He did, indeed. Said he thought you'd feel safer at my place. See there, the old far— . . . fella . . . does something right once in awhile."

"Fantastic! I asked him if I could . . . well . . . actually, I threw a fit . . . but he said no way, because he really, really hates you, no offense."

"None taken."

"I can't believe he said yes. This is just too cool!"

"Seems your father put your feelings and desires ahead of his own this time." Savannah nearly gagged on the words. It really grumped her butt to say anything nice about that s.o.b., but she sensed his daughter needed to have *some* positive thoughts toward the man who had sired her.

Margie started throwing her new clothes and makeup into shopping bags. "He's not letting me do this because he's a nice guy," she said, tossing in some teen magazines. "It's just that he was afraid that if he made me stay here another night by myself, I'd run away to Hollywood, become a hooker/drug addict on Sunset Boulevard."

"Now, where would he get an idea like that?" Savannah mused, stretching out on the bed. "How imaginative. A teenage, runaway, drugged-out hooker on the streets of Hollywood. How unique."

Margie giggled. "Okay, so it might not have been the most creative threat in the world, but —"

"It was right up there with holding your breath until you turn blue."

She hurried into the bathroom where she scooped miniature shampoos, conditioners and lotions into the bag. "Well, it worked, didn't it?"

"Only because you have a dumb dad. Leave the towels."

203

Sheepishly, she hung them back on the rack. "What would you do if your kid threatened to run away to Hollywood?"

"I'd tell them to go right ahead . . . everybody's entitled to follow their dreams of stardom. Then I'd follow them every step of the way, sneaking around behind shrubs and hiding behind lampposts to make sure they didn't get in real trouble. But my kid wouldn't take it that far, and neither would you. You're much too smart a woman for that."

Margie halted in midstep and studied Savannah carefully. "You think of me as a woman?"

"Usually, unless you're throwing a hissy fit. Don't you?"

"I guess not, because I was surprised to hear you say it."

"Well, maybe you'd better start thinking of yourself in terms of adulthood. You'll be twenty-one so fast it'll make your head spin."

"And you think I'm smart?"

"Except for opening the door without looking through the peep first, absolutely."

Margie beamed.

"So, don't use a lame threat like that Hollywood hooker malarkey on me, 'cause I won't buy it," Savannah said as she rose from the bed and grabbed one of the full bags. "Let's blow this joint. We've got two pints of Chunky Monkey waiting in my freezer with

204

our names on them."

"Hit me! Come on, land a good one!"

Ryan Stone — all 6'3" and 200 muscular pounds of his gorgeous self — stood in the middle of the mat, encouraging a dainty, Sunday school teacher type to kick the crap out of him. Only the Stone rocks were covered with extra padding in the form of a discreet, but industrial-sized cup.

Finally, the lady gave him a kick that was slightly more than half-hearted. Savannah sighed, knowing that was all he was going to get out of that student.

She had asked her close friend, Ryan Stone, former FBI agent, present bodyguard of some of the richest and most famous bodies in Los Angeles, to demonstrate self-defense techniques to a class that had suddenly tripled since the last attack.

At first, the ladies had been too enchanted by the tall, dark, gorgeous guy to do more than gaze at him. Finally, they were getting into the act.

"That's right. Another one!" he shouted at his wannabe attacker. "Another!" She landed a solid kick to his shin. Savannah saw him wince. "Hey, that hurt," he told the student. "Good job!"

Savannah motioned for the next combatant

to step onto the mat. "Okay, Angie," she said. "It's your turn. Front and center." Less timid than her predecessor, Angie rushed to get into place. Having seen the result of Charlene Yardley's attack, she seemed especially motivated.

"He's coming at you," Savannah yelled to her. "What are you going to do?"

"Scream."

"Scream what?"

"No-o-o-o!"

Ryan grabbed her by the forearm and held tightly, towering over her. She seemed momentarily frozen, her bravado gone.

"Again!" Savannah jumped onto the mat beside her and shouted into her ear. "Tell him *no!* Mean it!"

"No-o-o!" she shrieked. "No-o-o! No-o-o! No-o-o!"

"That's it! Knee him in the groin! Stomp his instep! Gouge out his eyes!"

Ryan effortlessly blocked each punch and thrust, but the girl's aim was excellent and her delivery enthusiastic.

"Yes!" Savannah yelled. "Now run! Run! Run!"

Angie flew off the mat and didn't stop running until she hit the figurative safety of the far wall.

"Fantastic!" Savannah said. "Now . . . Margie, step lively, darlin.' You're next."

Margie backed away from the mat as

though it were covered with burning coals and Ryan were some sort of fire-breathing monster. "I don't want to do it."

"I know you don't," Savannah said gently as she put her hand on the teenager's back and gave her a firm push forward. "But you need to, of all people. Get in there and show him what for!"

Margie walked up to Ryan and gave him little more than a nudge with her foot.

He laughed at her and shoved her hard, taunting her. "Ah, what kind of lousy kick was that?" he said. "I didn't feel a thing."

Savannah stood at her back, too close for comfort, deliberately invading her space. "Hit him again," she told her. "You know you want to. Pretend he's the bastard that nabbed you and let him have it."

Margie hit him this time with her fist in his chest. A second later her foot met his shin with a blow hard enough they could all feel it.

"Come on, break something," he said. She punched and kicked him again, much harder than before and she began to sob . . . but her crying sounded, not like a victim, but like someone enraged.

"Atta girl!" Savannah shouted. "Again!"

Margie attacked him with a vengeance, tears streaming down her cheeks, pummeling him for all she was worth. He could only ward off so many of the blows. Others hit, hard and solid.

"Ow-w-w," he yelled. "Okay, okay."

"That's enough," Savannah said, pulling the girl away from him and into her arms.

She clung to Savannah, her face buried against her shoulder, crying out the pain and fear she had been hiding since her abduction.

"That's my girl," Savannah said, stroking her hair. "That's my brave girl. You did great, sweetie. You showed that sonofabitch he was messin' with the wrong woman."

Finally, when the girl's sobs quieted down to simple, silent weeping, Savannah turned to Ryan. "Hey, buddy, are you okay?"

"It's nothing a quick trip to the emergency room won't put right. Congratulations, Margie. I pity the next guy who tries to take advantage of you."

"I didn't hurt you, did I?" Margie asked between hiccups.

"Not really, but I'm glad to see that you can turn into a tiger when you need to. That's what the class is all about."

"Okay, ladies," Savannah said. "I think we — especially Mr. Stone — have had enough for one night."

As she watched them leave, pausing to fawn over Ryan, she prayed they would all remain safe until the next time she saw them. "Just remember," she coached them as they walked out the door . . . together. "Avoid trouble, run from confrontation, but if you have to fight . . . whup the everlovin' shit out of 'im!"

★ ★ ★

One of the many things Savannah loved most about her friends, Ryan Stone and John Gibson, was their uncanny ability to know exactly when she needed a pleasant diversion from life's challenges. And dinner at Chez Antoine was as pleasing a pastime as could be afforded.

Of course, on a seldom-employed private detective's income, Savannah couldn't possibly afford Chez Antoine, but being the quintessential gentlemen, neither Ryan nor Gibson would dream of allowing her to pay.

Another thing she loved about them.

Like the hosts who had invited her, the establishment was pure elegance. From its beveled glass screens between the tables, lush palms, glimmering brass accents and teak paneling, to its celebrated chef, Chez Antoine was a class act.

And it was Savannah's favorite place to hang out, pretend to be an adult, and act classy herself.

As she sat at the table, with its glistening white linens, sparkling silver and crystal, savoring the last bite of salmon mousse, she fell in love with the two stunningly handsome, completely debonair men. And, looking across at Margie, she could see that the young lady had fallen under their spell as well.

Every woman between the ages of four and ninety-four would fall in love with Ryan Stone. And the British silver-haired fox, John Gibson, was a treat for the eyes, as well. He might be pushing sixty, but Gibson was one of those men who only became more dashing with age.

Yes, women loved Ryan and Gibson. And they loved women. But only as friends. They were life partners and had been for years. But that didn't stop ladies everywhere — including Savannah — from fantasizing about ways to reorient their sexuality.

"I can't tell you what a delight this is, having not one, but two lovely ladies for company this evening," Gibson said, toasting them with a glass of Chardonnay.

Ryan raised his glass as well, looking like a cover model for *GQ*. "Hear, hear. To the most beautiful women in the room tonight and the men fortunate enough to be their escorts."

Margie blushed sweetly. She actually looked pretty and feminine tonight, having taken Savannah's advice and "spiffied up" for the occasion. Her cobalt blue shift was simple but elegant, and she wore an antique, marcasite choker and matching bracelet.

Savannah thought that, for once, the teenager seemed to be enjoying her own femininity. Ryan and Gibson seemed to have that effect on females.

"Thanks," Margie told Ryan, not quite

meeting his eyes. "This is a nice place." She sighed and looked a bit sad. "We used to go to restaurants like this when I was a kid," she added, "before my dad . . . well . . . before my mom kicked him out. Now, he doesn't sit down and eat at a table. He just grabs something and eats it at his desk or in his car."

Savannah, Ryan and Gibson sat silently for a long moment, digesting this information and what it revealed about Captain Bloss's grownup little girl.

Finally, Ryan said, "I'm sorry to hear that, Margie. We all get busy sometimes."

"But I haven't sat at a table and ate with him even once since then."

"Have you told him that you'd enjoy sharing a nice dinner with him sometime?" Savannah asked, unable to believe it . . . until she reminded herself this was Old Man Bloss they were talking about. Not so tough a stretch for the imagination after all.

"No, I don't tell him I want to eat with him," Margie replied, petulance covering her hurt. "He's a *dad*. He's supposed to just *know* stuff like that."

"He's a *man*, Margie," Ryan said softly. "And I'm ashamed to admit that we men don't know a lot of things we should. The ones we love have to teach us. Tell your father what you need and —"

"Oh, I do. I nag him for stuff all the time."

"I'm not talking about a new outfit at the

211

mall or the latest CD," Ryan told her. "I mean truly important things — things you really *need*, not just material things you *want* — like sitting down to a table, eating a nice meal and spending some time with him."

"Ryan is absolutely right," Gibson added. "We chaps are a bit thick-skulled at times. You must be frightfully blunt with us. Don't expect your father to know how much that would mean to you; tell him. Give him the opportunity to do the right thing."

Margie thought it over for a long time, staring down at her plate. "And if he doesn't?" she asked, tears puddling in her eyes.

"Then he really is a miserable asshole," Savannah mumbled under her breath. She looked around the table to see the three of them staring at her and realized they had heard. "Oh, sorry," she said. "I didn't mean that. It just sorta slipped out."

"You meant it," Margie said, but she was grinning.

"All right, I did, but I shouldn't have said it. He's your dad and Ryan and Gibson are right. You need to give your relationship with him all you've got. He might surprise you and come through for you. It's possible; it's worth a try."

"Excuse me for changing the subject," Ryan said, turning to Savannah, "but speaking of giving something your best effort,

I understand your partner is working night and day on this case of the missing officer. Has he come up with anything?"

"I talked to him on the phone right after the defense class, and he said there's nothing new. Titus's girlfriend, Christy, is coming back for a few days to see if she can help with the search for him. I don't know what she thinks she can do."

"She probably needs the comfort of being with those who love him, who are worried about him," Gibson said.

"You never know; she might come up with something." Savannah's enthusiasm was subdued at best. "Dirk's over at Titus's house right now, going through his papers and personal stuff, trying to find anything that might point to a motive for the attack."

"Does Detective Coulter believe the officer's disappearance is connected to this unfortunate rapist affair?" Gibson asked as he motioned for the waiter to bring the dessert tray.

"It may be related," Savannah said, perking up at the sight of chocolate cakes, berry tarts, Napoleons and eclairs, rolling toward her on a dainty, deliciously overburdened cart. "But Dirk doesn't know how. Titus answered the call when Charlene Yardley was found, and he helped search the scene. Why that would make him a target, we don't know."

"Well, we're terribly grateful that this young lady escaped that brute," Gibson said, patting Margie's hand. "You displayed extraordinary courage and resourcefulness in the face of danger. Your family must be enormously proud of you."

Margie's smile faded. "Not so's you'd notice," she replied.

Savannah pointed to a triple-layer fudge cake drizzled with raspberry sauce. "Have a slice or two of that heavenly concoction, Margie, and you'll forget al-l-l your troubles, guaranteed."

Before Savannah could make her own selection, a buzzing sounded from her purse. She reached inside it and pulled out her cell phone. "Excuse me," she told her fellow dinner guests. "Normally, I don't carry this thing to dinner with me, but I wanted to be available for Dirk."

"Go right ahead," Gibson told her. "I'm afraid it's one of those dubious technological *advances* that we have to accept."

"Hello," she said. "Hi, Dirk. Margie and I are having dinner at Chez Antoine with Ryan and Gibson. We're about to eat dessert, so this had better be good, buddy."

She listened to Dirk's reply as Ryan ordered for her and everyone else at the table, then excused the waiter. He, Margie, and Gibson politely pretended not to be listening to Savannah's conversation, until she said,

"What? Oh, no. When? Okay. I'll meet you there in twenty minutes."

She refolded the phone and put it back in her purse. All three were staring at her, sumptuous desserts forgotten.

"Well?" Ryan asked.

"I sense something foul is afoot," Gibson added in his best "Christopher Plummer Plays Sherlock Holmes" impression.

"Foul, indeed," Savannah said. "Ryan, Gibson, would you two enjoy Margie's company a bit longer this evening? Maybe she could go back to your apartment for an after-dinner soft drink?"

"Of course, we'd be delighted," Gibson replied.

Savannah turned to the girl. "Is that all right with you, Margie?"

The teenager gazed at Ryan, lovestruck, and mumbled, "Sure."

"What's up?" Ryan asked, less subtle than his dignified partner.

"Dirk wants me to join him out on Turner Canyon Road. Officer Joe McGivney was patrolling that area tonight. His radio car was found abandoned there in an orange grove. Now he's missing, too."

"I'm sorry to hear that," Ryan said softly, looking as worried as Savannah felt.

"That's bad news, indeed." Gibson cleared his throat and turned to Margie. "But don't worry about Miss Bloss. We would be pleased to entertain her for the remainder of the evening."

Ryan rose along with Savannah and helped her into her jacket. "I'll walk you to your car," he told her, then said to Gibson and Margie, "You two go ahead with your desserts. I'll be back in a minute."

When he and Savannah reached the foyer, he took her hand and slipped it comfortingly into the crook of his arm. "So, what's really going on?" he asked her.

"Is it that obvious?"

"You don't turn pale over a missing cop. Besides, you left without taking a doggy bag full of chocolate cake. That isn't like you at all."

She didn't laugh or even smile. "Dirk says there's blood spray all over the inside of the vehicle."

"Like Titus Dunn's apartment."

"Worse. There's brain matter, too."

FIFTEEN

"You know, I used to like orange groves," Savannah told Dirk as they stood several yards from the abandoned cruiser that was anything but empty now. Dr. Jennifer Liu and her technicians were at work again, taking photos, making sketches, collecting samples — bits and pieces, swabs and wipings — and combing the area surrounding the car.

"When I was a kid in Georgia," she continued, "I used to go for long, peaceful walks in the peach orchards."

"I know what you mean. When me and the old lady were breaking up, I spent a lot of time walkin' up and down rows like these, and it helped settle my nerves. After this mess, I don't think a citrus grove is ever gonna settle anything for me."

"I hear you. Why couldn't he just do his meanness in grungy back alleys?"

Savannah watched as Dr. Liu studied the gruesome splattering of blood and other gore on the upper portion of the driver's seat.

When she had first arrived, Savannah had taken a close look herself. She wouldn't be

217

eating rare steak for weeks.

At the edges of the cordoned area, a crowd was forming. Savannah recognized a few of the spectators, including Angie Perez and her worthless, jock boyfriend. Along with the amateur gawkers were the professionals, reporters from local media and a couple of camera crews from Los Angeles television stations.

Between the Santa Rapist's exploits and now the missing police officers, San Carmelita was losing its sterling image as a safe, law abiding, upper-middle-class community.

"That blond kid," she told Dirk, "the one standing with Angie Perez. He's her boyfriend, the one who didn't want to stop and help Charlene Yardley. And here he is again. Have you checked him out?"

"I've got my eye on him. He's a bit of a cop buff, listens to police bands. He probably heard the call go out and bopped over here."

"Do you consider him a suspect?"

"I haven't exactly cleared him yet. He says he was with Angie and some friends when Charlene was attacked, but they admit he was in and out of the party, supposedly making beer runs, but he was gone a long time."

"Long enough?" Savannah noticed the young man watching the coroner with ghoulish fascination. But then, a dozen others in the crowd were wearing the same expression.

"Long enough," Dirk replied. "He's a 'maybe' for the rapes, but the cops . . . I don't know what the hell they're all about."

"When did Joe come on duty?" she asked.

"At 1700 hours."

"Did he call out with anything suspicious?"

"Nope. His memo book is on the front seat. According to it, he'd written three tickets. We'll run them down, but I'm not expecting anything there."

A sudden disturbance at the rear of the crowd caught their attention as some loud, unhappy individual was pushing through to the front.

Savannah thought she recognized the voice and the colorful vocabulary. Yes, it was Donald DeCianni. As he burst through the crowd and climbed over the yellow tape, Savannah noticed he was out of uniform. Judging from the baggy sweats, his tousled hair, and the sheet-wrinkle lines on his face, she assumed DeCianni had recently been asleep.

Well-rested and wide awake, Donald DeCianni wasn't exactly Mr. Personality. He had been known to challenge his fellow officers to a fistfight over which pizza parlor had the crispiest crust and the coldest beer.

"DeCianni's not going to take this well," Dirk grumbled. "He and McGivney were partners for about five years."

"Were they close?"

219

"No, couldn't stand each other. About two months ago, McGivney asked to get transferred just to get away from DeCianni, got sick of his bullshit. But you wait and see; DeCianni's gonna act like they was blood brothers or twin sisters or somethin'."

"Hey, Coulter," DeCianni called out as he hurried from McGivney's abandoned car to where Dirk stood with Savannah. "Is this mess yours?"

"The Santa mess is mine," Dirk told him. "If this is part of the Santa mess, then it's mine, too."

"Is it?"

"Don't know yet."

"What happened to my brother?"

Dirk shot Savannah an "I Told You" look, then answered him, "Don't know yet."

DeCianni sniffed and hitched his thumbs in the waistband of his sweats, exposing several inches of hairy, roly-poly belly. Savannah decided to study the wayward sprigs of hair sprouting from his head — the sight being slightly less revolting.

"And what about Titus?" DeCianni snapped. "Have you got a line on him yet?"

"Nope. Nada," Dirk said.

"Sounds like you don't know a hell of a lot," DeCianni said.

Savannah winced. Dirk wasn't the best guy on the planet to mouth off to. She watched as he reined in his temper.

"Well, DeCianni, if you wanna help me out," he said slowly, sarcasm dripping, "play detective for a while, just jump right in. You'll probably have it all wrapped up by midnight, huh?"

DeCianni backed down a bit, coughed and ran his fingers through his mop of hair. "Well . . ." he mumbled, "somebody needs to catch this guy. I mean, first Titus, now Joe. Who's next?"

"Could be one of us," Savannah said. Why should the boys nitpick at each other without a girl joining in?

"Why us?" DeCianni snapped. He actually looked worried.

She snickered inwardly, but donned her straightest face. "Titus was the first to respond to the call on Charlene Yardley," she observed. "I noticed that Joe McGivney was one of the first to show up on the beach when we started searching for Titus's body. Now we're here. Apparently it isn't healthy to respond to a crime scene these days."

DeCianni stared at her long and hard for a few moments, then turned to Dirk. "Is she serious? Do you think that's what's behind this?"

Dirk chuckled and shook his head. "Come on, DeCianni. Cops were crawling all over both scenes. It's got nothin' to do with anything. Savannah was just yanking your chain."

DeCianni stuck his face so close to Savannah's that she could smell his booze and cigar breath. "Don't go bustin' a guy's balls," he said, "when his partner's missing. You haven't been off the force so long that you don't know what a low blow that is."

"Ex-partner," she quietly added.

"Same difference." He nodded toward her, then Dirk.

She considered that for a second, then agreed. "True. Sorry, it *was* a bit below the belt."

"I'd like to see how you'd feel if something bad happened to this guy . . ." He punched a thumb toward Dirk. ". . . or vice versa."

As he swaggered away, the butt of his baggy sweatpants sagging almost to the back of his knees, Savannah turned to Dirk. "Is it just my imagination, or did that sound a little like a threat?"

Dirk sniffed. "DeCianni likes to think he's a major threat to humanity. Personally, I think beneath the blowhard bull, he's a pussy."

Savannah propped her hands on her hips. "Excuse me. But as a woman and a cat lover, I take offense at that."

"The profanity?"

"The association."

December 15 — 5:32 p.m.

"Where else but Southern California can

you have a barbecue ten days before Christmas?" Tammy said as she danced around the gas grill on Savannah's patio, wearing a bright red bikini and a sappy grin.

Savannah noted, with only a twinge of bitterness, that the grin was wider than her assistant's cellulite-free rear end. "Southern Florida," she said, "the Caribbean, the French Riviera. Here, have another beer." She shoved a brew at her, determined to put some meat on the kid's bones.

"Nope. It's mineral water for me."

Savannah turned to Dirk, who was chug-a-lugging down his fifth Beck's. "Mineral water," she murmured, "how healthy . . . how virtuous."

He simply grunted and slid lower in the chaise longue, pulling his Dodgers cap down over his eyes.

It had been a tough week, and they all needed to kick back a bit. Even Margie was getting into the spirit of the cookout, sitting at the picnic table, stripping the shucks from a dozen ears of corn. Except for the outlandish hair coloring, the unconventional piercings, and the metal studs sprouting from her black jeans and T-shirt, she might have been any other suburban kid.

Ten minutes before, she had reached into the cooler for a beer and gotten her hand smacked; Savannah was a vigilant big sister. Five minutes after that, the two of them had been squeezing lemons in Savannah's kitchen, and now a pitcher brimming with icy lemonade sat on the picnic table beside the baked beans and potato salad. Margie was rapidly making the pitcher's contents disappear.

The sun was setting, casting a purple haze across the tawny foothills behind the neighborhood. A coyote yipped in the distance, prompting a chorus of yowls from his neighbors, who were as restless as he was over the recent brushfires. The occasional piece of white ash floated, like a dirty snowflake from the sky, and settled on the lawn.

"When are your sister and the kiddies supposed to get here?" Tammy asked as she watched Savannah turn the chicken breasts over the flame. The smell of the salsa marinade and hickory smoke filled the damp, evening air, making everyone's mouth water.

"My granny called this morning," Savannah said, "and told me they received a call from Vidalia yesterday. Seems the driver kicked them off the bus somewhere in Texas. They spent the night in a motel and caught another one the next morning."

"That's awful!" Margie said, nearly dropping her corn. "Your sister being pregnant and all. That driver should be ashamed of himself."

"Ashamed? He should be fired," Tammy added, equally scandalized.

Savannah chuckled. "I thought so, too. I

even went so far as to suggest a good, ol' fashioned horsewhipping . . . until I heard about the fire."

"The fire?" Dirk peeked out from under his cap brim.

"Yeah. The one my nephew set in an elderly gentleman's hat. Apparently the old fellow had suggested that the boy not hang upside down from the luggage racks . . . and we Reids have been known to hold a grudge . . ."

". . . and to take revenge," Dirk added.

Savannah nodded. "When appropriate." She popped the top on a beer can and generously sprinkled the ale over the chicken until it sizzled and steamed. "So, their ETA has been slightly delayed. They'll probably arrive tomorrow night, barring any other 'mishaps.' "

"You mean . . . arson, murder or mayhem?" Dirk added.

"Among other juvenile indiscretions."

From inside the house, they heard the phone ring; Margie jumped up from the picnic table and flew inside.

"Teenagers and phones," Savannah said, "there's some sort of biological connection."

"Her friends don't know she's here, do they?" Tammy whispered. "I mean . . . for security reasons."

"No, Bloss didn't want anyone to know." Savannah reached for a plate and began dishing up the beautifully browned, delicately smoked chicken. She could feel her tummy

225

growl in anticipation. "He was quite definite about it," she added. "Personally, I'm as security conscious as anybody, but I think he's wigging out about this a bit."

"Me, too," Dirk said. "I doubt the guy's gonna try to get her again when there's so many women in town who would give in to him without a tussle."

Margie bopped out of the house, the cordless phone in her hand. "It's for you," she said, thrusting it at Dirk.

"Great. And me with most of a six-pack under my belt," he told Savannah in a whispered aside before he answered, "Coulter here." He listened for a moment, then fumbled in his shirt pocket for a pen. Scribbling on one of Savannah's decorator paper napkins, he said, "Okay, thanks. I'll get right out there."

He pushed the Off button and hoisted his body off the chaise. "Say, Van . . . I know you're in the middle of cookin' here, but how do you feel about a drive in the country?"

She studied the sick look on his face. "Turner Canyon Road? An orange grove, maybe?"

"How did you know?"

"Call it a hunch. Another orange grove rape?"

Dirk sighed. "A simple rape would be better news . . . if you can believe that."

"A body?"

"Supposedly McGivney's. An anonymous tip came in a few minutes ago."

"The same caller who told us about Titus being on the jetty . . . even though he wasn't?"

"They think so."

"Gee. Helpful, though not very accurate."

Savannah turned to Tammy and Margie, who looked a bit disappointed, but Dirk needed to get to the scene, and once again, he'd had a few too many to drive. Besides, she had to admit, she wanted to be in the thick of things . . . even if the soup was pretty thin.

"Do you mind?" she asked Tammy, not wanting to say in plain English, "Will you baby-sit the kid for me?"

"Not at all. Margie and I are going to eat everything you cooked and then, if you're not back yet, we'll play a wild game of hearts." She turned to the teenager. "You do know how to play hearts, don't you?"

"Nope." She didn't sound too excited.

"Well, high time you learned." Tammy waved Savannah and Dirk away with an airy hand, just before nabbing a piece of Savannah's chicken. "You two get going. And good luck."

"Yeah," Dirk grumbled as they walked back into the house. "We can go not find Joe, just like we didn't find Titus."

"That's it," Savannah told him as they

strapped on their weapons and she grabbed her purse. "Hold onto those positive thoughts until they squeak."

"Yeah, yeah," he said as they walked out the front door and down the sidewalk to her car. "Don't piss into a stiff wind, and never say die."

"Words to live by."

6:05 p.m.

This time, when Dirk and Savannah arrived, they were the first on the scene.

A homicide scene.

No doubt about it.

No futile combing the beach and coming up empty. Not tonight. Tonight the caller had been right on. He had said they could find a dead cop in the ditch on the northwest corner of Turner Canyon Road and Santa Rosita Way.

Officer Joe McGivney was there, all right, and he was very dead, lying on his back, one arm twisted behind his back, the other flung out to one side.

His weapon was still in his holster.

When Savannah shone her flashlight in his face, his sightless eyes stared back, flat and dull. Rigor mortis was well-established, insect infestation had begun.

Cause of death had to be related to the small, black, perfectly round hole right in the center of his forehead, Savannah thought as she deliberately put her grief and anger on hold and mentally clicked into analytical mode. The star-shaped pattern of splits in the skin surrounding the hole showed that the muzzle of the gun had probably been held directly against his forehead when the trigger had been pulled.

His badge had been ripped off the front of his uniform, making a jagged tear in the fabric. Half the badge protruded from his mouth, as though his killer had been forcing him to eat it.

"Shit," Dirk said as he sat down hard on the dirt near the body.

Savannah felt her own knees go weak. "Exactly."

After a long moment of silence, Dirk said in a husky voice, "It's always bad. But it's different . . . you know . . . when it's a cop."

Resting her hand on his shoulder, she said, "Of course it is."

"Now, why the hell do you suppose they did that?" He pointed to the badge.

"Who knows? It's one sick individual."

"Well, I'm not going to leave him like that."

Dirk reached down, but Savannah grabbed his wrist and gave it a gentle squeeze. "You have to, buddy. You can't move anything like that until Dr. Jennifer sees it, photographs it; you know that."

Dirk shuddered and wiped his other hand across his eyes. Savannah knew it wouldn't help. They would both be seeing this — awake and in their dreams — for a long time.

"Are you all right?" she asked, slipping her hand into his, a gesture more familiar and intimate than they were accustomed to with each other. To her surprise, his fingers clasped hers tightly, and that told her more than any words.

No, Dirk wasn't all right.

He was a tough guy. An overgrown street kid. And tough guys didn't hold hands at a time like this if they were all right.

In all the years they had been partners, then friends, Savannah had known that Dirk liked her, trusted her, relied on her, maybe on a good day even loved her. But there hadn't been many times when she had felt this tough guy needed her . . . or anyone else for that matter.

She was very glad she was there.

Two hours later, the now-all-too-familiar crowd had assembled: Dr. Liu and her team, the media, the spectators, a brigade of cops.

Someone had finally removed the badge from Joe McGivney's mouth and covered his body with a cloth.

Bloss had arrived, even before the coroner's wagon, and Savannah knew he was deeply distressed by this development; he hadn't even harassed her for being present at a crime scene.

She was sitting on the fender of her Camaro, keeping a low profile when he finally approached her and asked in a flat, subdued monotone, "Where is my daughter?" He actually looked too tired for hostility.

"She's at my place, eating barbecue and playing hearts with my assistant, Tammy. In other words, she's safe and she's having fun."

"That's good. Thanks."

It was all Savannah could do not to reach over and place her hand on his forehead to check for a fever. Since when did Harvey Bloss converse with her like a normal human being?

He did look a bit "peaked around the gills," as Gran would say. He had deep, dark circles under his eyes, and his usually overly ruddy complexion had an unhealthy gray cast to it.

Nope. Captain Bloss didn't look so good these days.

He looked like he was going to say something else, but one of his flunkies came running up to him, a worried and urgent look on his face. They spoke in low tones for a moment, then Bloss hurried to his dark, cop-boss, generic sedan, and they both climbed inside.

Through the open window, Bloss called out

to Dirk, who was conversing with Dr. Jennifer. Dirk joined them in the car for a few minutes.

When Dirk emerged, he looked as upset as Bloss. He walked over to Savannah, practically dragging his tracks out — from fatigue, or discouragement, or a combination of both, she didn't know.

"What is it?" she asked.

"Not what," he said. "Who. We've got another one missing."

She had a feeling, but she had to ask. "Who?"

"Donald DeCianni."

SIXTEEN

"You sure find out who your friends are when something like this happens," Christy Melleby said as she twisted the soggy tissue around her forefinger, then dabbed at the end of her nose. "It's like they're a bunch of cockroaches who scramble for cover when the lights go on. A couple of the cops' wives have actually ducked behind shelves in the grocery store rather than talk to me. I don't understand it."

Savannah sat on the other end of Christy's wicker sofa with its dainty floral cushions. She was sipping jasmine tea from an equally dainty, flower-spangled, china cup. The sun porch was like a miniature arboretum, a testament to Christy's verdant thumb. Pots of paperwhite narcissus perfumed the air, along with poinsettias of every shade from ivory to crimson. In the corner of the glass-enclosed room a Victorian Christmas tree glistened with pink tinsel and a hundred whimsical angels.

It was definitely what Savannah called a "girlie-girl" room. And the woman/girl who had decorated it sat sobbing into her hanky, the picture of distressed femininity in linen and lace. Her long, blond hair was curved into a graceful French twist, and she actually wore a strand of pearls around her delicate neck.

With a pang of sadness, Savannah thought how Christy Melleby was as feminine as her boyfriend, Titus Dunn, was masculine.

Savannah also wondered if she should be thinking of Titus in the past tense. Dear God, she hoped not.

"People don't mean to disappear into the woodwork," Savannah told her as she handed her another tissue from a nearby box. "They just don't know what to say to someone who's going through difficult times. They feel they should come up with some magic words that will make your pain disappear, and of course, that's impossible. And since they can't think of anything, they don't say anything."

"But you called," Christy said with a sniff. "At least you phoned and asked if there was something you could do."

Savannah felt only a teeny bit guilty. She *had* been concerned over Christy's welfare. The hope that she might get some shred of information that would help Dirk . . . well, that had been only secondary as a motive for calling.

Hadn't it?

Yeah, sure.

"And is there anything I can do?" Savannah asked.

"Yes, help them find Titus. Before . . ." She choked back her tears. "Before he winds up like poor old Joe, in a ditch somewhere."

Savannah didn't have the heart to tell this grief-stricken woman — tender of narcissus bulbs and lover of Christmas angels — she would bet cold cash that poor ol' Titus was probably already lying in a ditch somewhere . . . or buried in an orange grove . . . or floating on the ocean floor somewhere between the San Carmelita beach and the Catalina Islands.

No, some things were better left unsaid.

"We're working on it, Christy. Really, we are." She took a long drink of the fragrant tea. "How is your mother in Seattle?" she asked, knowing that, too, would be a sensitive topic.

"Dying."

"So I heard. I'm really sorry."

"Thank you."

At that moment Savannah was very glad she had made that call. Christy was right; people did disappear like cockroaches when the going got tough. And feeling awkward was no excuse. A friend was a person who pushed past the awkwardness and called anyway. A friend reached out, whether it was comfortable or not.

But then, true friends were a rare commodity in almost everyone's life.

"Not an easy time for you, huh?" Savannah said. Moving closer to Christy on the sofa, she reached over and covered her hand with hers. She noticed how cold Christy's fingers were, how low her life energy felt.

"No, it isn't easy," Christy replied. "But I'm really, really grateful that you're here."

Originally, Savannah had planned to stay only fifteen minutes or half an hour. But that was when she decided to hang out a little longer.

Two hours, three cups of tea, and a half a box of tissues later, Savannah rose to leave.

"We're going to find your honey for you," she told Christy as they strolled through the house to the front door. "And — I know you're only human and can't help it — but there's no point in tormenting yourself over what 'might' have happened to him. My Gran always says, 'Prepare for the worst and hope for the best.' I'm still hoping we're going to find him alive and well."

Christy nodded but looked as doubtful as Savannah felt. Her eyes were swollen nearly closed and her nose was the perfect shade of red for the holiday season, but Savannah thought she had never seen her looking prettier.

"Gran also says that the people who grieve the deepest are people who love the most. Apparently, you love Titus very much."

More tears rolled down her cheeks. "He's a good man. And I already miss him."

As they passed through the living room, Savannah saw a collection of photos spread across the coffee table. They were all of Titus, some with Christy, some with other cops, some with friends and family.

"I guess it just made it worse, digging these out of storage," Christy said as they paused beside the table and Savannah studied the pictures. "But looking at them makes me feel closer to him."

"I'm sure it does."

Then Savannah saw it: a snapshot of Christy and Titus at what appeared to be an air show. He had his arm draped casually over her shoulder; both were wearing goofy, happy smiles.

Her pulse rate accelerated fifteen points on the spot, and she could feel the blood rush to her face.

"When was this taken?" she asked, trying to sound casual.

"At last year's Point Morro Air Show," Christy replied. "We got a little too much sun, had a bit too much to drink, but we had a really good time that day."

"It looks like it." Savannah picked up the photo and studied it closely, making sure she was seeing what she thought she was.

Yes. Yes. Yes. There it was, as clear as could be!

"May I borrow this?" she asked. "Just for a while."

Christy seemed confused, but eager to help. "Sure. As long as I get it back. Why do you want it?"

Savannah thought fast; she wasn't good at lying to someone she liked.

"It's a good picture of Titus . . . you know . . . if they want to make up a flyer, or put it in the paper, or something."

Christy looked a little suspicious. "They have his department ID photo. It was in yesterday's paper. But if you think they might want it . . ."

"Thanks. I'll take good care of it." She shoved the photo into her purse before Christy could change her mind and hurried to the front door.

"I'm glad you came over, Savannah." Christy gave her a hug and clung a bit longer than usual. "Visiting with you really helped. Thanks for coming."

"Call me anytime," Savannah told her. "Day or night, if you need to talk, just give me a ring. We'll talk on the phone, or if you'll make me a cup of that lovely tea, I'll be over here, pronto, with bells on."

Another hug good-bye and Savannah was on her way. As she hurried to her car that was parked on the street, she clutched her purse and thought of the picture inside.

One part of her wished she hadn't seen it

. . . for Christy Melleby's sake. But the larger part, the detective part was having to exercise the utmost self-discipline not to jump up and down in the middle of the street and yell, "Yipp-p-p-pee!"

She got into the Camaro, started her up, and headed straight for the police station. She couldn't wait to show Dirk!

4:41 p.m.

Oh, goodie, Savannah thought when she walked through the front door of the San Carmelita police station and saw Officer Kenny Bates was on desk duty.

She loathed Bates; he was madly in lust with her. It was a rocky relationship.

"Savannah, baby . . ." he said when she walked up to his desk to sign the clipboard. "You came to see me. Just can't stay away from me, huh?"

She grabbed the board and scribbled her name and the time. "If there was a back door to this place, believe me, I'd use it," she said, "if I could avoid seeing your vile mug."

He smirked, and she wanted to feed him his face, feature by ugly feature.

Savannah and a dozen other females associated with the S.C.P.D. would have brought Kenneth Bates up on sexual harassment charges long ago, except that would have meant having to tolerate his revolting presence in a hearing. The price was too high.

If Kenny Bates had practiced his annoying behavior in Savannah's small hometown just outside Atlanta, he might have been reprimanded in some dark alley by a congregation of the harassed women and their assorted male relatives. Baseball bats might or might not have been used, but, either way, Kenny's behavior would have undoubtedly improved.

She shoved the register at Bates and gave him what she was certain was her most baleful eye.

"When are you gonna come over to my place," he said, "for a little rest and relaxation? I've got some X-rated tapes we could watch together. Maybe 'bone' up on our lovemaking skills. Maybe get a couple of nice 'tips' on how it's done."

As he stared pointedly at her chest, drool practically oozing down his chin, Savannah wondered — not for the first time — why it was always the most repulsive members of the masculine gender who blatantly pursued women. Nice, good-looking guys who showered regularly and held steady jobs never invited you to: sit on their face and spin, or treat yourself to the culinary pleasure of blowing them.

Such invitations were almost always issued by some scuz-bucket you wouldn't share a sidewalk with, let alone an intimate encounter.

"Come on, Savannah." He leaned across

the desk and she was overcome with the pungent fumes of his cheap cologne. "Let's get together, get naked and horizonal. What do you think?"

"The only way I want to see you horizonal, Bates, is on Dr. Liu's autopsy table."

He lit up. "We could do that! She's going to be gone for a few hours tomorrow afternoon and we could —"

"No, you don't understand. This fantasy of mine isn't sexual in nature. In my scenario, your chest is splayed open, the top of your head has been sawed off and your face peeled down. Got the picture?"

He giggled and wagged one eyebrow at her. "There's no use in trying to hide it. I know what you think of me."

"You know that I consider you a festering boil on the hairy rump of humanity? And you still hit on me? Does that make you stupid or what, Bates? Think about it."

She left him sitting there, looking only moderately insulted — a disappointment, when she had been hoping to leave him outraged.

Oh well, maybe the baseball bat visitation wasn't such a bad idea even here in civilized Southern California.

She filed the thought away for future consideration and hurried down the hall to the squad room to find Dirk. The photo was burning a hole in her purse, and she couldn't wait to show it to him.

The bullpen hadn't changed much in the last three years since she had been off the force. A few more computer screens, fewer girlie pictures on walls behind desks . . . and definitely fewer chairs filled. Municipal cuts had slashed deep into the department budget.

Several years ago, there would have been a bevy of detectives working on a case as prominent as the Santa Rapist and the missing cops. But at a quarter to five, Dirk was the only one sitting at his desk, his face stained green by the light of his computer screen. He was staring at the thing, so bleary-eyed that she was glad she had taken a moment to drive past the donut shop window.

"Need a bear claw?" she asked, dropping the white sack on the desk in front of him. "I'll trade you for a cup of coffee."

Instantly, he was alert. "Deal." He fished a Styrofoam cup from between the stacks of files cluttering his desktop and handed it to her. She took a sip; it was bitter and cold.

"You don't mind if I get a cup of my own?" she asked, walking to the table in the corner where the industrial-sized pot held a day's worth of brew. Fresh was too much to hope for, but at least it was hot. She poured herself a cup and another one for him.

By the time she returned to his desk a minute and a half later, the bear claw had been already been dispatched to donut heaven. In Dirk's presence, food seldom enjoyed a long shelf life.

She pulled a chair up to his and sat down, nearly squirming with excitement.

"You're looking pretty frisky," he said, studying her as he licked the sugar crumbs from the corners of his mouth. "What's up?"

"I got somethin'."

"Obviously. Me, too."

He did look a mite frisky himself, she noted. "What have *you* got?"

"You first."

"Mine's the best."

"Don't be so sure."

"It is. Wait'll you see this."

She opened her purse and pulled out the snapshot. "I was visiting Christy Melleby . . . sort of paying my respects . . . and I saw this. I asked her if I could borrow it, gave her some song and dance about needing it for a missing poster shot."

He took the photo from her and glanced at it briefly. "So?"

"Look closer."

He did. "So?"

"Don't you see it?"

"See what? They're at an air show. Probably the one at Point Morro, right?"

"Right. But that's not important. Look . . . right there."

She pointed to Titus's hand, draped over Christy's shoulder.

"His ring," she said. "He's wearing a big

ring with a star on it."

Dirk squinted and nodded thoughtfully. "He is."

Losing her patience, she socked him on the shoulder. "Come on, let's have a bit of a re-action here! That's a big deal."

"It is a big deal," he replied, equally cool.

She sighed, deflated. "You're weird, Coulter. I swear, you got more excited over the bear claw."

"I'm excited."

"I can tell. You're positively giddy."

"It's just that . . ."

"What?"

He reached into his desk drawer and pulled out a small, manila envelope. Peeling it open, he said, "Hold out your hand."

She did as he said, and he dumped the contents into her open palm.

It was a large, man's gold ring with a prominent star protruding from the center. And the star was almost exactly the same size of the mark Savannah had seen on Charlene Yardley's face.

"Wow!" she said. A slight chill trickled through her as she fingered the ignominious piece of jewelry. "How did you get Titus's ring? Did you find him?"

"Nope." Dirk looked satisfied with himself, as he always did when he one-upped her. "I just got back from interviewing Joe McGivney's widow."

"And?"

"She let me look through some of his personal effects, his dresser drawer, a strongbox under his bed. That's where I found the ring. His wife confirmed it: That ring you're holding there . . . it was Joe's."

5:10 p.m.

"Thanks to this guy's anti-social activities . . . orange groves have lost their appeal for me, and now beaches aren't far behind," Savannah told Dirk as they stood on the beach and looked down on the very dead body of the recently departed Donald DeCianni.

Dirk had received word only a minute after showing Savannah Joe McGivney's ring: An anonymous caller had told the 911 dispatcher that DeCianni's body could be found near the water's edge in Harrington State Park. As with the tip about Joe McGivney, the informant had been morbidly accurate.

DeCianni was still wearing the sweatpants and shirt he had worn the last time Savannah and Dirk had seen him, in the orange grove, when they had been checking out McGivney's abandoned unit.

Like his ex-partner, DeCianni had a neat bullet hole in the center of his forehead and his badge was sticking out of his slack, open mouth. No other wounds were immediately obvious.

DeCianni's body was sprawled on its back at the water's edge. Incoming waves licked at the sneakers on his feet. Vermin-infested seaweed was wrapped around his legs, and the tiny scavengers were already hard at work, recycling the remains of Donald DeCianni.

While DeCianni hadn't been Savannah's favorite person, she cringed, seeing a human being reduced to crab bait. She thought of what DeCianni had said about how difficult it was to see an ex-partner come to a bad end. If that were Dirk, lying dead on the sand, she knew she would be insane with grief.

Officers Jake McMurtry and Mike Farnon had arrived at the scene immediately after Savannah and Dirk. They were setting up a perimeter as everyone waited for Dr. Liu and her team to appear. Then the macabre circus would begin all over again. It was a performance that was getting old, fast.

"It's gotta be the same guy," Savannah said as she knelt on the sand and studied the hole in DeCianni's forehead. Just like McGivney.

"Yep, gotta be," Dirk replied. "We didn't mention the badge in the mouth to the papers, so it ain't some well-read copycat."

A dark sedan pulled into the nearby parking lot, and Savannah made a face. "Bloss. I suppose he'll give me hell for not baby-sitting his kid."

"Where is she?"

"On Rodeo Drive with Tammy and Ryan . . . Christmas shopping. There are a lot worse ways for a teenager to spend an afternoon, huh?"

Dirk sniffed. "Oh, I don't know. Piddlin' around in phoo-phoo stores with a fairy and a bimbo ain't my idea of a good time."

Savannah gave him a dirty look. "We can't all spend our time in manly man pursuits — like watching wrestling matches, demolition derbies and monster truck rallies on the tube while swigging beer and eating stale chips and cheap pizza."

He shrugged. "Some of us know how to have a good time; some don't."

"What the hell are you doing here?" Bloss demanded as he strode up to them, his face flushed from the exertion of trudging through the loose sand.

"It's my job," Dirk muttered.

"I wasn't talking to you, and you know it." He pointed to Savannah. "I'm talking to your mascot here, who's always hanging around when —"

"Hey, hold it a damned minute!" Dirk took a step toward his captain, fists clenched.

Savannah grabbed his arm. "It's okay, Dirk," she said quietly.

"No, it's not okay." He shook off her hand and stepped closer to Bloss, who looked temporarily nonplussed by the intensity of his detective's anger.

"I need all the help I can get on this fuckin' case," he shouted in Bloss's face. "And you give me nothin'! Nobody! I'm tryin' to catch a damned cop killer and a nut job who's assaulting another woman every couple of days. And you won't assign me one other detective to help me out, when I oughta have a friggin' task force workin' on this with me."

"I've explained to you about my budget and —"

"Screw your budget. We got cops dyin' here and I don't think you give a damn!"

Bloss's nostrils flared and the blood vessels on his forehead bulged. "Of course I give a damn! What are you accusing me of, Detective?"

"Being a damned fool and a jackass to boot."

"Dirk!" Savannah grabbed him again.

"No! I've had enough of this horseshit."

He stuck his finger in Bloss's face, and Savannah had instant visions of her friend standing in the unemployment line.

But Bloss's anger seemed to be changing to fear as spit flew from Dirk's mouth when he said, "This woman . . ." He jammed a thumb in Savannah's direction. ". . . has been working with me day and night, on her own time, for free, tryin' to solve this case. And then you walk up here and insult her . . . in front of me, knowing she's my friend.

In my book that makes you dumb and rude . . . whether you're a captain or not."

"And how intelligent are you," Bloss said quietly, "to address your superior in that way?"

Savannah didn't like the deadly calm in Bloss's voice. The last time she had heard him use that tone, he had been two minutes away from firing her.

"Dirk," she said, "I appreciate what you said, and I'm sure the captain would have appreciated my efforts . . . if he'd only been aware of them. And now that you've told him, I'm sure he'll be a wee bit more courteous if he sees me hanging around."

She sidled up to Bloss and looked him up and down as though evaluating his shanks and withers. "After all," she said smoothly, "it's to the good captain's advantage to get this guy behind bars as soon as possible. Who knows, he could be next."

She had said it flippantly, meaning nothing more than to make a mildly irritating, smartaleck remark.

But her statement's impact couldn't have been more dramatic if someone had touched the captain's hind quarters with an electric prod. His eyes bulged and turned blood red, sweat seemed to materialize across his forehead and upper lip, and his chin began to shake.

"What do you mean by that?" he demanded. "Why did you say that?"

"Why? Well, no reason in particular," she said, backing up until she was nearly stepping on poor DeCianni.

"No! You meant something! What do you know?"

Bloss looked like he was about to have a stroke or go into cardiac arrest, but Savannah figured it was only wishful thinking on her part.

"I just meant that, with cops dropping right and left, any one of us could be next." She couldn't resist one more little jab. "Except me, that is," she added with a smile. "I suppose, under the present circumstances, I should thank you for firing me."

Bloss turned on his heel and stomped away. Or at least he tried to stomp, although it was difficult to make much of a statement in the loose sand.

"My, my," she said, watching his less than graceful exit, "if I didn't know better, I'd say our brave captain is a Nervous Nellie these days. Wonder why?"

"I wonder, too," Dirk said, throwing his arm around her shoulder and giving her a companionable squeeze. "Hell, from the way his eyes popped out of their sockets, you'd think *he* was next."

SEVENTEEN

Savannah hung another ornament — a miniature, jeweled carousel horse — on the Christmas tree and stood back to survey the effect. Ah-h-h. Christmas. With all the glimmer and sparkle, the good food and camaraderie, it was her favorite time of year. The time when the child inside her came out to play. And even if there was no snow in the yard for snowmen when she trimmed the tree, Savannah was seven years old, feeling the magic and the love.

"This is dumb."

Okay, so Margie wasn't feeling the magic. She was being a bit of a Scrooge this morning, moping around the house in a black T-shirt and sagging, bagging shorts of the same colorful hue.

Savannah had threatened to withhold food and water from her if she didn't help trim the tree. So she had tossed some tinsel in its general direction, and now she was expressing her sentiments about the festivities from her seat on Savannah's freshly polished mahogany coffee table.

"This sucks. It's dumb. And it sucks."

"I see. And while you're expressing your opinion in such an articulate, erudite manner, why don't you tell me how you really feel."

Savannah readjusted the teddy bear with the bright green vest, hanging him closer to the girl teddy bear with the crimson bow. Okay, she was a bit sappy, but only for a few weeks each year. The rest of the time she was reasonably cynical and hardbitten, so she figured she was entitled to a little Yuletide levity.

And any killjoy teenager who wouldn't get into the swing of things could just go enjoy the holidays with her brimming-with-cheer father.

Naw, she wouldn't do that to the kid, but she did expect her to make a small effort toward holiday spirit. Even if it wasn't "cool."

"Listen you," she told her. "I like Christmas. And one of my favorite Christmas activities is decorating my tree. So, get off your butt — and more importantly, off my coffee table — and pretend to enjoy doing this with me."

"Or else?"

"Or I won't teach you how to make fudge later."

Margie eyed her skeptically. "Is it, like, *real* fudge? The kind you buy in a candy store?"

"Of course it's the real thing." She pointed

to her ample rear. "Does this look like the butt of a woman who doesn't know her sweets? I wear only the best."

Margie giggled and dropped some of her "disgruntled adolescent" act. "Can we put nuts in it, too?"

"Not just nuts . . . Georgia papershell pecans, sent to me by my own dear grandmother for exactly that purpose. String on some more of that tinsel and hang it straight. It's supposed to be icicles, for heaven's sake. And they hang straight down."

Margie actually got into the spirit of the activity, until she was even adjusting and readjusting the ornaments Savannah had hung. "Wow, it's really pretty," she said as they plugged in the lights and sat down on the sofa to admire their handiwork. "I never did that before."

"Did what?"

"You know . . ." She waved a hand toward the tree and looked a bit embarrassed. ". . . like, put things on a tree that way."

Savannah caught herself just before blurting out "What? You mean you never trimmed a Christmas tree before?" Instead, she swallowed the question and silently cursed Harvey Bloss and his ex-wife. What was wrong with those people? As poor as Savannah had been, growing up in a family of nine kids, raised by an aging grandmother, there had always been this shining symbol of

Christmas, a celebration of hope and love.

"Is your family Jewish?" Savannah asked.

"Nope. We aren't anything."

"Well, now you know how to decorate a tree yourself if you want to," Savannah said softly, understanding some of the girl's previous crankiness. "And next year, wherever you are, you can bring one into your home — even if it's just a tiny one that sits on a table — and decorate it."

Margie said nothing for a long moment, then surprised Savannah by reaching over and nudging her shoulder. "When I do that . . . next year and the year after that . . . I'll remember you and how we did this today."

Savannah smiled, more than pleased, then she stood and walked over to the tree. Picking the carousel horse off its branch, she said, "Then I want you to have this fellow for your tree. My grandmother gave him to me the Christmas I turned sixteen. And one of these days you can give it to some sixteen-year-old who has touched your heart."

Margie took the horse in her hand and stared down at it without looking up for a long time. When she did, Savannah saw that her eyes were bright with unshed tears.

"That's like . . . you know . . . really cool," the girl said. "Thanks."

"You're . . . like . . . really welcome. Is it time to make fudge?"

Margie jumped up from the sofa, all

smiles. "Any time is fudge time!"

"A woman after my own appetites!"

But they were only halfway to the kitchen when the doorbell rang.

Before Savannah had time to open the door, the bell rang several more times.

"All right, all right, I'm coming already," she called. "Don't wet your britches."

When she flung open the door, it was like lifting the lid on Pandora's box. A flurry of munchkins charged past her and into the living room, a swirling tornado of chaos and commotion. It took her several seconds to realize the crowd consisted of only two youngsters — her beloved niece and nephew, Jack and his twin sister, Jillian.

She scooped them up, one under each arm, just as they were beginning to scale the limbs of the Christmas tree. "Oh no, you don't, you little monkeys!" she told them, planting a kiss on the top of each one's golden curls. "No tree climbing in Aunt Savannah's house. Where's your sweet mama?"

"Outside," chimed Jack.

"Paying the taxi man for the window," added his sister.

Savannah set them on their feet but kept a tight hold on each collar.

"Paying for the *window?*" Margie asked. She stood in the kitchen doorway, her eyes wide with amazement.

"Don't ask," Savannah told her. "It's probably a long, sad story. Vi pays for a lot of things."

She took the children by their hands. "Come on, let's go help your mommy with the bags. Margie, you want to give us a hand here?"

"Sure." She shot the kids a doubtful look. "With the suitcases, that is, not with . . . them, right?"

"Right."

"I want some grape juice," Jillian said in a whiny, singsong voice that grated on Savannah's last nerve strand that was still intact, but strained from the week's miscellaneous stresses.

"I don't have any grape juice," Savannah told her as she walked them out to the taxi, where an extremely rotund, somewhat younger, but less well-groomed version of Savannah, was haggling with an irate cabby. "I only have grapes. But as soon as we get you all settled, I'll go to the grocery store and get you some grape juice. Apple, too."

"I want it *now!*" A tiny foot came down hard on Savannah's instep with a ferocity that she would have loved to have seen demonstrated in one of her defense classes.

But on her front lawn . . . on her own foot . . . by an irate five-year-old . . . was a bit much.

With one hand under each arm, she lifted her angelic niece until they were face to face.

"And I," she said, "want you to walk on your own feet, not mine. Because if you stomp on me again like that, I'll buy broccoli-and-liver-flavored juice instead of grape. Do you understand?"

Momentarily quelled, the girl nodded, and Savannah set her on the ground again. A second later, her arms were full of Vidalia and her tummy.

"Sis! I can't believe we're finally here!" she cried, hugging Savannah so tightly that she could hardly breathe. "This is a big ol' country! My tail end was practically rooted to that bus seat."

"I'll bet it was."

Savannah was a bit shocked to see what a difference seven and a half months of pregnancy had made in her younger sister. Vidalia hadn't gained any more weight than would be expected, but she was in desperate need of a haircut, and no Reid gal — pregnant or otherwise — would have been seen in such a shabby, shapeless outfit, outside of Gran's rose garden.

Savannah decided to chalk it up to Vidalia having spent several days on a bus with a couple of rambunctious kids with a tummy full of another one. Either that, or the once vain, fastidious Vidalia was in a downhill slide of depression.

"Here, let me get those suitcases for you." Savannah grabbed a couple of bags, but she hardly made a dent in the pile heaped on the curb. "Vidalia, meet Margie Bloss, a house-guest of mine. Margie, in case you hadn't already guessed, this is my sister Vidalia and her family."

"Houseguest?" Vidalia looked positively put out — *too* put out for a deeply depressed ragamuffin, Savannah noted. "You invited another houseguest when you knew we were comin' callin'?"

Savannah glanced at Margie and saw the stud in her left nostril twitch with irritation. "Margie is more than welcome in my home, and so are you and the twins," she added quickly. "The more the merrier, ho, ho, ho. Right?" She smiled weakly.

"I guess so." Vidalia shoved one of her bags into Margie's hands, and for a long, awful second, Savannah thought Margie might shove it back at her.

That was what she needed, a scene from a Jerry Springer show erupting right here on her front lawn.

"Let's go inside and stir up a pitcher of lemonade," Savannah offered. "Jillian was saying she wants grape juice, and maybe that would . . . oh, no . . . Vi." She looked frantically around the deserted yard. "Where are those precious young'uns of yours?"

They found the dreadful duo in Savannah's kitchen. Savannah stood, looking, but unable

258

to believe her eyes. Jack was balanced precariously on her countertop, searching the cupboard.

"I want a hot dog," he said. "Where are your buns, Aunt S'vannah?"

Every burner on her stove was blazing. Savannah hurried to turn them off, but slipped on something slick and had to grab the edge of the counter to keep from falling. "Who . . . what . . . ?"

"I turned the stove on all by myself," Jack said proudly as he dragged a loaf of bread from the cupboard. "I want to make the hot dog hot."

"Hot? Hot!" Savannah said, her temper soaring along with the heat on the top of her stove. She grabbed the boy, hauled him off the counter and set him on the floor.

Behind her, Savannah could hear Vidalia make a couple of whimpering noises that sounded like muffled protestations, but she ignored her. She also chose to disregard the giggling she heard coming from Margie's general direction.

She dropped to one knee, eye level with her nephew. "So, big boy, you want a hot dog. Is that right?" she asked him.

He nodded.

"Well, next time, you ask for one and some grown-up person will turn on the stove and make it hot for you. Do you understand?"

Another nod.

"Because if you ever touch my stove knobs again, young man, I'll turn you over my knee and when I get finished with you, your hind end will be hotter than a pepper sprout. Got it?"

"Got it, Aunt S'vannah." He nodded again vigorously, blond curls bobbing, but the mischievous twinkle in his eyes didn't quite portray the picture of the vanquished spirit she had hoped for.

She turned her attention to her niece who was hanging, half in, half out of the open refrigerator. "And what are you doing there, young lady?"

"Making grape juice."

"Making grape . . . ?" Ah, the mystery of the slimy object — correction, objects — on the floor had been solved. Savannah watched, as though in slow motion, as her darling niece tossed yet another red grape on the floor and stomped it with her shiny, black, patent leather shoe.

"See?" the girl announced. "Grape juice. And we don't have to go to the store!"

Savannah turned to her younger sister. The cherubim were, after all, her offspring and theoretically her responsibility.

"See why I'm so tired all the time?" Vidalia said wearily. "If you don't mind watching them for a few hours, I'm going to go take a nice, long nap."

Savannah watched as her sister lumbered

away into the living room and collapsed across the sofa. She *did* look exhausted, but . . .

Looking back at the twins and their bright, beaming countenances, Savannah remembered hearing once in Sunday school that evil spirits sometimes disguise themselves as angels of light.

Well, these two hellions weren't demons, just undisciplined, lovable kids who had been allowed to get away with murder for the past five years. It shouldn't be that hard to get them under control, right?

She reached for the roll of paper towels on the counter and pulled off half a dozen. She handed several to Jillian and the rest to Jack. "Okay, you two," she said. "On your hands and knees. You're at Fort Reid now, and we're gonna learn a little game called KP."

"I don't think I'm going to like this game," she said, sticking out her lower lip in an adorable pout.

"You don't have to like it," Savannah told her, ruffling her curls. "You just have to do it."

7:28 p.m.

Dirk walked into Savannah's kitchen, sniffed the sugar-cookie-scented air and walked over to the table where Savannah, Margie, the twins and a refreshed Vidalia were decorating the latest ones to come from the oven.

261

"Well, if this isn't cozy," he said, eyeing the platter brimming with goodies. "The picture of holiday family bliss."

"Looks can be deceiving," Savannah muttered. "Sit down and decorate with us."

After being introduced to Vidalia and the children, and giving Margie a high five, he pulled out a chair and reached for the platter. "I'll eat 'em, but I don't want to decorate nothin'," he said. "That decorating's girl stuff."

"It ain't neither girl stuff," Jack said, looking as indignant as he could, considering the green frosting smeared across one cheek and the chocolate sprinkles stuck to his chin. "I'm doin' it, and I ain't no girl! And my cookie ain't no girl neither!"

He pointed to the cookie man in front of him who was sporting an icing penis of monumental proportions. Jack had recently reached the age where the anatomical differences between the genders was consuming most of his waking thoughts. A state of mind that would typically last for the next eighty-plus years of his life.

Dirk chuckled. "You're all boy, that's for sure," he told the child, tweaking some of the chocolate off his chin. "And so's that cookie you're working on. Hand me one of those and some frosting, and I'll see what I can do with it."

"Nothing obscene," Savannah whispered.

"But he —"

"He's five years old. *You* know better. At least, you should."

"Hel— . . . heck. You take all the fun out of everything."

A few minutes later, Savannah leaned over his shoulder and studied his creation, a cookie man wearing a white beard and a red hat.

"Mmmm . . ." she said softly, ". . . anybody we know?"

"After the business with the rings, I'm beginning to wonder," he replied.

"What's that?" Margie said, glancing up from her reindeer, who had a silver stud in his red nose and several others in his ears.

"Nothing," Savannah told her, "just shop talk."

"Speaking of shop talk," Dirk said as he began to chew the legs off his Santa. "Do you mind if we take a walk around the block? I don't want to bore these guys with the details, but I had something I wanted to run by you."

Savannah doubted that any "details" would be boring. Quite the contrary. She appreciated Dirk's discretion; he could be sensitive when he had a mind to be.

"Let's go," she said, grabbing a couple of bells and a star for herself. "Will you be okay, Vi, if I'm gone for a few minutes?"

Vidalia instantly deflated. "Well . . . I was

hoping you'd watch the kids while I take another nap, but I guess I don't have to. It's just that my back hurts so bad and . . ."

Savannah glanced at Margie, whose eyes widened with horror at the very thought. And Savannah couldn't really blame her.

"I'm only going to be gone ten minutes, Vi," she said in her most authoritative, but gentle, big sister voice. "I'm sure you can stay awake and watch your kids that long. When I get back, I'll give them baths and put them to bed."

"Oh . . . all right . . . I guess . . ."

As Savannah walked out the front door with Dirk she could almost hear the crackling of the flames around the stake where Saint Vidalia suffered. And her final words rang in her ears, "I just can't get any help with my children . . . not from my sister . . . not from that sorry excuse of a husband of mine . . . not from . . ."

Savannah and Dirk hit the sidewalk and turned north, taking their time as they strolled through the quaint neighborhood of tiny Spanish-style bungalows, palm trees and bougainvillea-covered fences. The smells of evening meals and the sounds of television, conversations and music drifted from her neighbors' houses and filled the cool, moist air.

Christmas decorations glistened on most houses. Some had only a simple strand of lights, hurriedly tacked to eaves. Other yards looked like miniature Las Vegas casinos with animated Santas, elves, reindeer and angels, flashing Nativity scenes, and myriad lights twinkling in every tree and bush.

Dirk walked along, his face solemn and thoughtful, his hands shoved deep into his jeans pockets. Savannah slipped her arm through his, enjoying the peaceful, easy moment. One of the nicest things about Dirk was that he was as comfortable as an old slipper and required so little effort.

It was one of the few times this holiday season that Savannah had taken a moment to feel the Christmas spirit. But a sideways glance at Dirk told her that he wasn't sharing the moment with her. His mind was elsewhere. She didn't have to think hard or long to figure out where.

"What did you want to talk to me about?" she asked. "Is there anything new on the case?"

"Well, maybe. I just found out this evening, Edward Stipp was released from San Quentin a couple of months ago."

"He got paroled? What are those stupid boards thinking, letting a cop killer —"

"He wasn't paroled; he'd served his time. They had to let him out."

"I don't remember hearing about this."

"And that ain't just because you're gettin' senile. They kept it quiet, let him out and shipped him down to San Diego. Unfortunately, he didn't stay there."

Savannah stopped in the middle of the sidewalk and stared at him. "Don't tell me . . ."

Dirk gave her a tired, grim smile. "We've got us a new neighbor. He's living in one of those rundown shacks on the east end."

"By the oil fields?"

"He's been holed up there for the past six weeks. Prison officials knew he was here, knew we were missing cops, but do you think anybody bothered to drop a dime?"

"Those stupid peckerheads!"

"My thoughts exactly."

"How did you find out he's here?"

"Brenda Lally's working traffic out on the east end now. He left this shit heap of a car parked right in the middle of the street while he ran into a liquor store for smokes and booze late this morning. She wrote him up, he threw a fit, and she recognized him. Of course, he's twenty-some years older now, but he's ugly as ever."

"You've seen him?"

"Of course. She called me this afternoon and I was out there ten minutes later."

Impatient, she nudged his ribs. "And . . . ?"

"He wouldn't talk to me."

"So you . . . ?"

"Hauled his ugly butt down to the station, hassled him for a couple of hours. Nothin'."

"The thumbscrews wouldn't work?"

"Nope, the bamboo skewers either."

"Maybe you weren't shoving them in the right orifice."

They continued their walk, but the joy of the season was lost on Savannah, due to the bad taste in her mouth and the filthy, creeping sensation she felt when she thought of an animal like Edward Stipp, who never should have seen the light of day after killing a young cop, execution-style in a lettuce field. Stipp had the good fortune of committing his murder before the death penalty had been reinstated in California. He had been in his twenties at the time. Thirty years later, he was still plenty young enough to be dangerous.

"Is he still spouting hatred for anybody with a badge?" Savannah asked.

"He offered to shove mine up my ass for me."

Savannah did an instant replay on the dead cops and caught her breath. "I suppose that's a commonly expressed sentiment. Probably doesn't mean anything."

"Probably not."

They rounded the corner and headed back to Savannah's house. She noticed how boring her home was, compared to her festive neighbors' places. She decided she should at least string a few bulbs on Bogey the Bougainvillea . . . for the kids' sake, if not for hers.

"So, the 'interview' wasn't particularly fruitful, huh? Did you get a search warrant

267

for his dump?" she asked.

"Nope. That bleedin' heart liberal, Judge Burrell, said I didn't have nothin'. Wouldn't give me one."

"You want me to check it out? Us P.I.s aren't that picky about the paperwork."

He laughed. "Naw, you're gettin' quite a rap sheet full of suspected B&E's, thanks to me. Liberal-hearted Burrell might actually send you away next time."

"Mmmmm. Where does Stipp hang out these days?" she asked as a plan formed in her head.

"Mostly at the Shoreline Club, late at night. Why?"

She shrugged. "Just thinking that I haven't breathed my quota of stale smoke and beer fumes this month. I've got a black leather skirt and some fishnet hose that are getting dusty in a bottom dresser drawer."

He gave her an amused, grateful look. "You're a pisser, Van, you know that? You'd wear leather and fishnets for me?"

"I'd do anything for you, big boy," she said, giving him a quick peck on the cheek.

"Anything?"

She gouged him with her elbow. "Get real."

He sighed. "That's what I thought. You're just messin' with me again."

As they sauntered up the sidewalk to her front door, Savannah savored her last few seconds of peace and quiet, while one part of her brain tried to recall if she had any Winnie the Pooh bubble bath stashed beneath her bathroom sink.

"By the way," she said, her hand on the doorknob. "Exactly what happened . . . the minute after Stipp told you to shove your badge where the sun don't shine?"

Dirk sniffed. "Funny thing. At that very moment, Stipp lost his balance and fell. Banged his right eye on a door frame. Got himself a nasty shiner."

"Really? Imagine that." She reached down for his hand, held it up to the porch light, and studied his slightly skinned knuckles. "How did this happen? Did you, ah, hit the door frame, too?"

"I was trying to grab him, keep him from fallin'." He shrugged and shook his head sadly. "Damn . . . I guess I missed."

EIGHTEEN

Savannah picked up the phone in her bedroom and punched out Tammy's number. Any young woman as attractive as Tam should be out at this time of night, sharing a meal . . . and maybe even dessert . . . with an equally attractive male.

But Savannah knew she would be home.

Long ago, Savannah had formulated the theory that the more attractive a woman was, the less likely she was to be asked out on a date. Super homely gals didn't seem to receive a lot of invitations either. But those ladies in the middle, the girl-next-door types — they were scarfing up on the men.

At least, that was the reason Savannah preferred to explain why she was seldom asked . . . unless you counted dinner with a couple of gay gentlemen or happy hour beer and pretzels with Dirk.

She didn't count those.

"Hi, babycakes," she said when Tammy picked up the phone. "What 'cha doin'?"

Tammy sounded so out of breath that, for a second, Savannah reconsidered. Maybe her assistant wasn't that lonely after all.

Then Tammy answered Savannah's question with a panted, "Working out. Floor exercises. Sit-ups and —"

"Never mind, you make me tired just thinking about it. Have you got a pair of five-inch heels?"

Tammy was quiet for a moment, thinking. "I think so. Why? Do you want to borrow them?"

"No, I want *you* to wear them. I'll be wearing my own, five and a half inches, bright red."

"Me? Why? Are we going to play Hookers on the Stroll?"

"No, just Loose Ladies on the Town."

"What's the difference?"

"About four inches of leg and three inches of cleavage. We just want them to drool, not shove money in our garter belt. Get ready. I'll pick you up around 2200 hours."

9:12 p.m.

"Your sister doesn't like me, and I have to tell you, I'm not too crazy about her either," Margie said as she stood in the doorway of Savannah's bedroom and watched her pulling her "fallen woman garb" from various dresser drawers.

"Oh?" Savannah studied the small rip in the hem of her leather skirt — thanks to a

271

tussle she had been in with a porn shop robber . . . another assignment of Dirk's. It wasn't that big a tear. She doubted that Edward Stipp, after all those years in San Quentin, would even notice, let alone give a hoot. "Did something happen between you two while I was walking with Dirk?" she asked.

"Kinda." Margie walked into the room, gave a furtive glance down the hall, and quietly closed the door behind her.

"You don't have to sneak," Savannah told her. "Vi once slept right through a Georgia twister. The tornado tore most of the roof off, but when it had moved on down the road, we found Vidalia still snoring away in her bed. So, tell me . . . what's up?"

Margie walked over to Savannah's bed and plopped down on her tummy, her black-booted feet waving in the air. "She got mad because she said I hollered at her kids. That was the word she used, 'hollered.' "

"I see." Savannah searched through her closet until she found the disco-era red satin blouse with the deep vee neckline. Then she took the assorted garments into the adjoining bathroom and went inside to dress. She left the door open while she changed so they could continue their conversation. "Well," she said as she slipped off her sweater and slacks, "did you . . . holler, that is?"

"Kinda. I told Jack he was a rotten little

booger rat and I said it pretty loud. I guess that was hollering."

Savannah stuck her head out of the bathroom and gave Margie a curious grin. "Booger rat? Where did you get that?"

Margie giggled. "I don't know. Just sorta made it up on the spot."

"Mmmm . . . different." Savannah ducked back inside and began to slip on the garters and fishnets. "And what had he done to earn such an auspicious title?"

"He made some nasty comments about my hair and my nose ring. And I'd already told him two or three times to shut up . . . nicely, of course."

"Of course." Savannah grunted, trying to contain her burgeoning bosom in a push-up bra. Might as well give ol' Ed the cop killer an eyeful. If he was up to his nasty former habits, she would use any wiles, feminine or otherwise, to find him out.

"And I waited for Vidalia to tell him to be nice," Margie continued, "you know, like a mom's supposed to do, but she didn't. So I got mad and . . ."

"And hollered, 'Booger rat!' "

"Something like that."

Having put on the rest of the outfit, Savannah stepped out of the bathroom. She had transformed herself into what she hoped was a poor man's version of a femme fatale.

"Whoa!" Margie bolted up off the bed,

her eyes wide with amazement. "You look fantastic!"

"Oh, you think so?" Savannah decided that the kid had been insulted sufficiently in one evening, so she swallowed any wisecracks about her lack of taste.

"Yeah, but you need some metal."

"I was going to put on earrings. Big, hanging down ones."

"No, no, no. Here, you can borrow some of my stuff."

The girl hurried over to her and began to unbuckle her own paraphernalia and transfer it to Savannah. A minute later, Savannah was looking at herself in the mirror, wearing a metal-studded dog collar around her neck, a bracelet to match, a heavy chain around her waist and on her thumb, an enormous skull-shaped ring with rhinestone eyes.

"Now, sit down there . . ." Margie pointed to the dressing table. ". . . and I'll do your hair."

After the cloud of hair spray had settled, Savannah emerged with bigger hair than she had ever imagined possible. Margie had given her a modified version of her own spiked do, and Savannah had to admit, it was wild, but fun.

"You look perfect," Margie exclaimed, as proud as any Hollywood makeover expert. "Except for the tatoos."

"Tattoos? I don't have any tattoos."

"Exactly. That's what's missing."

"Oh well, Edward will just have to do without."

"Is that who you're going out with? Somebody named Edward?"

"Sort of. It's not really a date but —"

A shriek cut through the air, scaring them both witless. They turned around to see Vidalia standing in the doorway, wearing a nightgown that resembled a burlap sack, her hands clasped over her mouth, her eyes bugged.

"What is it?" Savannah said as she jumped up from her stool in front of the dressing table and hurried to her sister. "What's wrong with you?"

Visions of a premature delivery danced through her head, nightmare fantasies of the baby falling right out of Vidalia, and rolling across the floor, before anyone could catch it.

"What's wrong with me?" Vidalia said, gasping like the quintessential Southern belle with a case of the "vapors." "What's wrong with *you?* My lord, Savannah, wait until I tell Gran."

"Tell Gran what?"

"Don't you act all innocent with me." Vidalia shook her finger in Savannah's face. It was all Savannah could do not to bite it. Hard. "I know what sort of a git up that is."

"What git up?"

"The one you're wearing. You've moved out here to this California . . . this land of sin . . . this Sodom and Gomorrah and you've become a . . . a . . . a streetwalker!"

Savannah laughed and gave her horrified sister a hug and a kiss on the cheek. "Don't worry, Vi. I'm not a hooker . . . far from it." She sighed. "Hookers get a lot more money and respect than us lowly private detectives."

If the Shoreline Club had been a little classier, it might have been called a dive. If the clientele had been a tad more discriminating they might have been called the sludge of the earth.

But the place would have to be renovated and every occupant would need to bathe and shave — including the women — to reach such lofty aspirations.

Most of the lost souls holding down stools at the bar looked like they had just been released from San Quentin. Edward Stipp might be hard to spot.

Savannah had been here many times before in the pursuit of law and justice. She never failed to marvel at the genius of the decor.

The bar was decorated in a nautical theme with the usual assortment of mangy, stuffed, marlin on the wall, a rusty anchor hanging from the ceiling, and a tacky mural that featured a grotesquely busty and slightly cross-eyed mermaid. But no self-respecting sailor would be caught dead hefting a pint in the Shoreline.

"I want you to notice," Savannah told Tammy as the two of them took their lives in their hands and strolled through the joint, "that I take you to only the best places."

"I'm noticing. I'm noticing," Tammy replied, moving a little closer to Savannah for protection.

Savannah couldn't blame Tammy for being a bit uneasy. They had created quite a stir among the patrons, Savannah with her punk/metal look and Tammy who was shrink-wrapped in a black latex top and pants and high-heeled slides.

"Over here," Savannah said, guiding her to a cozy, U-shaped booth in the back . . . one where they could both sit with their backs to the wall. Strategy was everything.

As they slipped in, Savannah said, "I'll get in the middle, you on one side. Don't let anybody sit next to you; we need an escape route."

"Gotcha." Tammy glanced around at a dozen faces, all looking like mug shots, who were ogling them. "Do you see him?"

"Don't know. I don't want to look around yet and be too obvious about it."

Tammy flinched. "Oh, yeah . . . sorry."

"No problem."

A heavyset guy with sweat stains under his pits and booze stains on his long-ago-white apron came out from behind the bar and sauntered over to them. "What'll you ladies be having tonight?"

Tammy perked up at the mention of refreshment. "I'll be having a min—"

"A couple of beers," Savannah said, squeezing Tammy's knee under the table. "Whatever you have on draft will be fine."

"Beer? Why did you order me a beer?" Tammy whispered as he turned to walk away. "You know I don't like to drink anything but —"

"Mineral water. Yes, I know. Come on, Tammy. You're undercover here. You can't sip Perrier in a place like this. Dirk's right; you *are* a fluff head."

"A healthy one."

"Obnoxiously healthy . . . so one beer won't hurt you. You gotta nurse it all evening anyway. We have to stay alert, just in case this Edward fellow turns out to be a rocket scientist and we have to outwit him."

At that moment, a skinny, emaciated fellow who looked fifty-something going on eighty walked through the door. Edward Stipp was only a shell of the man he had been in his early twenties when he had made that police officer kneel and beg for his life . . . the life Stipp had taken anyway.

Savannah resisted the urge to pull her Beretta out of her purse and shove it in his left ear . . . although she did play with the fantasy for a few seconds before turning to Tammy.

"That's our date for the evening. The William Holden over there in the gray sweatshirt with the swollen black eye."

Tammy's nose wrinkled in distaste. "William? I thought you said his name was Ed something."

"It is. William Holden was an old . . . oh, man . . . sometimes you make me feel like an Edsel."

"Ed who?"

"Forget it and look seductive. We've got a pigeon to pluck."

Fifteen minutes later, the "pigeon" was sitting at their table, already missing a few tail feathers. Having bolted several shots of whiskey, Edward Stipp had succumbed to Savannah's considerable down-homey charms and was pouring out his life story to her and Tammy. All except the San Quentin part, which he had edited from his narrative.

"So, you've been a legal advisor for the past thirty years," she mused. "How interesting. Where did you get your law degree?"

"I don't have a degree," he said proudly as he studied his empty shot glass with his one good eye. Dirk — or rather, the door frame at the station — had done a real number on the other one. "I've just had a lot of spare time on my hands, so I studied law and gave advice to my buddies who needed it."

Savannah bit her tongue and painted a sweet smile on her lips so that she wouldn't spit on him. Scum like this kept the legal system mired down with ridiculous lawsuits about the fat content of their prison menu and the thickness of their pillow. Furnished with a law library that most pre-law students would envy, these jailhouse "lawyers" spent hours poring over texts that would instruct them how to bring such asinine charges.

"I wish you'd been around yesterday for me and my friend here," Savannah said, nodding toward Tammy, who was trying not to make a wry face every time she took a sip of her now lukewarm beer. "The cops were hassling us . . . picked us up at the corner of Lester and Oak . . . seemed to think we were working girls."

Ed looked them up and down with his good eye. "Well, aren't you?"

"Yeah," Tammy said, "but we weren't then. Once in a while, even pros have to go grocery shopping."

Ed waved to the barkeeper for another round of drinks. Having consumed his, he didn't seem to notice that the ladies hadn't finished theirs yet. That was the way Savannah liked her pigeons . . . soused.

"Those cops are always hassling innocent people," he said after the bartender had brought another transfusion for him and had removed the women's barely touched drinks and replaced them with cold brews. "They picked me up yesterday, too, for no good reason and gave me hell for more than an hour."

"You? An upstanding legal advisor?" Savannah looked adequately shocked. Tammy grinned and buried her nose in the suds, pretending to drink. "You too? Don't tell me you were hanging out at Lester and Oak."

"Naw, this detective guy, a real jerk, wanted to ask me some questions about these missing cops."

Tammy licked her lips. "Really? Why would they ask you about something like that?"

Edward smiled, but it looked more like a grimace. "Let's just say I'm not known for being a fan of law enforcement."

"So, this cop — the guy who questioned you — was a real creep, huh?" Savannah said, coaxing as gently as possible. Even drunk, he could get spooked and clam up before she heard anything good.

But, thankfully, Ed seemed to be in a chatty mood. "Yeah," he said. "He bounced me off a wall; that's how I got this." He pointed to his shiner. "I could have ended the talk right away, told him what he wanted to know, but I wasn't going to make life any easier for him or any other cop, not if I can help it."

Savannah glanced over at Tammy, who was all ears.

"What do you mean?" Savannah leaned closer to him and lowered her voice. "What could you have told him that he wanted to hear?"

"Oh, like that I couldn't possibly have had anything to do with those cops getting burned. I've been in a Vegas slammer for the past two weeks. I mixed it up with one of those rent-a-cops in a casino there. I just got back in town day before yesterday."

"I see." Savannah felt her spirits plummet. He was telling her the truth; she could see the sincerity shining in his one good eye. They were back to square one.

She nudged Tammy. "I think we'd better get going. I've got some Christmas stuff to do."

Instantly, Ed turned indignant. "What do you mean? I thought we were getting along great here. I thought . . . you know . . . this was a date or something."

Savannah waited until she and Tammy were well out of the booth and had their purses tucked under their arms, her car keys in her hand before she said, "Sorry, Ed. But like we told you when you first sat down, we're off duty."

"That's right," Tammy added. "Even working girls have Christmas presents to wrap."

NINETEEN

December 18 — 7:40 p.m.

"Are you all right, Savannah?" Ryan Stone asked as he stood beside her in her kitchen and watched as she arranged slices of apple, chunks of banana, strawberries, oranges and cubes of pound cake on a silver platter. "You seem tired or preoccupied. Is there anything we can do to help?"

She stood on tiptoe and gave him a kiss on the cheek. "I'm fine, Ryan. Thanks for asking. It's just that . . . going to a funeral in the afternoon, then giving a Christmas party in the evening . . . it doesn't seem right somehow."

"Of course not. There's nothing right about murder, ever." He took a slice of apple and nibbled on it. "If a person dies of natural causes or even a simple accident, it's easier to believe that their passing was part of a divine plan. But homicide. Never."

She walked over to the stove and stirred the chocolate mixture that was heating in the double boiler. The rich aroma filled the air. For Savannah, the scent of chocolate was as much a part of Christmas as the smell of pine or bayberry. At times like this, she missed her Gran's homemade fudge and walnut divinity. Mostly, she just missed her Gran.

"Joe McGivney's widow was a mess," she told him as she added a bit of cream to the mix. "Not that the rest of us were much better. When they played 'Amazing Grace' on the bagpipes, there wasn't a dry eye in sight."

"I know what you mean. The bagpipes always get me, too."

John Gibson had entered the kitchen in time to hear their last exchange. "I saw the procession going down Harrington Boulevard," he said. "There must have been peace officers there from all over the state."

"And some from Arizona and Nevada." She poured the chocolate into a large fondue pot as Ryan steadied it for her. "Nothing like a show of strength and support to make a public statement. The sight of acres of squad cars, rolling silently down the street, lights flashing, should be enough to make John Q. Public think twice before he takes out a cop."

"One would think so," Gibson said. "But it appears a certain Mr. Public hasn't gotten the message yet."

Savannah handed the platter to Ryan and the pot in its wrought iron stand to Gibson. "If you gentlemen would kindly transfer that to the dining room table, I'll get some plates.

And then we can all consume far more calories and saturated fat than the surgeon general would recommend."

"And savor every morsel, I'm sure," Gibson said, sniffing the chocolate.

The moment food appeared on the table, Dirk materialized. "I was out there in the living room," he told Savannah, "trying to entertain your depressed sister and be Christmasy, like you asked me to. And I could hear you guys in here talking about my case."

"How's it coming?" Ryan asked as Savannah motioned for them to take seats around the table. "Any good leads?"

"Hardly any leads, good or rotten," Dirk replied as he started to load his plate with fruit and cake.

Savannah noticed that, for once, Dirk was too discouraged, tired and hungry to care that he was talking to someone with a different sexual orientation. He seemed to welcome input from a professional, and although Ryan and Gibson had left the Bureau years ago, they had lent their expertise to several of Savannah's investigations.

With Dirk's case effectively stalled, he was eager for help from any and all quarters.

She left them to their discussions and walked into the living room, where she had her third True Spirit of Christmas experience this season. Her sister was sitting in Savannah's favorite chair, the overstuffed wingbacked affair with the wide, comfy footstool. The two cats, Cleopatra and Diamante, had rolled themselves into black, furry balls on either side of Vidalia's feet. All three were asleep.

On the end of the sofa, beside the twinkling Christmas tree, Margie had curled up with the twins, their heads bent over Savannah's ancient copy of *The Night Before Christmas*. The teenager was reading to them, and they were totally absorbed. Savannah could tell they were near the end of the story, so she decided not to disturb them with an invitation to the table.

She walked back into the kitchen/dining area and put on a pot of coffee to brew. Then she joined the men at the table. They were as involved with their discussion as the kids had been with their book. Though the subject matter was anything but festive.

"Anyone who would stick a cop's badge in his mouth has a lot of rage about something," Ryan said. "Whether his anger is over a particular issue, or if he lives his life in rage, that's the question."

"Among the chaps you've questioned," Gibson asked Dirk, "who do you consider most likely to be your fellow?"

"I really don't know. I've got a young guy, a football star, who I like for the rapes. But I don't know why he would come after the cops. No connection from him to them that I can see."

"And we had a possible on a recently released cop killer," Savannah said, helping herself to an orange slice and dipping it in the melted chocolate. "But, turns out, he's been in the Nevada system most of the time this has been going on. So, he's a bust."

"We've got a weird situation with some rings," Dirk said, reaching into his shirt pocket and pulling out a small evidence envelope. "Don't say anything about this, because we haven't released it to the public, but it seems our missing cop, and our two dead ones all owned rings like this."

"DeCianni, too?" Savannah said, surprised.

"I asked his grieving girlfriend about it today after McGivney's funeral. Says he's got one, but hardly ever wears it. Never told her where he got it. This one was McGivney's," he told Ryan. "And, even more interesting, our last rape victim had a bruise on her face that could have easily been made by a ring like this." He shook the star-studded ring out of the envelope and handed it to Ryan.

"Now that is interesting," Ryan said, examining it closely. "It's almost like a class ring, or . . ."

He handed it to Gibson, who fingered it thoughtfully. "Or some sort of fraternity."

"I've talked to all three women: Titus's girlfriend, McGivney's wife, and DeCianni's girl. They say the men almost never wore the rings and never said where they got them. In fact, DeCianni's girlfriend and him had a big fight about his. She thought maybe some other girl gave it to him."

"I'm sure you've shown that to your rape victims," Ryan said.

"Of course I did. And no, they don't particularly remember it. A couple gave me a weak 'maybe.' And Yardley was the only one with a star-shaped bruise."

"Have you shown this around your station house," Gibson asked, "to see if anybody has a clue as to what it might mean? They might even know if someone else wears such a thing."

"I wanted to." Dirk popped an apple slice into his mouth along with a chocolate-dipped banana hunk. "But the captain told me not to. Says he wants to keep that particular element under wraps for the moment."

Gibson continued to study the ring, turning it over and over in the light of Savannah's Tiffany-style lamp. "This isn't an especially good piece of jewelry. The workmanship is a bit amateurish. And there's no stamp to indicate the gold content, although I'd say it's low, probably about nine karat. It may have been cast by a local smith."

"I've already checked every jewelry shop in town," Dirk said. "They've never seen anything like it."

"I'll bet your captain is putting the pressure on," Ryan said, giving Dirk a look of sympathy mixed with a bit of respect. Dirk seemed to respond with a modicum of gratitude. Savannah smiled inwardly; maybe her best friends would learn to tolerate each other, after all.

"Pressure? Not really." Dirk glanced into the living room and lowered his voice. "To be honest, the captain's been a little weird about this, low key, like he doesn't give a damn if I wrap it up or not."

"Mm-m-m-m." Gibson handed back the ring. "That *is* rather strange. With his officers dropping like the proverbial flies, you'd think he'd have a burning desire to see this chap apprehended as soon as possible."

Savannah was about to ask every one if they were ready for coffee, when the doorbell rang. She glanced at the clock on her kitchen wall. "It's after eight. I wonder who that is?"

She stood and wiped the chocolate from her fingertips on her napkin. Quietly, she said, "Maybe it's Bloss, come to acknowledge his daughter's existence for a change. She's only received a couple of one-minute phone calls from him since she got here. And it being Christmas."

But when Savannah opened the door, she saw — not the hated Bloss — but another male who wasn't much higher on her list. "Butch!" she said. "What a shock . . . I mean, surprise!"

Looking over his shoulder, Savannah could see an ancient battleship of some sort sitting at the curb. She couldn't believe he had driven the thing all the way from Georgia without a breakdown.

Her brother-in-law pushed past her and into the small foyer. He was skinny, dirty-haired, slovenly dressed and in need of a shave. In Savannah's estimation, the epitome of "yahoo." Weekly she watched more upstanding-looking citizens arrested on the television show, *Cops*.

And he didn't appear to be in a very good mood.

"Where is she?" he demanded. She could smell the beer on his breath and the aroma of pot smoke on his clothes.

"Who? Vidalia?"

"Uh-huh. That so-called wife of mine. Took off with my kids and hauled 'em halfway to China. Where is she?"

She grabbed the sleeve of his rumpled T-shirt. "She's asleep. And your kids are having a story read to them, so why don't you keep your voice down and —"

"Who the hell are you to tell me to keep my voice down? You may be Vi's big sis, but you ain't mine."

"Listen, you," she said. "This is my home, and while you're in it you'll keep your voice down and behave yourself like a gentleman. Because if you don't, you're leaving . . . before you even catch a glimpse of your family."

"And who's gonna throw me out on my ear, you?"

Savannah gave him her dirtiest look and shoved her face close to his. "Think about it, Butch. My right thigh weighs more than your scrawny ass, and the rest of you, too. Now, do you really want to wrestle?"

He thought that one over for a moment and reconsidered. "I want to see my kids. I want to have a word . . . a nice, quiet, talkin' to . . . with my wife. That's all."

"Then you stay right here and I'll send the kids out to you," she told him, releasing his sleeve. "And I'll ask Vidalia if she wants to receive a nice, quiet talkin' from you."

Savannah walked into the living room and told the half-asleep children in Margie's lap that someone wanted to see them in the hall. Then she walked over to her snoring sister, sprawled in her easy chair.

"Vi," she said, shaking her arm. "Vidalia, wake up."

"Huh? Wh— . . . what?" The dead stirred to life.

"I'm sorry to wake you, but it seems your husband has driven all the way from Georgia, and he wants to talk to you."

She came wide awake. "Butch? Where?"

"He's in my front hall. I sent the kids out to him. But he wants to speak to you, swears he'll be calm."

Vidalia sat up straight and wiped the sleep spittle from the corner of her mouth. "You tell that sonofabitch that he can go straight to hell. He and me ain't talkin'."

Savannah stood there for a long moment, weighing the situation. She glanced at Margie and saw the sympathy in her eyes. Over the years, Savannah had done a lot for her siblings . . . probably way too much. They needed to be weaned and there was no time like the present.

"Tell me something," she said to her younger sister, who had already settled back down in the chair.

"What?"

"In all the time the two of you have been together, has Butch ever hit you?"

"Hit me? No, of course not."

"Not even a little bitty smack on the jaws?"

She laughed. "Are you crazy? He knows if he ever raised a hand to me, I'd stomp a mud hole in him."

"Okay, then that stuff about telling him to go to hell . . ."

"What about it?"

"You tell him yourself. I'm stayin' out of it."

TWENTY

December 19 — 10:54 a.m.

"I'm sure there must be a good reason why you would ask me to leave my loving home and spend my morning slumming with you," Savannah told Dirk as he drove her into the valley at the east end of town . . . not by any means the high rent district.

"I did it for you," he said proudly. "I took one look at you last night, after your sister and her old man had their run-in and knew you needed to get out of there."

He turned the corner and headed into the worst of the worst section. Every wall was covered with graffiti, every yard was littered with brokendown vehicles. Sagging porches supported old sofas and chairs that were bristling with rusty springs.

"Great neighborhood," Savannah said. "A German Shepherd would be afraid to walk these streets after dark without a pit bull on a leash. Why are we here? Is there a new donut shop opening and they're giving away samples?"

Dirk shot her an indignant look. "You're a bitter, cynical woman, Reid. And suspicious.

Did I mention suspicious?"

"Wherever we're going, we're probably just about there. Now why don't you tell me what you want me to do?"

"Will you do it?"

"Don't I always?"

He laughed. "You can't help yourself, Van. You're just a sucker for my pretty face."

"There must be a reason, but I'm sure that ain't it. What am I doing for you this time?"

Pulling the Buick over to the side of the road near a transmission-repair garage, he said, "I've got a lead and I think — you bein' a chick and all — that you'd be better at gettin' the information outta her than me."

"It's a 'her.' Ah, that says a lot."

"What do you mean? Are you sayin' I'm not good with women?"

Savannah raised one eyebrow and grinned at him. "Do *you* think you are?"

He shrugged. "Not particularly. But then, I'm not all that good with guys either, so . . ."

"Does this female lead of yours work at this transmission place?"

"No. She lives up the street." He pointed to some ramshackle apartments ahead on the corner. "She works at Ricky's, that new top-less joint in Two Trees. She's a stripper, and from what I hear, DeCianni was seeing her for the past few months."

"He was seeing more of her than the average customer at Ricky's got to see?"

"Apparently so. And I hear the two of them weren't gettin' along so good lately. Had a big fight a few days before he got it."

"You want me to just go in straight, as a P.I.?"

He laughed. "Well, of course. I wouldn't suggest you lie, or anything like that."

"Right. Or if she isn't home, you wouldn't want me to break in and check things out."

"Of course not. But if you get caught or killed, I'll disavow any knowledge of your actions."

"Thanks. Drive."

Moon Shadow looked just flaky enough that Savannah decided her name might actually *be* Moon Shadow. What a ridiculous name for an exotic dancer. She just had to get a lot of teasing about that one.

Moon stood in the doorway of her apartment, wearing a tube top and Daisy Mae shorts. Her body might once have been good, but it was long past its prime. The sad thing was, Moon wasn't much over thirty and her prime shouldn't have come and gone so quickly.

The cigarette in one hand, the glass of booze in the other, and the track marks on her arm provided clues as to why she had lost her youth early.

"Who are you?" she asked without preamble.

"My name is Savannah Reid," she told her. "I'm a private investigator and I'm looking

into the Donald DeCianni homicide. I understand you and he were good friends."

"Then you understand wrong. I hated his
guts, the lousy bastard."

"Did you kill him?"

Long ago, Savannah had decided that the
best way to find out something you wanted
to know was just to ask. Of course, the re-
plies were seldom truthful, but she could
read the answers she needed in the person's
eyes and their body language.

"No, I didn't kill him," Moon said. Her
eyes said the same. "But I'm glad he's dead.
Real glad."

"Do you know who did?"

"No, but I'd like to shake his hand. He did
the world, and me, a big favor."

"Boy, you really are mad. Do you want to
talk about it?"

Savannah had learned that, often, if a
person had no one to talk to, the thought of
unburdening themselves to a stranger was a
deep comfort. Everyone needed to talk to
someone; it was a basic human necessity. Savannah was betting that Moon Shadow was
as lonely and as in need of a listener as she
looked.

The bet paid off. She opened the rusty
screen door and said, "Come on in, lady. I'll
give you an earful."

And she did. An hour later, Savannah

walked out to the sidewalk, called Dirk on her cell phone, and told him to pick her up. She had more down and dirty gossip than she would have garnered if she had spent an entire Sunday afternoon sitting in the swing with Gran on her front porch in Georgia.

Dirk must have been waiting around the corner, because he picked her up within a minute.

"She's pregnant," Savannah announced the instant she climbed into the car. "Not as pregnant as Vidalia, but there's definitely a cinnamon bun in the oven. Ask me who the baker was?"

Dirk was as alert as Savannah's cats when they heard the whir of an electric can opener. "DeCianni, right?"

"Maybe. She doesn't know for sure. But she swears it was either him or the other guy she was seeing."

"Who?"

"Joe."

"McGivney? No way!"

"Yep. Seems she was having deep, mean-ingful, soul-centered relationships with both guys until two months ago when McGivney found out. That was also about the time she figured out she was pregnant."

"So she's about four months along?"

"Just starting to show a little. I guess her days of shaking it at Ricky's are numbered."

Dirk headed west, out of the valley and toward the ocean. In the distance they could see the white-capped waves glittering in the noonday sun. The temperature would probably reach eighty within the hour. A perfect Southern California day. Not very Christmas-like, but perfect.

"How did she stand with these guys," Dirk said, "once they found out they weren't her one and only?"

"They dumped her; she hated them. Pretty simple."

"Do you think she had anything to do with them being killed?"

"I don't think she did it herself. She mentioned an older brother. You might want to check him out. A guy named Star Shadow."

"You're kidding. That Shadow crap is for real? I assumed it was her stage name."

"Hippie parents."

"Oh. Figures."

"And one other possibility. She says that fooling around on their women wasn't their only vice. They were both in deep to Jorge Maldonado."

"The bookie out in Oak Creek?"

"I understand Jorge's special form of debt enforcement is kneecap displacement."

"Wonder how he feels about stuffing badges in dead cops' mouths?"

"Maybe you should pay him a visit and see if he strikes you as the creative type."

"First things first."

They had arrived at the beach, and he pulled the car into the parking lot beneath the pier. Seagulls swirled overhead. A couple of kids in bright pink and yellow bathing suits were playing on the swing set closer to the pier. An idyllic setting, but Savannah was suspicious.

"Why are we here?" she asked. "Don't tell me we're going to be looking for bodies again."

"Nope." He reached into the backseat and grabbed a couple of small white bags. "This visit is purely social. I've gotta pay you somehow for the good job you did for me just now, so . . ."

He opened the first sack and pulled out a couple of Styrofoam cups filled with coffee, some sugar, creamer and stir sticks. The second bag held half a dozen donuts.

"Coffee and donuts beside the bright, blue sea," he said proudly. "Now don't say I don't take care of my women."

"Women?" She laughed. "Like you've got more than one. I'm it, buddy. I'm all you got."

"All right. I take care of *you.*" He handed her a Boston cream filled and took out a big bear claw for himself.

"You do, indeed, big spender," she said, giving him a smile before she bit into the gooey pastry.

They munched and sipped in silence for a

while. Then she said, "These taste like the ones we used to get on midnight patrol out at Miguel's Quick Stop there in the valley."

He avoided her eyes, took another big bite and grunted.

"So," she said, "Miguel still gives you freebies, huh?"

"Just shut up and eat."

5:02 p.m.

Savannah and Margie stood at the kitchen sink, squeezing lemons for yet another gallon or so of lemonade. At the table, the twins were rolling Play-Doh into snakes and arguing whether theirs were girls or boys. Predictably, Jack had placed a penis and testicles on his.

From the window where she stood, Savannah could see Vidalia and Butch sitting on lawn chairs beneath the arbor in her backyard. The occasional angry word drifted back to the house. They hadn't stopped arguing since he had arrived last night.

He had spent the night on her sofa and Margie had bunked with Savannah again.

Ah . . . there was nothing like the bliss of having family home for the holidays.

"You guys go through a lot of this stuff," Margie said. "I've never squeezed so many lemons in my life."

"It's cheaper than soft drinks," Savannah

replied, dumping an obscene amount of sugar into the pitcher. "And with this many mouths to feed, I have to cut corners wherever I can."

An expression crossed Margie's face that looked a lot like guilt. "I'm sorry we've all barged in on you like this. You're used to living alone, all peaceful and then here come the troops. You must feel like you've been invaded."

"It's not that bad. And you don't have to feel guilty about how much you eat or how much lemonade you drink. You're the only paying guest in the house."

"You mean, my dad is paying you to let me stay here?"

"Well, he brought over that batch of groceries and . . ."

"And that's the last we saw of him." Her voice trailed away and Savannah could see the glint of tears in her eyes. Damn anyone who could bring a child into the world and then forget they exist.

"I'm glad you're here, kiddo," Savannah told her as she shoved the lemon rinds into the garbage disposal and rinsed her hands. "Really glad."

A few choice phrases floated through the open window from the backyard; it sounded like the fight was heating up.

A second later, Vidalia came storming through the house, muttering something about turning her husband into a gelding, and stomped upstairs. The bedroom door slammed so hard that the dishes in the kitchen cupboard rattled.

"Would you mind keeping an eye on those two?" Savannah said, nodding toward the twins who had graduated to curling their snakes into snails. "I'm going to go have a word with my dear brother-in-law."

"Sure, no problem. I still like messing with Play-Doh."

Savannah grabbed a cold beer from the refrigerator, poured a glass of icy lemonade from the pitcher, and joined Butch beneath the arbor.

It was a warm evening, and he had a glossy coat of sweat on his forehead . . . although she guessed the perspiration might be due to arguing with Vidalia. From experience she knew it was hard work.

"Your sister's bananas," he said, popping the top on the beer. "She's gone off the deep end this time. She says she's gonna divorce me, and I think she actually means it."

"I doubt she means it. It's probably just the hormones talking."

"She can't divorce me," he said, looking genuinely distressed. "She can't handle the twins by herself and with another one coming in a couple of months. She's plum crazy. How's she gonna feed herself and those kids if she throws me out?"

Savannah quietly studied her brother-in-law

and thought that, even though no one was particularly thrilled when he and Vidalia had gotten married, he wasn't a bad sort. Okay, he was a bit of a yahoo, but — whether Savannah wanted to admit it or not — so was Vidalia.

Butch might drink a little too much, but he was a sweet drunk and never got completely ripped or out of control. As a car mechanic he didn't make a lot of money, but they always seemed to pay the rent and have food on the table . . . when Vidalia bothered to cook. Otherwise, they spent a lot of evenings at the local fast-food joints.

All in all, he and Vi were a fairly good match . . . better than Vidalia realized. And although they had always bickered, this out-and-out warfare was a new thing. Something must be up.

"If you don't mind me asking," Savannah said, "what are you two fighting about?"

He looked embarrassed and uncomfortable as he stared down at his cowboy boots. "Oh, just some nonsense. It ain't worth goin' over."

She debated whether to push the issue and decided to throw out one more line. "If it's something big enough for her to divorce you over, maybe it's not just nonsense."

He drank about half the can in one gulp and toyed with the keys on the heavily laden ring on his belt before he replied. "She's all mad because she . . . well . . . about a month ago she found some stuff . . . you know . . . some magazines . . . that I had stashed under the bathroom sink behind the spare toilet paper rolls."

"Mmmm . . . I see."

"And she tore 'em all up and burned the scraps and made me promise I wouldn't bring anything else like that home ever again."

"Yes? And?"

"And . . . well, I sorta forgot my promise, and last week she found another one that had sorta slipped behind the toilet tank."

"That sucker just 'slipped' back there, huh? Imagine that."

He blushed. "Well, you know how it is. She ain't exactly been friendly lately and . . . well, guys gotta . . . you know. I don't know why she's makin' such an all-fired fuss about it. I mean, all men like that stuff. It ain't like I'm messin' around on her or nothin' like that. I'm not doin' nothin' nobody else don't do. I'm a good guy."

He began to sniff a little, and his bottom lip quivered. Savannah felt a rush of affection for him, knowing what this little talk of theirs was costing him. He really did care about Vi and his children.

"Of course you're a good guy, Butch," she said. "You're a *great* guy, and a fine husband. I know how difficult Vi — or any woman —

can be when she's expecting. And I know it's hard for a man to put himself in a pregnant woman's shoes. But let's think about this for a minute."

She considered her case long and hard before presenting it to him. "It's difficult to draw any kind of a parallel here that will help you understand, but let's pretend, just for a moment, that for some weird, medical reason, your pecker suddenly shrank to about half an inch long."

His eyes bugged out at the very thought. Yes, she had his full attention. "What?"

"Just pretend for a minute it could happen. And say this . . . condition . . . was going to last for about nine months."

"This is silly."

"I know. But I'm cheaper than a marriage counselor, so hush and listen." She took a deep breath. "And during this nine months, with this half-inch of equipment, you can't exactly do your husbandly duties to your wife . . . at least, not as effectively as you did before. Plus, you're probably not feeling too good about yourself, not feeling much like a stud. And maybe you're tired all the time and throwing up every morning to boot. Got the picture?"

He didn't look especially enchanted with the tale, but he nodded. "I guess so."

"Then one day, you're fishing around under the bathroom sink for a spare roll and you find a magazine full of good-looking dudes with twelve-inch wangs. And, all of a sudden, you realize that's why your old lady has been spending so much time in the john. And it's got nothing to do with constipation, like she said when you asked her."

He didn't reply, but grunted and rubbed the tips of his boots together.

"Now, even if your wife told you that all the other wives do it when their husbands go through one of those weird 'pecker-shrinking' periods, I still don't think you'd be too happy about it. Right?"

Another grunt.

"You'd probably tell her to get those damned mags out of your house, to wait and be patient until things were back to normal and you could take care of business again."

He choked and cleared his throat. "So, you think what I did was wrong, too?"

Savannah flashed back on the materials that Tammy had removed from the guest room. "Well . . . I'm not going to say what you do in your own bedroom . . . or bathroom, is right or wrong. That's between you and your own conscience. But the Golden Rule says, 'Do unto others as you would have them do unto you.' And I think it's a darned good rule . . . no matter what all the rest of the guys might be doing."

He wiped his eyes with the back of his hand and sniffed again.

"Also," she said, "I think it's really important, once you've made a promise to your mate, to keep it. But, like I said, it's free advice. You can take it or leave it."

She stood, leaned over and kissed him on the forehead. "And I meant what I said; you *are* a great guy. Vi's a lot luckier than she thinks she is."

"Thanks, Van." He gave her a weak smile and crushed his beer can in his hand. "I'll go talk to Vi. I want this to be a good Christmas for us all."

"It will be." She slapped him on the back. "Hell, just one big happy family, right?"

When Savannah walked back into the house, she found Margie and the twins still absorbed with their dough . . . the part that wasn't on her floor or chair seats. They were using her cookie cutters to make bells and stars. For once, Jack's creations were not genitally enhanced.

"We're gonna bake 'em in the oven," Jillian announced proudly.

"And hang them on the Christmas tree," her brother added.

Savannah gave Margie an affectionate smile. "Good going, Ms. Bloss."

"No problem, Ms. Reid."

In the living room, Savannah found Dirk sitting on her sofa, feet propped on the coffee table. *Gee,* she thought, *it must be about dinnertime.*

307

He was wearing a bedraggled expression, the one he wore most often these days. But she couldn't really blame him.

"I've seen cheerier faces on death row inmates," she told him as she sat beside him on the sofa and slipped a newspaper under his feet. "Need a beer?"

"No, I need an IV drip of morphine, but I'm still working. I just got back from that bookie's place, you know, Maldonado."

"Let me guess: Judging from the sourpuss you're wearing, it was a bust . . . and I don't mean the kind where you slap cuffs on him."

"You got that right. He's out of town, has been for over a month. Visiting some relatives in Atlantic City. And yes, it checks out. Completely. He's been very visible in the casinos there. About a zillion people saw him."

"Poop."

"My sentiments exactly. What's going on up there?" He pointed to the staircase. "I saw your brother-in-law going up, looking like a hanged dog."

"I laid a guilt trip on him. Hopefully, it'll lead to domestic tranquility."

"What had he done wrong?"

"He was born male."

"The bastard."

"Precisely."

The doorbell rang, and Savannah hauled herself to her feet. This was getting to be a bit much. "Grand Central Station," she muttered as she made her way to the door. "I'm beginning to long for the old days when I was suicidally lonely."

But it was a pleasant surprise — Ryan Stone in all his male glory, decorating her front porch. He was wearing a charcoal suit that was damned lucky to be draped across such a body. Savannah wished she were wearing something other than a faded T-shirt and jeans.

"Sorry I didn't call first," he said. "But I've got something interesting, and I couldn't wait."

"Come right in. Heaven knows, we could use something interesting."

"I saw Coulter's car out front," Ryan said as he walked inside. "This is for him, too."

"What's for me?" Dirk said, sitting up straight and taking his feet off the table.

Ryan glanced around. Seeing that the younger set was absorbed in their craft, he unbuttoned his jacket and sat in one of Savannah's easy chairs.

"As you know," he said, "I've still got friends in the bureau. And since I've left, they've acquired some pretty sophisticated toys."

"Like what?" Savannah said, sitting on the sofa next to Dirk.

"Like an extensive computer data bank that will cross-reference all sorts of goodies. Like similar crimes, comparable m.o.'s, facts in one case that parallel another."

"Sounds good," Dirk said. "Wish we had one."

"Well, for a few minutes this afternoon, you did. Without telling them why — because you told me to keep it under wraps — I asked them to run the star-studded ring through the files, just to see if we could come up with a match."

Savannah scooted out to the edge of her seat. "And . . . ?"

"Bingo." Ryan reached into his pocket and pulled out a computer printout. "Last year, on 21 July, a young Latino male was beaten to death in a junkyard in East L.A. The case is still open, no suspects. But the kid lived long enough to tell authorities that there were three assailants, white guys that he didn't recognize. They beat him with clubs and their fists. He said they were wearing big heavy rings that really hurt when they clocked him."

"Where does the 'star' reference come in?" Savannah asked.

"He died in a hospital about twelve hours after the beating. When they did the autopsy, they said it was from brain death due to inner cranial swelling. He had about a hundred significant bruises, but there were four that were particularly distinctive. They were on his head and face and one on his shoulder, the shape of a star."

They sat quietly for a few moments as Savannah and Dirk digested this new information that was possibly very helpful, though it wasn't immediately obvious how.

Finally, Savannah said, "July 21st . . . that date rings a bell." She walked to her purse that was lying on the table in the foyer and took out a small memo pad.

Bringing it back to the living room, she thumbed through the pages until she found what she was looking for. "Yep, that's what I thought."

"What?" Dirk said, trying to read over her shoulder.

"July 21st last year . . . that was the first day of the Point Morro Air Show."

Dirk nodded thoughtfully. "The ladies said their men didn't wear those rings very often. In fact, hardly at all. But we know one thing — that day, at least Titus Dunn was wearing his."

From the upstairs guest room came a sound, the rhythmic squeaking of bedsprings. Ryan smiled and gave Savannah a questioning look.

She shrugged and turned to Dirk. "Gee, things are looking up around here. It seems everybody's making a little progress."

TWENTY-ONE

December 20 — 11:37 a.m.

Savannah's feet were hurting, her spirits were flailing, she was cranky and hungry . . . and it wasn't even noon yet. Since early that morning she had been running around San Carmelita with the photo of the notorious ring in hand, asking every off-beat, garage, basement or backyard jeweler if they had ever seen such a piece.

She had never known how popular a hobby gold casting was. Sometime, when she wasn't so tired, cranky and hungry, she might check it out as a possible pastime herself. Considering the lack of men in her life, it might be the only way she would get her hands on any good jewelry.

This last shop was in the back of a tarot reading parlor, where they sold strange, esoteric jewelry with lots of crystals and Egyptian-looking hieroglyphics. The air was heavy with the scent of lavender incense and an aura of mysticism.

She rang the silver bell on the counter and a handsome, middle-aged black woman wearing a colorful batik caftan glided into the

312

room. "Good morning, child," she said in a lovely accent that Savannah guessed might have been from the Caribbean. "I am Mama Talula. And how may I help you today?"

Savannah smiled and said, "My name is Savannah, and you would make me a very happy woman, if you would just tell me that you've seen a ring like this before."

She laid the photo on the counter and waited for the usual negative response.

"Of course I have, dear girl. I have seen it. I made it. Are you a happy woman now?"

At first, neither Savannah nor her tired, aching feet could believe it. "Did you really? Or are you just trying to cheer me up?"

The woman laughed and the sound was like that of the silver bell on the counter. "I am glad that you are happy, and I am telling you the truth. I made that ring several years ago."

"Do you remember who it was for?"

"I don't believe he told me his name. He was a beautiful young man, with fine cut features and a strong, muscular body."

Savannah had pictures of Dunn, McGivney, and DeCianni in her purse. She pulled out the one of Dunn, as he was the one most likely to be described as "a beautiful young man."

"Is this him?"

Mama Talula looked at the picture and nodded. "That is him. I would remember his face anywhere. As I said, he was beautiful, but part of his aura was dark, very dark, as though there was evil around him. I was afraid for him."

Savannah thought of Titus's blood-splattered walls. Yes, evil had been very close to Titus Dunn.

"Have you read the newspapers lately, Mama?" Savannah asked, replacing the photo in her purse.

"No. I don't like to read such things. All the wicked doings in the world, they make me sad."

"I can understand that. The young man who bought your ring, he's missing."

"I'm sorry to hear that. Is that why you're asking about the ring?"

"Yes. That's right." She took McGivney's and DeCianni's pictures from her purse and held them out to the woman. "Have you seen either of these men?"

Mama studied them carefully. "This man, I have never seen," she said, pointing to McGivney's picture. "But this one, he came in with the first man and asked me to make him a ring, as well."

"And you did?"

"Of course. Just like his friend's."

"So, you made those two?"

"And another for a third friend of theirs. I never saw him. They told me his size, said it was to be a surprise, a gift for him."

"They didn't mention his name?"

"No. But I believe they were in military service of some sort."

"Why do you say that?"

Savannah could feel an area on the nape of her neck start to tingle, just the way it always did when she was about to get something good.

"Because when they came in the last time, to order the fourth ring, they —"

"A fourth ring? There were *four* rings? Are you sure about that, Mama?"

"Of course, I'm certain. My rings are like my children. I made four, exactly alike, except for size, of course."

"And what were you saying about the men being in the military?"

"I think they were. When they came back for the fourth ring, I remember the younger man said to the other, 'The captain's really going to like this. Now we've all got one.'"

Savannah resisted the urge to vault over the counter and give Mama Talula a kiss.

"Now, you are a very happy woman?" Mama asked, her face lit with a broad smile.

"Mama . . . I'm beyond happy. I'm ecstatic!"

12:25 p.m.

"This was a good idea," Savannah told Margie as they sat at the table in Burger Heaven and watched the twins happily

315

burying their faces in their ice cream cones — their rewards for having polished off their junior deluxes with cheese.

Margie lowered her voice and leaned closer to Savannah. "Anything's better than sitting around at your place, listening to Vidalia and Butch 'make up.'"

Savannah took a sip of her chocolate malted. "No kidding. I think I liked it better when they were fighting."

"Mommy and Daddy were playing bum-bum again this morning," Jack announced with an ice cream–smeared grin.

"Bum-bum?" Margie said.

"Maybe you shouldn't ask," Savannah whispered.

"Yeah!" Jillian nearly dropped her cone onto the table. "Jackie went in the bedroom to tell them he wanted some soda and guess what he saw . . ."

"I really don't think we should —" Savannah just had a feeling.

"He saw Daddy's bum-bum going up and down and up and down, and Mommy was under him, and she was laughing really hard."

"Yep, that's what I thought," Savannah muttered. She gave Margie the eye. "You just had to ask."

"And Daddy got all mad," Jack said. "He told me to knock next time, but I'm not gonna because I thought it was funny and I wanna see it again."

"Why don't you finish your ice cream there, young man," Savannah told him, ruffling his curls, "and then you and your pretty sister can go play in the balls."

She pointed to the cage full of red, orange and yellow, plastic balls where other children were diving in, screaming with glee.

"Oooo, neat! Hurry up, Jackie," Jillian exclaimed, then attacked her cone with renewed vigor.

Savannah looked up and saw Dirk walking toward them, a grimmer than grim expression on his face. The last time they had spoken on the phone, less than an hour ago, he had been down in the dumps. He had driven into Los Angeles and talked to the father of the young man who had been beaten by the guys wearing star rings. The trail was so stale, he hadn't gotten anywhere with it.

But once Savannah had told him about her conversation with Mama Talula, the fourth ring, and the "captain" reference, and he had been downright chipper. Apparently, something had happened to send him into another depression. Lately, he had been more moody than Vidalia.

Margie saw him, too, and took her cue. "I'll take the kids to the rest room and wash their hands," she said. "Then we'll play in the balls."

"Thanks a lot." She smiled at Margie and

delighted in the warmth of the smile she received in return. This tough, bratty kid was turning out to have a sweet soul after all. "You know," Savannah added, "you should have been a big sister. You're really good at it."

"Not as good as you."

"Actually, better."

Margie and the kids vacated the booth and Dirk took their place.

"Tracked me down, huh?" she said.

"I didn't exactly find this detective's badge in a Cracker Jack box, you know." He reached for some of Jillian's cold, leftover fries.

"Who ratted me out, Tammy or Vi?"

"Fluff head."

"That does it, I'm going to take away all those benefits of hers, all those fancy perks."

"Perks? She gets perks?"

Savannah laughed. "Heck, at the moment she does well to get paid. So, why did you track me down?"

"I wanted to give you the good news and the bad news."

She took another drink of her malt. "Okay, give me the bad first. I'm ready."

"Another cop is missing."

She nearly choked on her drink. "You're kidding. Shit. Who is it?"

"Well, that's what might be construed as the good news. Or maybe not . . ." He looked over at Margie, who was laughing, playing with the children, tossing them into the middle of the balls. "It's Bloss. He didn't come into the station this morning, or call in."

"Did anybody go out to the house?"

"We sent Farnon and McMurtry out. They looked the place over, said nothing seemed out of the ordinary."

"Wanna go look ourselves? See if *we* can find anything out of the ordinary?"

The very thought of getting to snoop through the high and mighty Captain Bloss's things brought a grin to her face. Dirk was wearing one just like hers.

"Sure," he said. "There are several things I'd like to look for."

"Like maybe a certain ring?"

"Exactly. Sh-h-h, we probably shouldn't tell her yet." He nodded toward Margie, who was coming back to the table.

"No, there's no point in worrying her any more than she needs to be, but . . ."

"I came back for my Coke," Margie said, reaching for the soda. "They're really having fun in there."

"I know," Savannah said, "but we're going to have to cut out of here in a few minutes. I have to go somewhere with Dirk. I'll drive you three back to the house first."

"Okay, but you have to drag them out of the balls. I can tell you right now, it won't be easy."

"I'm sure you're right." Savannah hesitated, then said as casually as possible. "Margie, does your father still have his wedding ring, the one he wore when he was married to your mom?"

She shrugged. "I don't know. I guess so. I never heard that he threw it away or gave it to anybody."

"If he did have it . . . or some other sentimental piece of jewelry . . . like maybe an old watch, where do you think he would keep it?"

"I'm not sure, but he has an old green box, like a little trunk with metal corners. I think it was from when he was in the Army. He's got some keepsake type things in there, like his Army medals and his birth certificate, stuff like that. He keeps it under the sleeping bag in his bedroom closet. Why?"

Savannah looked over at Dirk, but she could see he was going to let her handle this one.

"Savannah . . ." Margie sat down on the seat next to her, looking worried. ". . . is my dad in some kind of trouble?"

"I'm not going to lie to you, Margie," she said. "He may be. We aren't sure yet. Dirk is going to do everything he can for your dad because your father is Dirk's captain. And I'm going to do all I can because he's your dad and you're my friend."

"Thank you. Can you at least tell me what

kind of trouble it is?"

"I would, honey, but right now, I'm not sure myself."

"Is he going to die like those other policemen?"

Dirk cleared his throat, leaned across the table and patted the girl's hand. "Not if we can help it."

TWENTY-TWO

2:03 p.m.

Going into someone's house, when they weren't at home, without their knowledge or permission, had always given Savannah tingles along the spine. But entering Bloss's gave her a downright chill. She had been there before, when she had collected Margie's clothes for her. But that entry had been at the request of one of the house's occupants.

If Bloss knew they were there, he would have a fit; she had no doubt about that.

Unless, of course, he was as dead as the other missing cops and didn't care about anything.

"Not a bad place," Dirk remarked, looking around at the heavy, dark Spanish-style furniture set off against cool, white walls. Plants hung from the high, beamed ceilings and mint green and coral Oriental rugs covered the oak-planked floors. Everything was neat and tidy, obviously cleaned by a maid service, Savannah surmised. Captain Harvey Bloss wouldn't have the time to do much dusting or vacuuming on his workaholic schedule.

"Must have had it decorated by a professional," she said. "Anybody who wears hot pink, palm tree neckties and isn't couth enough to use a tissue for his nose wouldn't come up with this."

Dirk's own nose twitched, like it was out of joint. "I guess on a captain's salary, you can afford a pad like this. Too bad he doesn't deserve it."

"You go see if you can find that chest Margie was talking about," Savannah told him, "while I snoop around."

"How come you get to do the fun stuff?"

" 'Cause I'm a girl and I'm not getting paid."

"I'm not sure what that has to do with anything," he grumbled as he headed off toward bedroom to check out the closet.

Savannah made a beeline for the bathroom.

"What are you gonna do in there?" he called after her.

"Contrary to popular belief, it's the bathroom, not the bedroom, that's the best place to snoop. It's where you find the coolest stuff, every time."

A couple of minutes later, after Dirk had searched the bedroom closet and Savannah had finished with the bathroom and poked around the rest of the house, they met in the kitchen.

"Any sign of the ring?" she asked. Dirk was holding something behind his back.

"Nope," he said. "I'll bet whoever nabbed him took it, too. This was all that was in the chest, and I don't know for sure if it was for that ring."

He held out a small, black velvet, ring box that was empty, but it bore the imprint of a large ring on the nap of the fabric inside.

"At least I didn't see no blood," Dirk continued, "or nothin' that would make you think he got hisself killed here."

"Bloss didn't get nabbed," Savannah said, quite sure of herself. "He isn't missing, he's hiding."

"Why do you say that?"

"There's no suitcase or overnight bag in any of the closets, except a Barbie one in the second bedroom, which must have been Margie's, when she was a kid. A man who travels as much as Bloss does would have at least one handy."

Dirk shrugged. "Maybe he just throws his junk in a pillowcase like I do."

Savannah made a face and shook her head. "And . . . his shaving stuff is gone."

He thought that one over for a second, then nodded. "Gotcha."

Opening her purse, Savannah took out her memo book and cell phone. She consulted the book, then dialed a number.

"Mama Talula, this is Savannah Reid," she said brightly. "I was in your shop earlier today."

"Yes, of course," Mama replied in her charming, gracious accent. "The very happy woman. Are you still happy, child?"

"Oh yes." Savannah took the ring box from Dirk and turned it over and over in her hand. "Tell me one more thing, Mama. The rings you sold those men . . . the ones we were talking about today . . . did you put the rings in boxes when you gave them to them?"

"Of course. A work of art must be properly displayed."

Savannah smiled to herself. "Do you happen to recall what kind of boxes they were?"

"The same boxes I always use . . . just your standard ring box covered with black velvet."

"Thank you, Mama. Keep smilin'."

She switched off the phone and handed the tiny box back to Dirk.

"Well?" he said.

"No applause," she said, grinning from ear to ear, "just throw money."

On a built-in desk at the end of the kitchen counter, a telephone jingled. Savannah and Dirk looked at each other.

"Do you think we should . . . ?" he said.

"No, wait a minute. Let his machine pick it up."

They listened as Bloss's gruff voice basically demanded that the caller leave a message or else.

But after the long beep, instead of a human reply, they heard a series of beeps and clicks. Then the tape on the machine began to rewind.

"It's Bloss," Savannah said. "He's calling in to get his messages."

Dirk reached for the phone. "I think I'll answer it. Ask him where the hell he is and what's goin' on."

Savannah grabbed his hand. "If he's hiding, he probably won't tell us. Wait . . ."

They listened as two messages played, both from concerned personnel at the station, asking if he was intending to report to work today.

Savannah pointed to the caller identification box. "We don't have to ask him," she said. "That'll tell us."

They peered at the read-out.

"Jackson's Diner?" she said. "That sounds familiar. Where is that?"

"It used to be Angel's Taco Heaven. It's just down the street from the Blue Moon Motel."

Savannah's eyes sparkled. "Ah, ha! Figures. Let's get going."

2:25 p.m.

The rapist sat on the edge of the bed in the dark room, armed and waiting.

One more. Just one more, he told himself.

326

This one was a matter of principle. Nobody got away. Nobody. It was his code.

He gritted his teeth and promised himself that when this was over he was going to sleep, for days, weeks, for eternity.

At this point he didn't give a damn. His life was over anyway.

This wasn't fun anymore. Whatever charge he had gotten in the beginning — it was dead. As dead as he was inside.

He knew he was a corpse walking. But alive or dead, he would settle this last score. Yes. It was a matter of principle. And only a matter of seconds. Because he could hear footsteps approaching.

He wasn't the only corpse walking. No, he wasn't.

There were two.

2:30 p.m.

As Dirk drove toward the outskirts of town and the Blue Moon Motel, Savannah couldn't shake the uneasy feeling she had first experienced when she had driven Margie and the kids back to her house.

"Still bothering you?" Dirk asked her as they passed over the Rio Verde Bridge, marking the city's border.

"Yeah," she said. "And it's getting worse."

She pulled her cell phone from her purse and gave Tammy a call.

Briefly, she explained the situation to her assistant. "The kid's really worried about her old man," she told Tammy. "We had to ask her some questions and she's no dummy; she figured out that something's up."

"Do you want me to go over there?" Tammy offered. "I'll just keep her company until you get back."

"Would you mind? I'd really appreciate it. Vidalia and Butch are a bit too wrapped up in themselves right now to provide much support for her. She's been through a lot lately."

"No problem, I'm on my way."

"Thanks, Tam. I'll give you a raise in pay."

"Pay? You're going to start paying me? I don't have to work for love and personal fulfillment anymore?"

"Good-bye, smartass."

When Savannah hung up, Dirk said, "So, feel better now?"

Savannah shrugged. "I guess so. A little."

"We'll check out the motel and get you back as soon as we can," he said.

She continued to stare out the window and wonder. "Thanks."

He stepped on the gas.

2:37 p.m.

When the door opened and the intended victim stepped into the motel room, Officer Titus Dunn found that the feeble rush of

328

adrenaline wasn't enough to carry him this time. His hand shook violently as he lifted his gun from his lap and pointed it at Harvey Bloss.

The infection was too deep, the fever was too high, and his strength was almost gone.

But all he had to do was pull the trigger. Number Three would be properly dispatched. Vengeance complete. Mission accomplished.

He had anticipated the look of shock on Bloss's face when he flipped on the light and turned to see him sitting there. But he was disappointed. Bloss didn't even look surprised as he walked across the room to the dresser, picked up a whiskey bottle that had been sitting there and poured a plastic cup half full.

"Dunn," he said calmly as he drank about half of the amber fluid in one gulp. "I was wondering what took you so long."

A surge of anger shot through the killer, giving him the extra jolt of adrenaline he needed. He steadied his gun.

"With two fingers," he said, "pull your weapon and put it on the table there. Slowly. Now sit in that chair." He waved his gun toward a rusted contraption with a torn leatherette seat.

Reluctantly, the captain complied.

Dunn tossed him a pair of handcuffs. The simple gesture caused a pain like white lightning to shoot through him, but he pushed past the misery.

"Cuff your right hand to the chair arm," he said. "Do it! Now!"

Dunn studied his captive with eyes that burned. But it was a cold fire. "So, you were expecting me sooner?" he said as he watched Bloss struggle with the cuffs, trying to put them on with his left hand. "It's not easy, running around for days with two bullets lodged in you . . . bullets your 'brothers' gave you. Thanks a lot . . . Bro."

Finally, Bloss snapped the cuffs closed on his own wrist, then squinted at Dunn with those dark, slitted eyes that Dunn had come to hate.

"You came after my daughter," Bloss said. "My own kid! What the hell did you think I'd do?"

"What made you think it was me?"

"She saw your ring, you moron."

"It could've been DeCianni or McGivney. They're Marshals. They've got rings."

"I checked them out. They had alibis. Both were accounted for; you weren't." Bloss shook his head and gave Dunn a contemptuous look that made Dunn want to go ahead and blow his brains out on the spot. But he had waited for this a long time. The fantasy of carrying out this execution was the only thing that had gotten him through the night before, when the fever had been so high, the pain so bad.

And since this would be his last killing, he

330

didn't want to rush it.

"I can't believe you wore one of our rings to do shit like that," Bloss continued in that self-righteous tone that made Dunn furious. "Those rings were a symbol of justice and the power of the law. But rape? What kind of lowlife are you? I can't believe you were even a cop, let alone that we let you join the Marshals."

Titus laughed, but the movement caused an agony in his ribs. One of the bullets had struck there, in his side, and passed on through. The other was still lodged in his left shoulder. A bucketful of stolen antibiotics and driving rage had kept him going so far, but he had just about reached the end.

"You didn't mind us wearing those rings when we took care of dirty business for you . . ." he said, ". . . like that pimp in Oak Creek, the coke dealer in the valley, or that kid in East L.A. All that boy did was steal your wallet and whack you around a little. But you couldn't report it because you got robbed with your pants down, bangin' a hooker."

"That kid was trouble, had been all his life." Bloss passed his left hand over his forehead that was slimy with a film of sweat.

"And you decided he had to die," Dunn said, "so we killed him for you."

"I told you to rough him up, not kill him."

"Sometimes things don't go as planned; he

had a gun in his boot and he drew it on us. Of course, you didn't exactly shed any tears when we told you he was dead."

"That was different. It was justice. That's why I formed the Marshals in the first place, why I invited you guys in . . . to administer justice when the system broke down and let a criminal slip through the cracks. And that's a long way from raping and beating innocent women."

While Dunn silently seethed, the only sound was that of the clock ticking on the nightstand. Dunn felt a wave of weakness and nausea sweep through him. He could taste the saltiness of his own sweat that ran down into his eyes and the corners of his mouth. He allowed the rage to build to a crescendo inside him.

The more fury he felt, the more steady his hand became, but the more difficult it was to breathe.

"And is that what you thought you were doing when you sent McGivney and DeCianni after me?" he said. "My so-called brothers, coming to murder me in my own home? Did you think you were administering justice?"

Bloss glowered at him, not bothering to hide his hatred; not a smart move for a man staring down the barrel of a gun, Titus decided. This guy deserved to die, because he was stupid, if for no other reason.

"It *was* justice," Bloss said. "And if you'd gotten what you deserved, you'd be dead and McGivney and DeCianni would still be alive. They were good men, not scum like you."

"Well, this is what I call justice. Marshal Dunn strikes a blow for law and order and takes out the brother who betrayed him. Maybe they'll carve that on my tombstone."

"Your tombstone? You're the one holding the gun."

"We're both dead. But you're goin' to get to hell first, buddy . . . just a few seconds before me."

TWENTY-THREE

When Dunn made the comment about the tombstones, Savannah and Dirk knew it was time. For the longest four minutes she could remember, they had been standing outside the slightly ajar motel door, listening to the exchange inside.

The case was solved; now all they had to do was get their least favorite police captain out of the room, hopefully without having his hide or vital organs perforated.

Dirk gave Savannah a nod, she pushed the door open, and he rushed inside, weapon drawn and trained on Titus. Savannah did the same.

Titus hardly even flinched. He glanced over his shoulder at them, but immediately turned back to Bloss.

Even under the stress of the moment, Savannah was shocked at Titus's appearance. She had never seen anyone — at least, not anyone living — who was so gray, so bloated, so miserably ill. She couldn't believe he was still conscious and functioning.

The golf shirt he wore was crusted with

black, dried blood over his torso. His slacks were just as badly stained, and a swath of clumsily applied, filthy bandages were wrapped around his left shoulder.

"Coulter, Savannah, this is between Bloss and me," Titus said. "Just turn around, the both of you, and walk out that door."

"That's not the way it's going to happen," Dirk said quietly. "You know that. You know what we've got to do here."

"Yeah, and I know what I'm going to do," he said. His voice sounded a bit quivery, but his resolve was solid.

Savannah braced herself, holding the Beretta in her right hand, her left beneath to steady the weapon. In all her years on the force, she had only been forced a couple of times to sight down that barrel at anything other than a paper target.

And now, her finger on the trigger, every muscle flexed, she couldn't believe she was sighted on Titus Dunn.

This couldn't be happening. The inevitable wouldn't occur. Not if she could stop it.

She took a step closer to him. "Titus, don't . . ." she said, pleading. "This isn't the way any of us wants this to end. Put down the gun. We don't want to hurt you, but you know we will if we have to."

"We all gotta do what we gotta do," he said with a wry chuckle. "And I know what I've going to do: I'm going to shoot this sonofabitch here, and then you two will shoot me . . . unless, of course, I get one of you, too."

As in other moments of high drama, Savannah experienced a surreal slowing of time passage. Titus was raising his gun slightly, his finger tightening on the trigger. And in that split second, a series of thoughts raced through her mind: Titus sharing pancakes with them at the restaurant, Christy weeping on her sunporch with the Christmas angel tree, Charlene Yardley's bruised face and broken spirit, weeping for her dead mother with the sweet, Southern accent, and Margie crouching, terrified, behind a pile of dirty tires in a dark service station lot.

Then three shots exploded, filling the room with smoke and the smell of cordite.

Three bullets seared burning paths through living flesh.

Two bodies hit the floor.

And when the smoke had cleared and the noise was only a roar in their ears, another thought went through Savannah's head.

Titus was right. It had gone down just the way he'd called it.

TWENTY-FOUR

2:45 p.m.

Both Titus Dunn and Harvey Bloss lay on the floor of the motel room. Bloss's hand was still cuffed to the chair. Both shot. Neither one breathing. Neither had a pulse.

Just a quick examination told Savannah and Dirk that Titus Dunn was beyond resuscitation. They had fired one bullet each. Both had struck him in the region of the heart. His death had been almost instantaneous.

Bloss was a different story. Titus's aim had been low, nicking him on the inside of his thigh. While it was a bit more than the proverbial flesh wound, the injury shouldn't have been fatal.

Quickly, they ripped his shirt open, yanked down his trousers, and looked for another wound. But there was none.

"What's wrong with him?" Dirk asked, shaking his captain by the shoulders. "Why doesn't he have a pulse for cryin' out loud?"

"I guess he had a heart attack or maybe it just scared him to death," Savannah said as she dialed 911 and requested an ambulance.

Dirk knelt over his inert captain, listening

for respiration, but, for all practical purposes, Bloss was as dead as his counterpart.

Looking up at Savannah, Dirk said, "You know what this means?"

"What?" Savannah bristled. *No, don't even think about it,* she thought. *No way.*

"If we don't give him mouth to mouth," Dirk said, "he's going to die."

"And your point is . . . ?"

"You've got to do it. I can't."

"What do you mean, you can't? He's your boss, your responsibility. Pucker up, babycakes, he's all yours."

"I can't. I can thump on his chest, maybe get his heart started. But I can't do the breathing part. I just can't."

"Why not?"

"He's a dude."

"Are you telling me that you're such a friggin' homophobe that you can't give a dying man the breath of life? Is that what you're telling me?"

Dirk shrugged and looked miserable. "Maybe I could . . . if he was some other guy, but . . . Bloss. I just . . . I can't. You do it."

"Hell no! I'm not touching him. I'd rather eat a maggot."

Then she thought of all the rotten things this man on the floor had done to her. The loss of her job, the time he'd had her falsely arrested for murder, all the snide remarks and . . . and the look that would be on Margie Bloss's face when she heard her father was dead.

"Come on, Van," Dirk begged. "You gotta do it. If he dies, I won't get to bust him for the vigilante shit!"

Savannah dropped to her knees, pinched Bloss's big, red nose between her fingers, bent over him and said, "Boy, oh, boy, Coulter. You are gonna owe me so big for this! There aren't enough donuts or pizzas in the world to pay for this!"

December 21 — 3:39 a.m.

Savannah sat at her kitchen table, sipping a mug of hot chocolate, wishing that she, like the rest of the world, was asleep.

There was nothing quite like killing someone to keep you awake at night — someone whose home you had visited, whose barbecue you had eaten, whose sweetheart you had consoled. The mental picture of Titus lying on the floor, staring up at her with dead eyes didn't lend itself to a peaceful night's sleep.

She wondered whose bullet, hers or Dirk's, had actually killed him. Maybe both. Dr. Jen was good; she would find out during the autopsy. A ballistics test would tell them for sure.

But did it matter?

No. Not really.

Titus was dead. He wasn't coming back. And while that was, no doubt, a comfort to his many victims, their loved ones, and even the community at large . . . Savannah didn't feel all that good about it.

If she had it to do all over again, she wouldn't change a thing. Titus had given them no choice.

But it still sucked. And no amount of hot chocolate or soul searching was going to put it right tonight.

In the living room, the children snoozed away on the sofa. Vidalia and Butch were in the guest room, the bedsprings having finished squeaking a couple of hours ago.

Margie was nestled all snug in Savannah's bed, having come home from the hospital where her father was still in Intensive Care, but his condition was stabilized. He had suffered a heart attack, but the damage appeared to have been minimal. Dirk could hardly wait for him to recuperate sufficiently so that he could place him under arrest. He had promised Savannah that she could be present for the auspicious occasion. She had already decided to wear rings on her fingers and bells on her toes.

While at the hospital this evening, Savannah had dropped by Charlene Yardley's room to find that she had been discharged. The nurse said she had gone home and would be spending time with her children. Savannah wondered if she had heard the news before she went to bed.

If she had, at least *she* would sleep better.

But Savannah wasn't the only one having trouble counting sheep tonight, she realized when she heard footsteps for at least the fifth time in an hour, traipsing down the upstairs hall to the bathroom. At first she figured it was Butch, getting rid of the beer he had consumed this evening. But she heard a cough that sounded more female. Maybe it was Vidalia, and maybe she was sick.

Leaving her hot chocolate, which had passed from lukewarm to decidedly cool anyway, Savannah quietly made her way through the living room, past the sleeping children, and up the stairs to the bathroom.

She knocked softly on the door. "Vi, is that you, honey?" she asked.

After a few moments of rustling sounds, the door opened and a very tired looking Vidalia stuck her nose out. "It's me."

"You keep getting up. Is everything okay?"

"No. That's why I keep getting up."

"What's wrong? As Gran would say, 'A case of the green apple quick step'?"

Vidalia sighed and sagged against the door frame. "No, I wish I *did* have diarrhea. I've never been so constipated in my life."

"That's pretty common with pregnancy, isn't it?"

341

"But not this bad. I feel all shivery and sick, and it's coming in waves. I . . . oh . . . here it comes again."

She closed the door, leaving Savannah standing there with a feeling that a drama of a different kind might be starting.

Savannah opened the door to see her sister sitting on the pot, her face red from straining. In a family of nine kids, modesty and privacy had been abandoned long ago. "Vi, how long has this been going on?"

"For the last four hours, I guess. Why?"

"Did you say it's coming in waves?"

"Yeah."

"And you're feeling the urge to push?"

"Well, sure. I told you, I've never been so cons— . . ."

Vidalia looked up at Savannah, comprehension dawning on her face. "Oh, no. You don't think it's labor, do you? The baby ain't supposed to come for another six weeks or so."

"Are you sure about your due date?"

"Not real sure. I wasn't keepin' track of my periods, so we don't know exactly when I got pregnant. The doctor was guessin'. I . . . oh . . . here it comes again."

Savannah did a quick mental count. "Those were only about two minutes apart."

"Do you think I might be in labor?"

Savannah wasn't sure how to break it to her, other than bluntly. "Kiddo, I think your baby's about to be born. Come on, let's get you back to bed, and I'll call the hospital."

Supporting her under the arms, Savannah helped her sister down the hall to the guest bedroom. "Butch!" she called. "Butch, wake up! We need you here."

When she flipped on the light, her brother-in-law sat up in bed and looked around him, completely disoriented. "What? Vi, what's the matter?" he said when his wife waddled to the opposite side of the bed and collapsed on it.

"We think the baby's coming," Savannah said. "Call 911 and tell them to send an ambulance."

He still looked dazed.

"Now!" she yelled.

He bolted out of bed, as naked as a jaybird and headed for the door.

"Butch! You might want to put some jeans on that scrawny butt of yours first, if you don't want to frighten the rest of the household," she suggested.

"Oh, yeah . . . okay." He scrambled into his pants, then flew out the door.

Savannah wondered if he was too scattered to find the phone, but she had more immediate concerns. She turned her attention to Vidalia. "Make yourself as comfortable as you can, and I'll be right back."

She ran to the bathroom and washed her hands thoroughly, then rushed back to her bedside. "Let's see what we've got going down there, sugar," she said as she pulled up her sister's nightgown.

"O-o-o-kay, that's what I thought."

"What is it?" Vidalia asked, her breathing hard and ragged.

"It's either a bowling ball, a purple watermelon, or a baby's head, right there."

"Oh no! Can we wait until the ambulance gets here?"

"*We* could, but I think the baby's got other plans. It's crowning right now, Vi."

"What are we going to do?"

"I'm going to deliver it. We're certainly not going to try to send it back to where it came from."

"Have you done that before? Have you delivered babies?"

"Lots. No sweat."

Savannah could almost feel her nose growing and her tongue turning black. It would probably fall out of her mouth any moment. At least, that's what Gran had always told her would happen if you told a whopper.

But she'd watched Dirk deliver a baby once about five years ago . . . so, it wasn't that big a lie, right? She gave her labored sister a nervous grin. "Constipated, huh?"

"Hey, I didn't know. It doesn't hurt so bad this time, not like it did with the twins." She screwed up her face and began straining again. "Or maybe it does," she added between pants.

Butch came stumbling back into the room, tripping over his own feet. "I called them. They said they'd be here lickety split."

Yeah, right, Savannah thought. She knew all too well how "lickety split" the emergency services were in this town.

"Go wake up Margie," she said. "We need as many hands as we can get. The baby's almost here."

"What?"

"Go!"

By the time he returned with a sleepy-eyed Margie, Savannah had her hands full with a frantic, squalling Vidalia. "I can't stand this!" she was screaming. "It's never coming."

"It's coming," Savannah said, the evidence all too clear. "Believe me, it's coming." She turned to Butch. "Run down to the kitchen and get a turkey baster, a pair of scissors, and that ball of string from Jack's kite."

Butch nodded. "Baster, scissors, kite."

"No! The string from the kite. And Margie, grab an armful of clean towels from the bathroom closet. Throw about half of them into the dryer and turn it on. Then bring the rest back here."

"Got it."

"And you, Vi, I think we can deliver the baby's head with the next contraction or two. Are you ready?"

"N-n-n-o-o."

"Me either, but let's do it anyway."

Butch and Margie arrived at the same time, arms laden with the requested supplies. The ball of string was still attached to the kite, and Jack was at his father's heels, squalling something about his daddy breaking it. His sister wasn't far behind.

"Oh, great," Savannah mumbled when she saw her niece and nephew. "That's all we need now."

"I'll take care of them," Margie said grabbing each one by the hand. "How would you guys like to have ice cream for breakfast?"

"We can't have breakfast yet!" Jillian said, starting to cry. "It's still dark out."

"That's when you're supposed to eat ice cream for breakfast." She pulled them out the door and said over her shoulder, "I'll get them settled, then I'll come right back."

Savannah nodded, without looking up. "When you do, bring me those warm towels from the dryer. Pile them in the wicker laundry basket."

"What are the towels for?" Butch asked, looking like he was about to start crying himself.

"For the baby," Savannah said. "If it *is* coming early, it'll need to be kept nice and warm."

"Early, you mean premature, like the twins were?"

Savannah recalled how touch-and-go it had been with the twins those first few weeks.

They had nearly lost little Jillian.

Her stress level went through the roof as she felt the baby's head pushing against the palm of her hand.

"It'll be okay, Butch," she said. "Just get up there by your wife's head and try to comfort her."

Butch moved into position and began stroking Vidalia's hair. "Don't worry, baby," he told her as she panted, sweated and strained. "Don't worry about it being premature and all that. It probably won't be near as bad as it was with the twins."

Vidalia's eyes widened, and she began to cry even louder.

"Thanks, Butch," Savanna murmured, listening for the blessed sound of the sirens above her sister's wails . . . and hearing nothing. "Thanks a lot."

Halfway up the staircase, laundry basket and warm towels in hand, Margie heard something that sounded like a puppy's yelp or kitten's mew. Could it be?

Yes?

She ran into the bedroom just in time to see Savannah gently suctioning a tiny baby's mouth and nose with the turkey baster.

"Wow! It's here already!" she said, hurrying to the bed.

"And you're just in time with those towels," Savannah said. "How hot are they?"

"Just nice and warm."

Savannah checked with her hand before grabbing one and winding it snugly around the wriggling infant. Vidalia was still huffing; Butch looked ecstatic.

"It's okay," he said proudly. "It's another boy, and he's little, but he's breathing okay."

"You did it," Margie told Savannah proudly.

She wondered why Savannah didn't look so relieved.

Margie moved closer to the bed. "What's the matter?"

"Nothing. The baby's fine," Savannah said. "It's just that . . . I think maybe . . ."

Vidalia bore down again, her face purple, pushing, straining.

"Yep, that's what I thought," Savannah said. "We did it . . . but now we get to do it all over again."

7:12 a.m.

Unable to sleep, Dirk had driven to the hospital at dawn to check on Bloss's condition.

Weak. Stable. Still unconscious.

So, other than making sure that Officer Morton O'Leary was stationed at the door of the I.C.U., Dirk couldn't do much about arresting him yet.

As he was leaving through the emergency

348

entrance, he heard the news . . . and promptly headed for the maternity ward on the third floor.

That was where he found Savannah, sprawled across five seats in the waiting room, looking like a semi truck had run over her.

"Hey, Auntie!" he said, "I hear congratulations are in order."

"Uh, huh," she mumbled without moving or even turning her head to look at him. She was staring at the ceiling, for all practical appearances, brain dead.

"I hear it's twins, a boy and a girl, and you delivered them."

"Uh, huh."

"So, are they checking mom and the kids in? They'll be here for a few days, I guess."

"Huh, uh."

He leaned closer. "Was that a no?"

"The babies were born outside the sterile environment of the hospital," she said, so low he could hardly hear her. "They're contaminated. They can't stay in the nursery with the other newborns."

"And?"

"And Vidalia won't stay in the hospital without her babies. So, they're all coming home with me. All. Home. My home. With me."

"Oh, Van . . . I'm so sorry," he said.

"Me, too. So, so sorry."

December 25 — 2:15 p.m.

Eighty degrees. Not a cloud in the sky. Just your typical Christmas Day, Savannah thought as she watched her friends and family celebrating the holiday in her backyard. The twins were running around in bathing suits, squirting each other with the garden hose, screaming like miniature banshees.

Tammy was catching some rays in her polka-dotted bikini, stretched out on a Betty Boop beach towel. Why, Savannah wasn't sure, because she'd seen her slathering on a heavy-duty sunscreen just before lying down. Go figure.

Maybe it was because Ryan Stone was sitting beneath the arbor, sipping a champagne cocktail, looking incredible in charcoal slacks and a navy blue shirt. Tammy had never fully surrendered the fantasy of catching Ryan's attention.

Dirk sat in a chaise longue beneath the magnolia tree, holding one of the newest arrivals, Noel. Dirk didn't look especially at ease with his paternal role, but they were all taking turns keeping the newborns occupied, and it was his shift, so he wasn't complaining.

Butch sat next to him on another longue, jostling Noel's sister, Merry, who wasn't happy and was intent upon the entire neighborhood knowing it. Like a typical Reid girl, she was cute beyond words, ate constantly, and was quite mouthy when things didn't go her way.

Vidalia was asleep in the hammock next to the house, Cleopatra curled into a ball on her now fairly flat tummy. She looked great in the dressy slacks set Savannah had bought for her. As one of her Christmas gifts, Savannah had treated her to a "Day of Beauty" at a local salon. The hair and facial makeover, along with massages and herbal steams had brought back her usual, lovely, vain self.

Yes, Savannah thought, *just a typical California Christmas.*

She walked back into the house where it was ninety-three degrees, thanks to the turkey roasting in the oven. The kitchen smelled of pumpkin and mince pies, mashed potatoes and gravy, freshly baked rolls, and the fragrance of sage, thanks to Savannah's aunt's wonderful dressing recipe. Aunt Gondi made the best dressing south of the Mason-Dixon line, and Savannah had been able to get it only by exchanging her own famous onion roll recipe.

She found Margie arranging pickles, olives, radish roses, and cherry tomatoes in decorative patterns on a platter.

"That looked great, kiddo," she told her as she stole an olive and popped it into her mouth. "How are you doing?"

A look of sadness crossed the girl's face, then she smiled. "Okay. The hospital says my dad's doing fine. He'll be able to leave tomorrow. Not that it makes much difference. He'll be going right to jail."

"I'm really sorry things turned out this way for you." Standing beside her, Savannah gave her a hug around the waist. She returned the embrace.

"It's all right. When I talked to my mom on the phone today, she says she thinks it'll work out for me to stay at home with them. She says if I'll behave myself, she'll tell her old man to lighten up on me."

"Are you going to, behave that is?"

"I guess. Mostly, he just didn't like the hair. He shouldn't mind this, huh?"

She pointed to her new do, which was now red, a red that a few women in the world might actually have naturally. Also, she had removed the ring from her eyebrow, the studs from her nose and tongue, and had exchanged her black and blue makeup for shades of dark red.

"You look beautiful," Savannah told her. "You were beautiful before, but I was so busy looking at all the 'stuff' that I didn't notice you as much."

"Thanks." She blushed and, for a moment, looked incredibly sweet and vulnerable.

"Are you about ready to eat?"

"I've been ready for hours. The smell of that turkey is making me crazy. But I think we're going to have a visitor first."

"A visitor? Who?" Savannah said.

"Just don't be scared when you see him," Margie replied. "Gibson asked me if I thought it was okay, under the circumstances, and I said, sure, because it's for the kids, you know?"

"No, I don't know. I have no idea what you're talking about."

"She's talking about a visit from old Father Christmas . . . or Saint Nicholas, as you Yanks call him," said a deep, deliciously refined, British voice behind her.

Savannah turned and got the start of her life. There was Santa, standing in her living room, a large bag of loot slung over his shoulder, a broad smile between his mustache and beard.

A few dozen images flooded her mind. All of them frightening and sad.

That was yet another evil Titus Dunn had committed. An entire community had lost its innocence, had lost a beloved icon and symbol of love and generosity.

But there was no time like the present to reclaim it.

Savannah strolled over to Santa, tweaked his rosy cheek and said, "Mr. Claus, I want you to know I've been far more nice than naughty this year. Not that I wouldn't have welcomed the opportunity to be naughty, but my social life being what it is . . .”

He threw back his head and gave a rather theatrical, “Ho, ho, ho . . . I understand completely. That's why Santa has brought you something special.”

Reaching into his pack, he pulled out a bright red envelope with her name written on it.

She tore it open and found airline tickets and prepaid vouchers for a deluxe, two-week vacation at a singles club in the Bahamas.

“Oh, Gibs— . . . I mean, Santa, you shouldn't have,” she said, “but I'm so glad you did!”

Santa tossed his bag over his shoulder once again and gave Margie a nod. “Come along with me, young lady,” he told her. “I've given my elves the afternoon off and I find myself in desperate need of a Santa's helper.”

Savannah followed the two of them into the backyard and watched the twins go crazy with delight at the sight of him.

She looked over at Dirk and Tammy and saw that their reactions were similar to hers. They would all need some time to heal.

But as she watched Jillian and Jack scampering around “Father Christmas” — opening their own gifts and joyfully distributing more to the adults, and their new brother and sister beneath the magnolia tree — she knew that the children were the balm that would aid in that healing.

Once again, she felt seven years old, and Christmas was the happiest, most magical, time of the year. At least for the moment, there was peace on this little bit of earth that was her backyard. And there was goodwill galore.

Down south, many people consider the dressing (stuffing) to be the best part of a holiday dinner. Traditionally, many Southern cooks don't stuff the turkey or goose, but bake the dressing separately in its own pan. Savannah's Aunt Gondi is known, far and wide, for her incredible dressing. We are proud to share it with you.

Aunt Gondi's Dressing

1	cup chopped onion
1	cup chopped celery
2	tablespoons butter

Lightly saute onions and celery in butter. Place onion/celery mixture in large bowl along with:

4	slices toasted, crumbled bread
4	cups crumbled cornbread (see recipe below)
1	teaspoon salt or to taste
1/4	teaspoon pepper
2	tablespoons sage (more if you like)
2	eggs lightly beaten

Add:

3–4	cans chicken broth heated
1	stick of butter, melted in broth

You will want the mixture to be very moist, almost soupy, as it will dry out while baking.

Put mixture into a greased (or sprayed) 9" x 13" pan, and bake at 350 degrees for 30 minutes.

The basis of any great Southern dressing is great cornbread. No one has ever made better cornbread than Ma Johnson. Her cornbread was wonderful in dressing or straight from the oven, served with a pat of butter. If you want an unusual, but distinctly Southern treat, crumble some cornbread into a glass of cold buttermilk, add a sprinkle of salt and pepper to taste.

Ma Johnson's Cornbread

In large bowl mix:

2   cups white, self-rising cornmeal
1/3 cup flour
1/3 cup sugar
3/4 teaspoon salt

To dry ingredients add:

2   eggs
1 3/4 cups milk
1/4 cup bacon grease, melted

Mix just enough to moisten all dry ingredients. Overmixing will make the bread hard.

Pour into greased, 10" round pan and bake at 425 degrees for 20–25 minutes.

Ma Johnson's secret: Fry a few pieces of bacon in a heavy, cast iron skillet, remove the bacon, measure the grease and add it, hot, as the last ingredient. This greases and preheats your pan and gives the bread a wonderful, crispy edge. And most old-fashioned, Southern cooks swear by their cast iron skillets for flavorful cornbread.

About the Author

G. A. McKevett is the pseudonym of a well-known author. She is the author of seven other Savannah Reid mysteries, *Just Desserts*, *Bitter Sweets*, *Killer Calories*, *Sugar and Spite*, *Sour Grapes*, *Peaches and Screams* and *Death by Chocolate*.

The employees of Thorndike Press hope you have enjoyed this Large Print book. All our Thorndike and Wheeler Large Print titles are designed for easy reading, and all our books are made to last. Other Thorndike Press Large Print books are available at your library, through selected bookstores, or directly from us.

For information about titles, please call:

(800) 223-1244

or visit our Web site at:

www.gale.com/thorndike
www.gale.com/wheeler

To share your comments, please write:

Publisher
Thorndike Press
295 Kennedy Memorial Drive
Waterville, ME   04901